I0596103

The Witch

Alterealm Series

Book 4

By J. Risk

Family tree at the end of The Empath

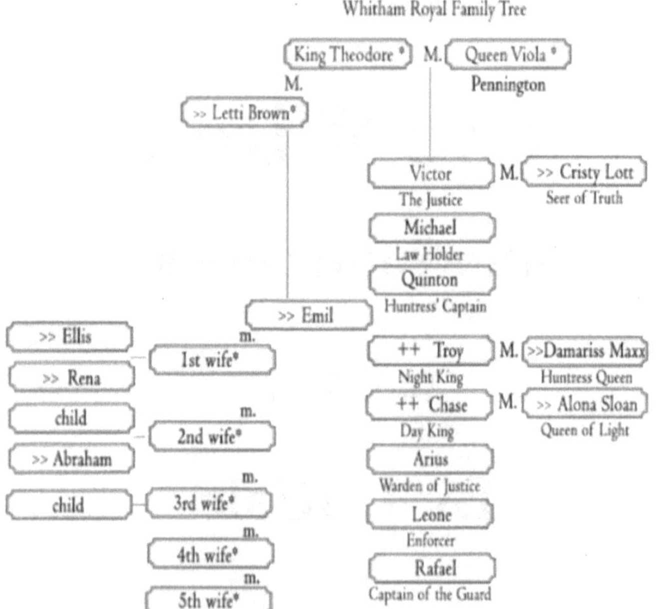

"You have news of my brother?"

I actually jumped when his voice filled my cube. I nodded. "Yes." I'd found his family.

"Where are you from?"

I frowned. "Pluto, what the hell does that matter?"

He turned and again I couldn't hear them.

"Seriously?" Reaching into my pocket I pulled out the chain and pendant Leone had said everyone knew was his. Holding it in my palm, I went over to the wall and slapped my hand against it. All eyes went wide. Oh, they knew that, I thought. "Figured that would get your attention," I said just in case they could hear me. I stared at the one with Leone's eyes. "I don't have time to screw around. Leone needs help. Now."

The door to my display cube opened. The guard that had put me in here motioned for me to come out. I did, hesitantly, then went where he pointed. Into the space with those ten anxious and angry looking people. Mostly angry.

"Talk quickly," the big scary one said, then waved his hand for me to speak.

"Oh yeah, you're definitely related to him." My hands tingled, my magic must not be blocked in this room. He was huge and scary as shit. He stepped toward me. I held up my hand, sparks and all toward him. "You stay right there." I shook my head. "I don't want to hurt anyone."

Someone snorted.

A dark-haired man with a scar on his face stepped in my direction. He didn't look happy at all. "Back off, Scarface. I'm here because I need help."

I felt this pressure inside my head and raised my hands further making sure all of them could see the energy sparking from them. "Whoever is trying to mess in my head, knock it off."

"Look, honey," A tall man with a baby face and serious eyes held his hands up toward me.

"Stay there, Tarzan, we don't have time for this."

"Oh gods. Can she stay? We need this in our lives. I need this in my life." The tall twin with the goatee said, a big grin on his face.

THE ALTEREALM SERIES

1 *The Huntress*
2 *The Seer*
3 *The Empath*
4 *The Witch*
5 *The Chronos*
6 *The Warrior*
7 *The Telepath*
8 *The Healer*
9 *The Kinetic* (coming soon)

Writing As: Jacqueline Paige

Dreams
Three steamy stories that started with a dream

Curses
Two tales of curses.

After the Silence
Volume 1 Bree

ANIMAL SENSES
1 *Heart*
2 *Scent*
3 *Passion*

MAGIC SEASONS ROMANCE
1 *Beltane Magic*
2 *Solstice Heat*
3 *Harvest Dreams*
4 *Autumn Dance*
5 *Winter Mist*

SINGLE TITLES
Solitary Witchling
Salvation
Café Serenity

Published by FRP
Copyright © 2018 Roxane Kerr
Edited by Gaele L. Hince
Cover art by: Off the Wall Creations

Updated 2020

Excerpts from *Beltane Magic* by Jacqueline Paige, *The Chronos* by J. Risk
copyright © 2015, 2018 by Roxane Kerr

All rights reserved. Including the right to reproduce this book, or portions thereof, in any form
without prior written consent of the author, except for brief quotes for use in reviews.

This is a work of fiction. All characters and events portrayed in this novel are fictitious or used fictitiously, and any resemblance to any actual persons, living or dead, events or locales, is entirely coincidental.

ISBN (paperback) 978-1-7773723-9-2
ISBN (digital) 978-1-7773723-8-5

Prologue

"Why are you just sitting here?"

I looked at the food on the plate in front of me, figuring it was self-explanatory, then back to Davis. "I need to eat and rest occasionally or I won't be able to do *crap*." I told him wishing he would just go away. He was a magic user himself, or I'd try to make that a reality. I didn't know enough about this mage stuff to be sure it would work, and worry that he would do something worse in retaliation. Then again, if he kept getting in my face I may have to find out what I could do to him.

If it hadn't been for him talking my best friend Erin into meeting all these power hungry, demented morons, she would be here still—then I could drag her, kicking and screaming if need be, far, far away. So yeah, Davis was at the top of my wish list to have something bad happen to him.

He gave me an unamused look.

Like I cared what he thought of me.

"It *is* working though, isn't it? You assured me you could work it from this distance."

It had been working for over a week, and he just thought to ask me that now? Sighing, I set down the sandwich I *really* wanted to eat, deciding if I answered him, he'd go away. "Yes. It took a few days to find one that I was *able* to get into." I'd never encountered so many closed minds as I had in that search. I was almost afraid to see the bodies that went with them. Good thing for me I didn't have to. Other than the one I was mesmerizing, I'd never have to see these royals Davis and his crew had so many issues with.

"Are you certain it's one of the royals? If you're tapped into some servant, it's completely useless."

My first thought was to pour my juice over his head and walk away—but then I'd be thirsty, and he'd probably just follow me. "You make it sound like it's as easy as scrolling through a list and picking one." I cocked my head to the side and gave him a blank stare. "People don't walk around thinking my name is Bethany. My name is Bethany. All day long." Great, now *my* appetite was gone. "Yes. It took me an entire day to find his name and reversing it. Just to do that, and *be* sure, cost me another day to recharge." I scowled at him. "Magic—*my* kind of magic comes with a price, using my magic too much, knocks me out." He continued to stand there and look at me like I wasn't even speaking. I sighed again. "His name is *Leone*." I waved my hand at the door. "What's his face said that was one of the royal brothers." I pointed a finger at him. "Are *you* sure they'll trade Erin for *him*?" A look of what may be described in a comic book as 'pure evil' appeared on his face. It was creepy, to say the least.

"Oh, they'll trade one of their brothers for anyone we say." He grinned. "Tomorrow we'll move you to the other side so you can draw him in."

I shrugged. "Sure. Just as long as I get Erin back, I'll," I made quotes marks in the air, "draw him in." Dropping my hands to the table, I gave him my best 'go away' look and held it, hoping he'd go be creepy in someone else's face.

He nodded and then turned to walk out of the room.

I exhaled, letting my shoulders sag. The sooner I was rid of that guy, the better it would be. Looking back at the plate,

I picked up the sandwich again. I wasn't hungry now, but I knew if I didn't keep up my strength, I'd never get Erin back.

Taking a bite, I chewed it slowly. It was like chewing cardboard, no flavor at all. I looked at the drab colored walls of the wrecked building they had some of us in. Talk about no flavor, this crumbling place had seen better days.

Pausing with the juice bottle raised to my mouth, I checked to see if Leone was still sleeping. He was and I was happy about that. I took a few sips and picked up the bread again. A mesmerizing spell could almost be left on autopilot when the person was sleeping, taking very little effort. But when he was awake, it took every ounce of my energy to stay in his head. If he hadn't had a weak moment, I never would have gotten in to begin with, so there was no way I was losing it and starting all over again. Usually when doing this spell, the person was within sight—I still didn't know how I'd managed to without even having a visual target, but somehow, I had.

I didn't know where we were going. The *other side* didn't tell me much. Other side of the city, other side of the lake? Who knew? If it was closer to him, it would take no time at all to draw this Leone into the trap creepo and his friends had been working on. I frowned at my juice bottle, I didn't have any more details than that. I should be asking more questions. Just like I should have dragged Erin out of here when she'd brought me to some of them. Any and every sixth sense alarm had been going off when she did. The warning bells in my head, a feeling of dread in my stomach, my skin crawling, and just about every other descriptive phrase that meant 'run the other way '.

These people were lunatics and should all be locked up. And *what* was with the weird colored contacts these people used? Sure, getting a bit freaky for a rave or party was doable, but they did it for no reason at all. To add to their complete weirdness, half of them were deep into medieval roleplay and dressed like they should be running a dungeon.

This crap about bringing down the gate, or wall, or whatever they called it, to allow people to cross over... I snorted out loud. Pretty insane. Dropping what was left of the sandwich, I rubbed my temples. My head had a dull ache that wasn't going to go away until this was over. Grabbing the juice, I got up and walked to the corner where my cot was. Laying down was the only way I could maintain contact when he woke up. If I tried standing, my legs would just give out and I'd do a face plant on the floor.

I thought of Erin for a .moment. She was going to owe me for a long, *long* time after this. Setting the juice on the crate, I sat down and rolled my shoulders. "Okay, Leone, lets pick up the intensity a bit." I lay on my back and looked at the cracked ceiling, that I knew every mark on now. "What am I saying to you today?" I closed my eyes, "not that it matters, all you want is me out of your head." I felt bad, but there were no other options.

Chapter One

I stood there staring at Davis, some creeper named Herman, and some big sweaty, bald guy whose name I couldn't remember. The bald one stood there watching the other two walk around the room waving their hands in the air. Usually, I was the strangest person in the room. I mean I could do magic, and that just wasn't something you ran around telling people. These guys here were mages and aside from waving their arms around like they were guiding planes to land...I really didn't know what it was they could do.

I glanced out the window and left them to do their thing in the bedroom. They'd already done their little dance in the hall and bathroom. I decided I was wasting my time watching and hoping they'd do something to jazz me. We'd *crossed over* last night and after I threw up, I realized we'd actually teleported. To where? No idea. A tiny little house in the middle of nowhere, was all I knew.

When my brain wasn't throbbing from staying connected to Leone, I'd have to find out a lot more about that. Imagine being able to get from one end of the city to the other without riding buses or subways full of people crammed together. Wouldn't that be something?

Lifting my arm, I looked at the strange watch thing they'd told me to keep on. When I asked what would happen if I didn't, they told me 'bad things', so I was wearing it.

"Are you sure he's coming out this morning?"

Davis practically yelled in my ear. Scared the crap out of me. I turned and stepped back, putting some space between us. "Yes. He'll be up shortly."

He nodded like a bobble-head. "Good. Draw him to you, then we'll sedate him to get him inside."

"And then what?" I watched the other two go out to the kitchen.

"Don't worry about that. All you have to do is stay here with him until we call you with the time for the trade."

I crossed my arms over my chest. "How am I supposed to make him stay here?"

He waved me off like I was an idiot. "He won't be able to leave the house."

My brain was prodding me to ask more, but right now I just wanted to get away from these guys. "I'm going outside to find somewhere to get comfortable before he wakes up."

"Fine, fine. Just let us know when he's close."

I watched him go to the kitchen. Shaking my head, I went out the door and then stopped and looked around. Endless fields, no matter what direction I looked. Turning I started walking to the one and only tree beside the house. Whoever lived here, they clearly didn't like people—or anything.

Sitting down, I leaned back against the rough bark and tried to relax. Staying tethered to Leone since we'd teleported had been a lot easier. I don't know where he lived, but he was much closer than before.

"Okay, Leone, time to wake up. Let's get this done so we can both get back to our regularly scheduled lives."

Not that I had a phenomenal life to return to. After bailing on my job when Erin was taken, I was definitely unemployed—which was no big deal. Being a cashier at the supermarket wasn't exactly my dream job. I had two weeks to come up with rent or Erin and I were homeless. Our one-

and-a-half-bedroom apartment wasn't the Ritz, but it was a roof over our heads. The creativity of calling a one bedroom with a room the size of a closet a one and half bedroom still got me.

I blew out a breath to focus. Maybe Leone's life was a little more interesting than mine. Closing my eyes, I reached for him. Suggesting he should wake up now. It was a beautiful day today. Perfect weather. Great time to get out for some fresh air…

I stood in the door listening to the commotion. Something crashed and hit the floor. I cringed at another sound that sounded like a yelp of pain.

"Did you give him the proper dose?" The bald one asked, sounding like he was doing some serious straining.

To me, it sounded like they were wrestling. Then again Leone turned out to be some kind of giant. I hadn't expected that at all. His thoughts and persona, internally, didn't come off as some sort of he-man body-builder.

"I gave him a full dose." That was Davis.

"Give him…." Creeper dude grunted, "*more.*"

Hurried footsteps echoed the hall. Davis came running into the room and opened his bag. He glanced at me, a panicked look on his face. "Come and help us."

I jolted like he'd slapped me. "Do what? Get trampled by a giant when I get in the way?" I'd always felt like my body had forgotten to grow. At five feet tall, there was no way I was going to try to help them 'tame the beast'.

He filled a syringe from the little bottle. "No. I'm going to give him more sedative. We need a sample of his blood."

"For?" Warning bells were chiming in my head again.

"Proof it's him we have."

As far as proof went, that was solid. I guess the one thing you can't fake would be someone's blood.

He held out a small vial and another needle. "Take these, stay out of the way until he's more compliant."

I snorted as I took them. "Good luck with that." I was really feeling like this was a bad plan, but still followed him to the bedroom.

The room was wrecked from the four of them wrestling. Leone had been groggy when they carried him in, but he was wide awake now.

I stood in the door as the three of them tried to hold him still so Davis could drug him again.

Baldy went flying into a wall as Leone snarled and shoved him with one arm. The Herman guy was trying to hold his other arm, unsuccessfully. Leone raised it up and Herman's feet left the floor, as he dangled from it.

If this was the drugged version of this man, how many did it take when he was alert? My mouth was probably hanging open—but seriously this guy was a brute.

Using his shoulder, Leone knocked Davis back again. Swinging he caught Baldy in the jaw. I stood there, eyes wide, waiting to see if he hit the floor from the force of that blow.

"Bastard, Davis," Leone growled.

Davis had gotten close enough to stab him and empty the contents of the syringe into him.

A few seconds later, Leone shook his head like he was trying to clear it. The three men dove on him and down he went. The cracking of the little table by the bed filled the silence in the room.

"Now." Davis looked over his shoulder at me.

I rushed in and held out the needle to him. There was no way I was sticking that in anyone.

Leone moaned and tied to swing his arm, but it ended up giving Davis the access he needed when Herman grabbed on and held it.

Leone kicked out when Davis started to draw his blood, I stepped back further.

Getting up, Davis came over. "Here." He nodded to the vial I held.

I pulled the stopper and held it out for him. He started emptying the blood into it. Leone kicked out again and bumped Davis, who squirted blood on my hand.

"Uh, watch it with the bodily fluids." I handed him the vial and wiped my hand on my jeans. Looking around him, the other two were lifting the rest of Leone's body onto the small bed. He didn't exactly fit. "Now what?" I looked back to Davis who stood looking at the vial of blood.

"He can't leave the area from the bathroom to the bedroom, so all you have to do is watch and feed him."

I nodded. "I can do that." I looked at Leone and again and the feelings of guilt started to hit me. "How-how long do you think?"

Davis glanced to Baldy and then looked back to me. "We're supposed to give them two days to panic and try to find him, then deliver the message and blood."

"Try to find him? What if they do?" My heart was beating so hard inside my chest I felt like a cartoon character-where you could *see* it beating.

"Don't worry," Herman said pushing past us, "this house is so well cloaked even people that know it's here can't find it."

I followed him. "Does that wear off?" This would teach me for not asking questions *before* I agreed to do things. If the people looking for Leone were even half the size he was… I would not stand a chance.

He shook his head, then stopped and shrugged. "In about fifty years."

I smirked, feeling relieved. "Okay. So-so, two days, no biggie."

Baldy came in wiping the sweat off his face. "Kitchen is fully stocked for you. We'll call you as soon as we have a time."

They headed to the door.

"Okay. See you in a few days."

They left without another word.

I closed the door and locked it. "Jerks." Turning, I leaned back against the door. The silence was a bit eerie after the last few weeks of being surrounded by the contact-wearing-role-playing crew. "So, Bethany, what would you say is the weirdest moment in your life?"

Pushing away from the door I went to check the kitchen. "Well, there was that time I was in an invisible house with an unconscious giant…" I nodded and opened the fridge. It was full. At least in all this bizarre crap, I'd fallen in with people that liked to eat. After too many times of living on gross handouts from soup kitchens and food banks—I wasn't going to complain.

Closing it, I looked toward the bedroom wondering how long he'd be out. The next few days were going to be awkward. I should check on him, right? They didn't exactly measure the dose they pumped into him. Wouldn't that be the worst move ever if they killed the hostage needed to get my friend back?

I looked around for a weapon and then stopped and shook my head. "Stupid, you *are* the weapon." With my hands raised in front of me, I walked cautiously to the bedroom. I stopped in the door. He was still out. His large chest was rising and falling. So, still alive. I glanced down at my own petite one and felt a bit inadequate. So what if his pecs were bigger than my breasts, he was a giant right? His everything was bigger than me. I stepped closer and looked down at him. His hand could probably wrap around my whole head.

With my hands on my hips I checked over the rest of him. He had red hair, not the bright orange-red, but a deep rust color. My own was a brighter, deep red, more like dark fire. His was cut into spikes of red all over his head. I wondered if it was meant to be that way, or if it was a brush cut left too long. Whatever, the style suited his jaw of steel. I wondered what color his eyes were. It had been a little hard to see them while he was wrestling three guys—and winning, for the most part.

He made sound and I almost tripped, stumbling backward. "Great, now you're turning into a creeper." Spinning on my heel, I went back out to the kitchen. For the first time in two weeks my head wasn't pulsing in time with my heartbeat. I could eat and rest without having to hurry back into his head.

They'd stocked the fridge well at least, so that was a bonus. One thing I appreciated was food. I'd gone too often without it, or very little of it. Most would binge after living the way I had, but I savoured the abundance and would make it last. Life could take odd turns without warning, and it was better to always be prepared.

I found a pan and figured out what to make. Scrambled eggs, couldn't go wrong there. As I waited for them to cook, I stared off into space.

That nagging feeling was back, the one that kept trying to tell me there was something wrong in all of this. Sighing, I stirred the eggs around. If I were being honest, I'd known from the moment I agreed, that it was all wrong. I didn't have a choice. If not for Erin getting me off the streets eleven years ago when I was fifteen, I'd probably be dead by now. I still remember when she offered to let me stay in that crumbling building she'd been squatting in. It was condemned and falling down, but it was dry and out of the weather. Not to mention, it kept me away from all the weirdos on the streets. We'd sealed it up, so no rodents could get in and that had been our home for a year. When they'd torn it down, we worked odd jobs, saved money, then lied about our age and found the one and a half bedroom apartment. I couldn't abandon her when she needed me.
Scraping the eggs onto the plate, I set the pan in the sink and sat down. Davis and his crew weren't telling me the truth, I knew that, but no one was getting hurt. Leone would be home again in a few days and Erin would be free. Then I was done with all of this, and if Erin thought for even a millisecond I was letting her see any of these douchebags again, she was in for a really big surprise.

Chapter Two

A loud sound startled me awake. Half-rolling, half-falling off the couch, I scrambled up and stumbled to the bedroom. Leone was awake and laying there with his hand over his face. The sound that had woken me was the leg of the small bed collapsing.

"What the hell," he murmured and rubbed his hand over his forehead, "am I hurt?" Holding his hand over his face he flexed it a few times. "Where am I? Was there an accident? Raf? Michael?"

I stood froze in the doorway, not sure if I should answer his questions or just tiptoe back out before he noticed me. "You'll be okay." I said quietly. "The drugs are probably making your head a bit wonky."

He turned his head and squinted at me. "Drugs?" Squeezing his eyes shut he blew out a breath. "For what?" Sitting slowly, he clutched his head between his hands and rested his elbows on his knees.

I opened my mouth to tell him, and then shut it. Probably not a good idea to explain that part. "Would you like some water or... something?" He continued to sit there, not moving or speaking. "Leone?"

His head snapped up and dark eyes glared at me. He blinked and then shook his head and looked at me again.

He'd just discovered the voice that had said his name a thousand times in his head, wasn't a hallucination.

"I'm a real live girl." I nodded at him.

The look of confusion faded, and his dark brown eyes locked on me with hatred, very plainly at me. "What the hell is going on?"

A shiver of dread moved down my spine. "I can explain." I offered, not sounding nearly as confident as I'd hoped to.

Moving cautiously, he turned and swung his legs off the bed. He must have been dizzy, because he paused and didn't stand. "You can explain why you've been fucking around in my head every day?" Hate-filled eyes looked to me again. He examined me from head to toe. "I don't know you."

I shook my head, not feeling as if there was anything I could say.

He exhaled slowly and braced his hands on his knees and stood up slowly.

I raised my hands from my side, just in case I needed to buy myself some time if he came at me. Pausing, I looked at them. Why couldn't I feel my magic? It dawned on me the mages hadn't used their power on him but had wrestled him instead. Whatever they'd done to this room to keep him here must block magic too. Well crap. I backed up a few feet when he stood to his full height.

His chest rose and fell a few times as he adjusted to being upright and then he looked at me again. "Answers." He snarled. "*Now.*"

I stepped back again when he took a few test steps toward me. Looking to my left, I tried to gauge how far the protection worked. "Just-just go slow. If you go down, there's no way I can get you up." I motioned up and down my small form. "I don't know what they gave you." He kept moving in my direction. I shuffled back further. I was almost past the bathroom door now.

"They? Where are we?"

His tone sent goosebumps all over me, not the happy kind but most definitely the run-away kind. "I don't know." I checked to see if my magic was back, it wasn't. I stepped back again.

"What side are we on?" He glanced to the watch thing on my wrist.

I stepped back two steps. "I don't know." Still no magic.

"When are *they* coming back?"

The drugs must have been wearing off fast, he was at his full height now. At least a foot and a half taller than I was. "I-I don't know that either." I felt a familiar tingle in my hands and almost cried in relief.

He stopped and braced a hand on either side of the wall. He probably had the spins. That stance made him look even larger. I couldn't reach both walls along the hall at the same time. "What *do* you know?"

Leone looked down at me and I froze, unable to think for a moment. The past few weeks, no months, suddenly seemed like the dumbest plan I'd ever had in my life—and I'd had some pretty stupid moments. "They're going to trade you…"

He growled out like a wounded animal and smashed his fist against the wall. The sound of cracking plaster and crumbling followed.

Shit.

"Son of a…" He looked back to me. "Move," he growled between clenched teeth.

I stepped back and hoped, like really, *really* hoped that Herman guy knew his stuff, because if their magic didn't stop him, there was no way on earth I was going to even try. I loved Erin, but I was attached to being alive almost more than as I was to her.

Leone took two steps and then purple sparks were flying as he hit whatever they'd erected to keep him contained. "What the hell." He smacked it with his hand creating more sparks, then glared at me. "Take it down."

I opened my mouth, then lifted my hands. "I didn't do it."

He gave me a blank look. "You've been fucking around in my head, don't tell me you're not a mage and can't remove this."

Frowning. I gave him my own hard glare. "I am not a mage. From what I've seen those that are should be dropped in some deep hole and forgotten."

He made a noise that could have been one of agreement, but I wasn't sure. "So you're a telepath?"

My eyes opened as wide as they could. "A what?" I shook my head. "No." I hugged my arms around my waist trying to stop my stomach from churning with that feeling of dread. "I have magic... skills." Trying to explain it never sounded right.

Huffing out a breath he put a large hand to his forehead and squeezed either temple. "Are you still fucking around in my head? I can't think straight."

"No. No, I-I'm not." I went to step forward and remembered the crumbling wall. "It's probably from whatever they gave you. I don't think a body is meant to get two doses..." His hand dropped, and he gave me an unamused look. "I can," I motioned over my shoulder, "make coffee or get you some juice?"

He closed his eyes and sighed. "Fine." His eyes popped open again. "*Then* you're going to explain what *the fuck* is going on."

I opened my mouth, then closed it and nodded as I backed down the rest of the hallway.

Going around the corner into the kitchen I leaned on the table and dropped my head down. This was a great idea. Leave the expendable tiny woman to deal with the pissed off giant. "You are such a moron, Beth." I whispered to myself and then straightened up to make coffee.

Carrying the coffee and a bottle of juice I stopped in the hall where he'd hit the invisible barrier. Did I want to go across it?

Leone was standing in the room looking out the window. He gave me a distasteful glance. "Don't worry, as much as I'd like to crush your throat in my hand I won't. You have answers I need."

I didn't move. "That's reassuring." The look I gave him said the opposite.

He waved his hand at me. "Set it on the floor."

Deciding that was the best solution, I knelt and set it on the floor just inside the barrier. Getting up, I went back to the kitchen and got my cup.   When I turned the corner, he stood in the middle of the hall holding the cup. "It's black." I said, sitting on the floor.

He took a sip and said nothing for several minutes.

I stared into my cup, not knowing how to start a conversation in this circumstance.

"What's your name?"

Startled I looked up at him.

He pointed to his head, "you've been in my head every moment for weeks, I think telling me your name is the least you can do."

He did have a point. "Beth." I answered quickly.

His dark eyes stayed on mine. "Okay, Elizabeth…"

I shook my head. "Not Elizabeth. Bethany."

"Fine, Beth*any*, why are we here?" His jaw clenched a few times. "I'm the prize to be traded for that scum Marcus. I got that part."

I set the cup down and crossed my arms. "And Erin. I don't give a crap about that freak Marcus."

He gave me a surprised look. "The Witch?"

I shrugged, "my friend. They told me the royals, or whoever, would exchange one of their brothers for my friend and that idiot she's been duped by."

It was his turn to stare into the dark liquid he held. "That's not going to happen."

"What? Why not?" I stood up, unable to stay sitting now.

He took a big gulp of the coffee. I winced when he should have by how hot it was. When he lowered the cup, he had a bland expression on his face. "Because the royals, *my* family, will find me and there won't be any exchange."

I snorted, "Sorry to burst your bubble *Leone Royal*, but I've been told no one will be able to track you down." The look he gave me had me replaying what I'd said to see if it was anything to warrant the strange expression on his face.

"You have no idea, do you?" His jaw clenched.

Crossing my arms, I tried to look bored. "About?" I flung my hand out to emphasize he should continue.

"Who I am, what your involved with, *who* you're working with?" He tipped the cup back and emptied it, then bent and set it on the floor.

I just stood there, feeling stupid because he was right. I didn't know. Most of what I thought I knew was from me fitting the pieces together—which had never been my strong suit. "Okay then, enlighten me." I snapped, clinging to the hope that I had done the right thing.

He stepped closer but stopped before he reached the barrier. With a smug look on his face he glared down at me. "My last name is not Royal, I am part of the *royal* family—" he titled his head, "like my father was a king and mother a queen."

If there was ever a moment I looked stupefied, now would have been it. "You're royalty, like *royalty*? I thought it was a family name or gang or…" Oh my God I'd high-jacked a prince's mind!

He shook his head slowly.

I spun around and looked at the doorway to the kitchen, because I just couldn't stand there with what I knew to be the stupidest expression on my face, with him watching me.

"Do you know what they're trying to do?"

I didn't want to answer. I wanted to grab my phone, walk out the door, and never look back. I shook my head, only because I didn't know where I was or how to get home. "Some crap about bringing down a wall and freeing a nation, or something." I sighed and slumped my shoulders. "I just wanted to get my friend back and get the hell away from them."

His quiet laugh was brief. "Well, at least you know you shouldn't be near them."

I turned and looked at him. "Ya think?" I rolled my eyes at him. "They all gave me the creeps. I have no idea what Erin seen in them."

"That's not what I meant." He shrugged, "but yes, they're the sort that should never see the light of day."

I frowned. "What do you mean?"

Crossing his arms over that large chest, he looked at the floor. "Your *food* to most of them." He said in a low, scary as hell tone then lifted his chin to look at me.

His eyes were red!

Red!

There was no way he had put contacts in. I would have seen it. I stumbled backwards and almost tripped over my own feet. "They're not contacts." I whispered aloud.

He blinked and looked at me again and his eyes were brown.

"What the..." I felt like my eyes were bulging out of my head and didn't care.

Tilting his head, he studied me. "They kept you in the dark." He glanced to the bottle of juice and then bent and picked it up. Opening it, he watched me. "That thing on your wrist," he motioned with his chin, "tells me we're on my side..."

Something inside me snapped. "Side. Of. What?" I waved my hands around, pacing in a little circle. "No one explains that—*ever.*"

"Your *friend* Erin didn't explain anything? She knew enough. She tried to kill my brothers and I."

I stopped and looked at him. He wasn't joking. I closed my eyes. "That stupid staff Marcus gave her." I whispered. Opening my eyes, I looked at him, without really seeing him, "I could feel the power in it. It was wrong, I told her to burn the damn thing. It was like she was possessed, or something, whenever she was around Marcus."

"Well she didn't." He gave me a smug look, "she'll never see the light of day again."

I rushed forward and jabbed him in the chest with my hand. "She better be all right." I jabbed him again. "I didn't do all this only to find out she's dead." My words sunk in. I covered my mouth and looked up at him, waiting to hear if my friend was dead or alive.

His dark eyes studied me briefly. "She's alive."

The breath I'd been holding whooshed out in relief. Then I realized I'd crossed the barrier and turned to go back.

He grabbed my arm and held me, so I couldn't.

I spun back to him. "You are so lucky I can't use my magic right now."

"Oh?" He leaned down so his face was an inch from mine. Anger etched his face. "What would you do? Dance around in my fucking head some more?"

I jerked my arm trying to get out of his grasp. "No, I'd knock you on your ass."

He snorted and released me.

Like a coward I jumped to the other side of the invisible line again. "Don't ever touch me again."

Leone stepped as close as he could without setting off the purple sparks. "After all the time we've spent together inside my head, I think that gives me the right to do whatever I want where you're concerned."

"I had no choice." I spat at him.

"You did." He clenched his teeth. "There is *always* a choice."

"Yeah, easy to say if you're royalty. I'm not that lucky." I wanted to scream in frustration.

Sliding down the wall, Leone squatted with his back against it. "Can you bring down this barrier or not?"

I looked at him and then the air between us. "Even if I could, you are my ticket to getting Erin…"

He shook his head slowly. "Not going to happen. Accept that now, and let's find a way out of this."

I slid down the opposite wall and stared at him.

"Get me out of here and I will take you to see the witch." His tone was soft, and he seemed sincere. "You have my word."

I raised one eye brow. "Your word means nothing to me..."

Reaching, he pulled a chain over his head and held it out to me. "This is my royal amulet. It is mine and only mine, and the all of Alterealm knows it." He raised his hand further. "Take it. My entire family will honor any pact I make with you if you hold that."

Hesitantly I reached across and took it from his hand. Holding it in front of my face I studied it. It was two swords crossed with a sun on one side and moon on the other.

"I'm the enforcer." He offered.

I looked at him then back to the pendant dangling in my hand. "And this means you have to take me to see Erin?"

"Yes. You have my word." He shrugged, "I have several brothers that would kick my ass if I didn't keep my word after it's given."

Just as I knew those with Marcus were insane, something told me Leone was telling the truth. "Okay." Getting up, I tucked the chain and pendant into my jeans pocket. Backing away from where I had sat, I raised my hands. "You might want to get back." I shrugged. "I have no idea if I can do this. I don't do spells with waving my hands around and stuff, like the mages."

Leone stood up and went and stood in the bedroom door. "Wait, will it work from that side?"

I took a deep breath. "Has to, my magic won't work if I cross it."

He nodded. "Okay. Do it."

Closing my eyes, I connected with what I called my spark. As I opened my eyes, I raised my hands up and watched the arc bounce between my hands. It was like a fire, I'd always thought it was so cool that I could manipulate it enough it would look like an explosion of reds and yellow flames, an energy.

Stepping toward the barrier, I lowered my hands until there were purple sparks combining with my red ones. I pushed and tried to force the barrier to part. My hands started shaking. Stepping back, I dropped them, and the flames were gone. I looked up to Leone. "Move in case these go through."

He nodded and stepped out to stand in the bathroom doorway.

Taking a step back, I blew out a breath and reached for it again. Bringing my hands almost together in front of my body I moved them, watching the bright ball form. With a quick jerk I sent it at the barrier. It hit it with enough force it sounded like a small explosion. The floor beneath my feet shook. Gritting my teeth, I did it again and this time the blow-back almost knocked me off my feet. I was using a lot of power and knew I'd pay for it, but I gave it one more attempt. This time I did get knocked back and landed on my butt because of my weakened state.

I looked to Leone. "That's all I've got until I recharge a bit." I huffed out a breath and dragged myself over to lean against the wall.

Leone came back to the barrier and sat down. "I get the knocking me on my ass line now."

I shrugged. "I don't know what this is they've done, but my blast should have broken though." I slid over to be close enough to pick up my coffee. Energy was energy, regardless of temperature.

Leone was quiet for a few moments. "Your transporter device, it is just a stabilizer, or do you have buttons?"

I gave him a 'huh' look.

"Does it open?"

Setting the coffee down I lifted my wrist and looked at it. "I don't think so." I pried on the edges gently and then shook my head. "I don't see any buttons." Sighing, I turned my wrist over and undid it and tossed it toward him. "You look."

He scrambled to his knees and caught it, then gave me a horrified look, concern etched on his face. "Are you okay?"

I sighed. "I feel like a zombie from using that much magic, but after a nap and snack, I'll be fine."

He gave me a look and sat down again, glancing from me to the device I'd tossed at him.

"Davis and his idiot friends said," I made quotes in the air, "'bad things would happen' if I took that off." I huffed out a breath. "Is *anything* I've been told the truth?"

He turned the device over in his hand. "Actually, in that they weren't lying. Very few people can cross over and survive without wearing one of these."

I gaped at him. "I could have died taking that off just now?" I put my hand over my fast beating heart. "Should I put it back on?"

Leone looked at me for a long moment, the silence almost suffocating. Finally, he shook his head. "It's not necessary, for you." His blank look turned to a confused one. "Your eyes didn't change color when you were using your magic."

I studied him. "And that means?"

"You're completely human." He whispered so low I barely heard him.

I snorted, "Uh, last time I checked, yeah."

"I wasn't sure, whatever they gave me messed with my sense of smell for a bit." Dropping the device, he covered his face and started mumbling. "Could this get any more fucked up?" He stood up and paced down the hall. "That's fucking brilliant. Trap me somewhere with a *human* female." He raised his face and looked at the ceiling. "What could I have possibly done to piss off the fates this much?"

I pulled myself up, so I was sitting straighter. "You want me to come back and explain after you're done having your meltdown?"

He turned and glared at me. "You're going to have to get help."

"I have my phone. We can call someone?"

His look brightened, then he shook his head. "I don't know any numbers, because they're in my phone. Which is on my horse. Do you have him? My horse."

I shook my head.

"Can you call someone?"

I raised my eyebrows. "I don't know where we are." I motioned in the direction of the kitchen. "I see nothing for miles outside. Fields, a few trees, just nothing."

Standing there with his hands on his hips he closed his eyes. "How long was I out?" He looked into the room toward the window.

"A few hours."

He nodded slowly. "Okay, so it's hasn't been a full day." He shrugged. "Porting out probably won't work. They're blocking magic. Probably using some kind of cloak too…"

I had no idea what he was talking about as he continued murmuring quietly to himself.

"When are they supposed to negotiate with my family?"

"Two days they said."

He started to pace. "From now. or is today day one?"

I shrugged. "From today I think."

"Fuck. Three days. I can't do three days. I don't even think I can go two." He stopped moving. "Shit. I'm screwed." He glanced to me then shook his head. "You might be as well. Fuck." He growled his annoyance. "Did they tell you to pick me or was it random?"

I looked at him for a moment trying to decide what his problem was. "They brought me a bunch of stuff to use to try to zero in on one person." I gave him a hard look. "I couldn't even get in to any but your head, and that almost knocked me out trying."

His brows drew together, and he looked at me for a moment, then clenched his jaw. "So they don't know, it's totally random, and my dumb fucking luck that it's me here." Leone went into the bedroom and stopped in the door with his back to me. "Fuck." He said again.

"Am I supposed to have any clue what you're talking about?"

He spun around and smirked at me. "What," he waved his hand around, "did they tell you to do for the next few days while you guarded me?"

I laughed. "I'm not *guarding* you."

"Whatever. What did they say?" He lifted his hand in a regal way to tell me it was my turn to speak.

"To make you food?" I'm sure my confusion was showing on my face.

He looked at the floor then to me. "They used those words?"

I thought back to what Davis had said. "Um, all you have to do is watch him and feed him."

Leone snorted. "Yeah." He nodded and walked into the bedroom.

I stood up, then felt light-headed and leaned against the wall. "Leone? What am I missing here?"

Coming back to the door, he gave me a curious look, probably because I was holding up the wall.

I waved it off. "Just wobbly after using magic. I'll go get some juice, then you can fill in more blanks, because as usual I've missed a lot." I turned and walked to the kitchen. When I got there, I grabbed an orange juice and sat in the closest chair. My head was pounding, and this day wasn't turning out to be what I'd hoped for. I hadn't known it was going to be three days before this was over. I thought they'd contact them as soon as they had Leone. I reached up and pulled the scrunchie from my hair and then immediately regretting it when all I could see was my hair hanging in front of my face. Brushing it back, I took another drink, and then grabbed an apple off the table and got up.

He stood right where I left him, looking off into space. "So." I stopped at the spot of the barrier and looked at him. "What are you freaking out about?" I cringed at my own words. "Besides being held against your will, obviously."

"Obviously." He said in a droll tone. Huffing out a breath he walked slowly toward me.

It sent chills up my spine, he moved like a predator.

"Your random," he motioned to his head, "mind whatever…"

"Mesmerizing." I supplied for him and got a blank stare in return.

"The problem with your random mesmerizing stunt is, it has landed you here with," he held up one finger, "one, a younger royal that can't go three days without feeding." He put up two fingers, "two, a younger royal that can't feed off humans." Three fingers. "Three, your human."

The only one I understood was the last. "I don't…"

"That's the problem." He stopped just on the other side of the barrier and looked down at me. "You have *no* idea what you've walked into." Sighing, he rubbed his hand across his forehead. "By mid-day tomorrow I'm going to be," he paused for a moment, a look of contemplation on his face, "bordering on hard to manage." He nodded, "by tomorrow night I will not be pleasant to be around… and you *cannot* cross this invisible ward they've placed right here," He tapped his hand lightly on the barrier, causing sparks to fly. "After that it gets worse." His brown eyes searched my face.

I shook my head. "Still not…"

"Come over here." He took a step back.

Raising my eyebrows, I looked at him.

He raised his hands up. "I will not hurt you. You are my only way out of this."

Biting my lip, I weighed the pros and cons of stepping across. Pro, he was going to explain something, and considering he'd filled in more blanks in the half hour then Davis ever did… Con, I'd be within his reach in case he was some whack-job like the rest of them.

Sighing, I stepped across the stupid barrier and stood in front of him. Something moved through his eyes as he looked down at me, but I couldn't make out what the look meant. For a second, I thought he looked afraid of me, which was all wrong, and probably me projecting my own fear to think dumb things.

"I'm going to try to explain this, without scaring you." He paused his jaw stiffened, "you said something about contacts when my eyes changed."

I nodded. His voice was quiet, almost soothing, as long as I didn't think of how it sounded when he was angry.

"I'm assuming if you dealt with mages, you've seen purple eyes…"

I nodded again, almost mesmerized myself by his quiet tone.

"Okay, mages are purple and there are other eye colors where I'm from… red, yellow, white, green…"

I frowned. "Where you're from?"

He held up his hand. "We'll get there in a moment. I'm trying to stay calm and not remember you are the reason I am here."

My lips formed an o, my eyes wider, I nodded. "Different colored eyes. Got it."

"Red," he lowered his lashes just enough I couldn't see his eyes for a second, then he grasped my arm lightly and looked at me, "like mine are now, means we feed on essence."

His eyes were a deep, blood red, and appeared to glow as well. My heart raced, but I was determined not to run the other way. I swallowed the lump in my throat.

"Red eyes also come with," he opened his mouth, "fangs."

I did try to step back when I saw he wasn't lying, but his grip tightened just enough that I couldn't. Fangs. Glowing red eyes and fangs. What. The. Hell.

"Are you good?"

I shook my head and couldn't find a word to describe how not good I was.

Inhaling through his nose, he cringed like he was in pain and then squeezed his eyes shut. "Don't move. Don't speak." He said softly. Blowing out a breath, he looked like he was trying to stay strong. Which made no sense. After several deep breaths, he opened his eyes and they were brown again.

"For years I have struggled against an addiction to human essence…"

I knew I probably looked like a deer in headlights right then, but the pieces were fitting together about him freaking out, and I really wasn't liking the picture forming in my head. "Oh." Was the only thing I said.

"Yes. Oh." He nodded.

"I-I don't know what essence is—but I'm thinking if fangs go with…bad for me, huh?"

He tilted his head, "in this case, bad for both of us." He released my arm and put his hands in his pockets. "I don't want to feed off you…"

I was okay with that.

Rubbing his hand on the back of his neck, he gave me a hard look.

"I sense a but." I stared up at him.

"I can't go without feeding for three days."

I pointed to the kitchen. "There's plenty of food, will that," I clasped the apple in both hands in front of my chest, "help?"

He shook his head. "Yes, we eat as well, but that's not feeding."

"Oh." I was fitting more pieces together, I couldn't break the barrier, he couldn't feed off me—which was okay on that front, but apparently not. "What happens if you don't feed?"

"What happens if you starve?" He asked back in the same tone I'd used.

"Right." He could be ill, and then the trade might now happen. The idea of him dying, of me being here with a dead giant when they came back, that scared me more than the idea of his fangs biting. "What," I couldn't believe I was asking this, "what is essence, I mean the fangs…"

"I don't drink your blood." He looked bored, which meant I wasn't the first to ask.

I was relieved to hear that. "Uh, but you still bite… with the fangs…"

He inclined his head. "Yes."

"Oh." I wrapped my arms around my waist. "Right, cuz' why would you have *fangs* if you didn't? That wouldn't be evolutionarily necessary." I nodded, knowing I was babbling. I licked my lips, nerves kicking in all over again. "So—*if* as a last resort you *had* to feed, uh, what…" He wasn't moving, hadn't blinked in at least a minute…

Reaching, he brushed my hair back from my neck and then tilted my jaw gently moving my head to the side. Leaning down, closer, his breath brushed against my skin at the base of my neck. "Right here."

Vampire was my first thought, but he'd assured me he didn't drink blood. Was I being conned—again?

"Bethany?" He whispered.

The apple I held dropped to the floor. "Yes?"

"Move back across the line." His voice was shaky.

I immediately stepped back not one, but two steps. When I looked back at him, his eyes were red. He didn't speak. I didn't speak, just stood there looking at each other. I could see his jaw clenched and wondered how close I'd just come to being bitten. The fact that it was appealing for a quick second, scared the hell out of me. I swallowed and then remembered my apple, which was now halfway down the hall in the wrong direction. "Essence, got it." I said quietly. He still hadn't moved. "I need food. Do you want me to make you something and then we can," I waved my hand around, "figure this out?"

"Sure."

That was it, he continued to stand there staring at me. Nodding, I backed up, "I'll be back shortly." I turned and went to the kitchen then sat down on the floor against the cupboard. I looked at my phone on the table and thought about calling Davis and telling him to find someone else to come and watch Leone. I didn't know what had just happened, and I didn't want to know. If I did that though, then how would I get Erin back? If what Leone said was right, my best bet to get to her was stick with him. So many if's…

Getting up, I opened the fridge to figure out what to make. I hoped he wasn't a fussy eater, because I wasn't the greatest in the kitchen, by anyone's standards.

Chapter Three

When the sun was bright enough that I wished for sunglasses, I knew I'd been walking for a few hours. It was day three. No call from Davis. For all I knew they were never coming back.

Days one and two also involved walking in other directions yet thinking of nothing.

Leone hadn't been lying about his disposition, it had deteriorated rapidly. When I'd returned yesterday, he'd picked up the bed and beaten it against the wall. Needless to say, the bed didn't make it. He'd dropped down on the mattress on the floor and hadn't gotten back up again.

When he'd been sleeping for a while, I tiptoed past the barrier and left him some food, water, my phone and the biggest knife I could find in the kitchen. If Davis returned, I wanted him to have some way of defending himself.

Stopping, I turned. I'd been leaving a faint trail of magic, so I could find my way back. Then again, I could be lost out here forever. Or, worse, return without help again. I didn't want to think about either outcome. Both meant Leone may not survive, and then I would die inside, knowing I was responsible.

My feet were throbbing, legs like rubber, but I'd be in great shape after this—so that was a plus. You could walk all day in the city and never feel quite like this. Then again, there you had to stop for cars, buildings and people. Here there were endless flat fields on uneven ground. I'd almost broken my leg in a hole in the ground a while ago. At least potholes in the street weren't camouflaged by grass and weeds.

I hadn't found a single house, or even a road, the whole time. Was it possible to miss the city I thought I hated? It hadn't come to that yet, but I'd kill for a convenience store right about now for some munchies and a slushy.

I'd come upon a large herd—at least I think they're a heard, of cattle not long after I'd started walking today. I'd got excited thinking there would be a farm nearby but hadn't seen a single building. Where are all the people?

You would think after walking for three days I'd have come to terms with the information Leone had dumped on me that first night. I hadn't. There were just some things your mind rejected, and you had to force feed the information over and over, until it was accepted. Most of what he told me fell into that category.

It turns out the 'other side' is an actual freaking other realm! Which brought the whole eye color change, fangs, and extra-large people into perspective.

I stopped and stood there. I was in another realm. I still couldn't get past that. Shaking my head, I started walking again.

Leone told me to find a guard, that there would be patrols, they'd take me to his brothers—all seven of them. Seven. He had eight apparently, but one lived on my side of the other-sideness. How crazy was that, having that many brothers? I grunted when I tripped over the uneven ground. I wonder if they're all giants.

Turning around I left another magic trace. I had to be careful how much I used, or I'd have to stop and rest. The way Leone was when I left, I didn't have time to stop and take a break. I had to find him help.

I stopped again and looked at the ground. A man—was he a man? I was going to have to think of him as a regular person. Well, regular with something extra, like fangs eyes that glow red. I wasn't exactly the norm for a person either. I had sparks and energy shooting out of my hands. Right, so a *man* was trapped in a spellbound and warded house, starving to death, and couldn't get out because of me. Sighing I looked back across the field. I had to find help, I was the only chance he had.

I looked at the bottle of water I was carrying. I didn't want to bring a bag, so in all my brilliance I left with a single bottle to walk with for who knew how long. Opening it I took a tiny sip and then capped it again. I froze and then looked around. I thought I heard voices. I waited, listened, and didn't hear anything again. Great, now I was hearing things, too.

I stumbled again.

There were the voices again. Turning, I looked all around me. There were people. I'd found people. Moving quickly in case they vanished, I didn't even blink for fear I was hallucinating. As I got closer one of them stopped and looked at me. There were four teens. I'd found someone.

Three boys and a girl were all looking at me by the time I reached them. Later I'd digest the fact they were taller than I was.

"You okay, lady?" The girl asked.

I shook my head. "No, I need help. I have to find a royal guard."

The tallest boy pointed down the hill. "They patrol down there every half hour the last few days."

I turned and looked, "where down there?"

"If you go down that hill, you'll see the trail they've trampled." The girl added.

I nodded. "Okay, okay."

"Do you want us to wait with you?"

I looked to where they'd pointed. "No. No. I'll be fine."

"Okay See ya." The girl smiled, and they started going in the other direction.

I ran, almost eating dirt a few times as I slid down the slope. I almost cried when I saw the path. "Half an hour." I panted. I'd done it.

I glared at the clear wall. I'd done it all right. The royal guard had called someone when I told him I had news of Leone, and now I was standing in a large glass box. I touched it, I wasn't even sure if it was glass, but whatever it was I was surrounded. I couldn't even see out, so how it was possible to not see through clear glass, I had no idea. I paced around trying not to scream. I'd already tried magic to no avail. It was blocked in here.

Something changed on one side of my cube and a man stood looking at me through the glass. Another giant. He had long black hair and haunting grey eyes. He didn't look anything like Leone. He just stood there legs apart, arms crossed over his large chest, just looking at me like I was a bug.

I didn't know if he could hear me or not, but I didn't have time for a staring contest. "As much as I appreciate being chosen to be part of your display case Barbie dolls, I don't have time for games. I need to find Leone's brothers."

He turned his head and then two more men stood there. Twin giants. Holy crap was all I could think.

"Guys, this isn't going to help Leone. Find me someone in charge. Do you guys speak English or is all that muscle blocking off your voice boxes?" I sighed. No reaction at all.

Two women appeared and then in the span of a few moments ten pairs of eyes were staring right at me. They were talking, but I couldn't read lips. I looked for any resemblance to Leone. One had the same brown eyes, and another had the same hair color as Leone, but neither looked very approachable. The one with the I-will-kill-you-and-not-think-twice aura and the same hair color as Leone moved to the side.

"You have news of my brother?"

I actually jumped when his voice filled my cube. I nodded. "Yes." I'd found his family.

"Where are you from?"

I frowned. "Pluto, what the hell does that matter?"

He turned and again I couldn't hear them.

"Seriously?" Reaching into my pocket I pulled out the chain and pendant Leone had said everyone knew was his. Holding it in my palm, I went over to the wall and slapped my hand against it. All eyes went wide. Oh, they knew that, I thought. "Figured that would get your attention," I said just in case they could hear me. I stared at the one with Leone's eyes. "I don't have time to screw around. Leone needs help. Now."

The door to my display cube opened. The guard that had put me in here motioned for me to come out. I did, hesitantly, then went where he pointed. Into the space with those ten anxious and angry looking people. Mostly angry.

"Talk quickly," the big scary one said, then waved his hand for me to speak.

"Oh yeah, you're definitely related to him." My hands tingled, my magic must not be blocked in this room. He was huge and scary as shit. He stepped toward me. I held up my hand, sparks and all toward him. "You stay right there." I shook my head. "I don't want to hurt anyone."

Someone snorted.

A dark-haired man with a scar on his face stepped in my direction. He didn't look happy at all. "Back off, Scarface. I'm here because I need help."

I felt this pressure inside my head and raised my hands further making sure all of them could see the energy sparking from them. "Whoever is trying to mess in my head, knock it off."

"Look, honey," A tall man with a baby face and serious eyes held his hands up toward me.

"Stay there, Tarzan, we don't have time for this."

"Oh gods. Can she stay? We need this in our lives. I need this in my life." The tall twin with the goatee said, a big grin on his face.

"Excuse me?" The tall dark-haired woman with drool-worthy boots said glaring at him.

He shook his head. "Beloved, for entertainment purposes only. She knew Troy was messing in her head, Rafael is Tarzan, and she's going to hurt Victor? Come on, it's awesome!"

My nerves were winding tighter and tighter inside me. Soon I was going to start blasting anyone that moved.

A woman stepped out, she could have been a schoolgirl, wearing a backpack, and all but bounded toward me and grabbed my wrist. I was too shocked to react. "It's the daisy!" She said excitedly.

I looked at the heliopsis flower tattooed on my wrist. "Heliopsis." I said, even while knowing clarification of the flower inked in my skin wasn't really important right now.

"Cristy." The one with the scary aura said.

She dropped my wrist and hurried back to him.

"Okay." The blonde woman said with her hands raised so I could see them. "I think we've gotten off on the wrong foot. Why do you have Leone's amulet?"

I lowered my hand slightly. "It's a long story we don't have time for. He needs help. *Now*." I said slowly.

"Where is he?" The one with eyes that looked so much like Leone's asked me.

"I don't know exactly. I left a trail of magic to find my way back." They didn't even blink at that, come to think of it my sparks didn't deter them either.

The man with the scar stepped forward again, looking very hesitant. "Is he hurt?"

I shook my head. "He's being held in a house by some kind of barrier. I can't break through it."

He turned to the one with long black hair. "Go get Romulus and Clairee. Meet us at the stables."

The man turned and ran down the narrow corridor. He looked back to me and held his hands up. "I'm Michael, Leone's brother. Is he all right?"

"I don't know. He's really out of it right now. He hadn't gotten up or moved for hours so I left when it was still dark to find him help." I looked around trying to assess if I could lower my hands now. "He needs to feed," I waited to see if they understood me, "he said he won't from me…"

"Fuck." The one with the goatee wasn't joking now.

The man with the eyes like Leone's came closer and sniffed me. "She's human."

"Shit." The other twin hissed.

"How many days has it been?" The scary one asked.

I shrugged. "Since he was taken?" I felt like I needed to offer them something. "I made him food, he ate that first day, than was," I glanced to the blonde woman, "irritated after that." I looked back to Michael, "last night he just laid in the bed, and wouldn't get up, and won't let me anywhere near him."

Michael rubbed his hand down the back of his neck while his blue eyes moved up and down me. "How long will it take to get back there?"

"I don't know what time it is, but I've been walking nonstop." I dropped my hand finally. "We don't have time to waste, they said two days and they'd be back. It's three now."

"Two days?"

He didn't know what I was talking about. Davis hadn't contacted them. I nodded and took a step back knowing how the next part would go. "Yes, they were going to contact his family in two days and negotiate a trade…"

All the men rushed toward me, Michael turned, placing himself in front of me and held up his hands. "First, we find Leone, *then* we'll sort this out."

I remembered my phone. "I left him my phone. You can call him."

Michael turned, pulling his phone out and handed it to me.

I took it and with shaking hands dialled my number. I put it on speaker. It rang, once, twice, by the third time my stomach started to churn. If he didn't answer, there was going to be no placating these people glaring at the phone.

"Yeah." Leone's hushed voice came on the line.

I huffed out a relieved breath. "Leone, I got here." I told him quickly.

"Find Michael."

Michael took the phone. "She did, brother. How are you holding out?"

"Been better. Been worse." He sounded so hollow.

"We're getting Romulus and Clairee to come and get you out. Just hang in there. Call me if it gets worse…"

"Michael," there was a long silent pause, "Bethany is safe." He was panting like he was in pain. "I gave my word."

"I'm fine, Leone." I said loud enough he'd hear.

"I will ensure this, brother." Michael said in a formal way.

"Yeah, okay."

"We'll be there soon, brother." Brown eyes assured him.

"Yeah." The phone went dead.

I wanted to say 'see', then realized every pair of eyes in the room were on me.

"Can you ride a horse?" Michael asked tucking the phone into his pocket.

I gave him a wide-eyed look. "Like yee-haw, horse?"

"More like giddy up." Tarzan said walking past us. "Meet you at the stables. I'm going to get changed."

The blonde woman glared at the one twin. "Don't even think it, we're going."

The dark-haired woman nodded. "I'll go get my riding boots."

I watched most of them leave and then turned to see Michael still studying me. "This may be a bit much to ask, but I need some juice and something to eat." I shrugged. "I used a lot of magic leaving a trail to follow back, if I don't recharge I will pass out before I can get us back."

He pulled his phone out of his pocket and dialled it. "Mitz can you send some juice and sandwiches to the stable?" He nodded. "Thank you." Shaking his head, he hung up and motioned down the hall of clear rooms.

I now knew how Jack felt after he climbed that beanstalk. I was in the land of giants, and their horses weren't cute little ponies like the ones at the petting zoo. I stood as far back as I could and watched as armed giant after armed giant returned. The medieval roleplaying wasn't playing after all. I was in a shogun nightmare, only they all wore pants and not those Japanese skirt things.

Michael, in black leather with large sharp weapons came over and stood beside me. "That amulet is not what's protecting you," he pointed to the little one with the backpack, "Crissy is. She says your aura is good and that tattoo on your wrist was shown to her for a reason."

I took a drink, not sure what I needed to say to that.

"I gave Leone my word I would keep you safe, and I will, but…"

I stopped eating and looked at him.

His blue eyes were locked on mine. "If anything happens to Leone, I don't think even I will be able to save you."

I swallowed and then huffed out a breath. "Yeah I got that." Putting what was left of the sandwich back into the bag, I pulled the amulet out and handed it to him. "He gave me this as his word to take me to see my friend, Erin."

His expression hardened. "The witch?"

I nodded. "Yeah. The stupid shit you do to help friends—even when they don't want to be helped." I waved my hand around. "All of this other side, other realm stuff is news to me. It's like I woke up in the Land of Oz."

His look softened a bit, then he looked at both my hands, his brows drawing together. "You're not wearing a device."

I sighed. "No, I tossed that at Leone. Apparently, I could have died taking it off."

"Mmm." He said quietly and then turned and walked over to a short woman and held out the amulet. She took it and held it up, closing her eyes.

The guard that had put me in the cube stepped in front of me holding the reins of a large horse. "This is your horse."

I looked up at it, my heart stuck in my throat. "Does it have a baby I can ride?" I squeaked.

He shook his head, not looking amused.

"Shit. Help me get up there." I had ridden a pony once, when I was ten—that was tied to a big wheel that turned as it walked. This creature was definitely not going to walk in a calm, slow circle.

Once on, I looked down and decided it was a good thing I wasn't afraid of heights. I looked at the guard still holding onto the animals' head. "You need to take us back to where you found me, so I can pick up my trail."

He nodded and let go. Just let go and walked away. I gripped the leather straps so hard my knuckles were white. I had no idea how to drive this beast.

Michael appeared beside me on another large animal. "Maybe you should ride with me, so we don't have to walk."

I nodded, even afraid to turn my head to look at him.

His horse nudged my leg and I almost yelped. Leaning over, he wrapped his arm around my waist and lifted me, so I could straddle his horse behind him. I wrapped my arms around him and held on, regardless of weapons pushing into me, not caring that I could be holding onto the man that would end me if his brother didn't survive until we reached him.

"Hold on."

Was the only warning I got before we took off following the guard on his horse.

Chapter Four

Traveling by horse was a much faster return trip then stumbling on foot. I almost fell off Michael's horse when I spotted the tree and little house. "We're here." He stopped the horse and I fell to the ground with all my usual grace.

Getting up, I ran to the house, then turned to see everyone giving me the strangest look. The greasy looking man they called Romulus came up beside me and waved his hands around. Turning back to the others he nodded.

I realized then they couldn't *see* the house, only I could. I really needed to find out more about this mage stuff.

Several of them came over and stood behind the mage.

"Can you bring it down?" The scary one, whose name I found out was Victor, asked.

"It will take me a few minutes." Romulus mumbled.

I gaped at him then turned to Michael. "We don't have minutes."

Romulus turned to me and gave me an unamused look. "I have to find a door at least. Maybe I can open it enough to get through."

I sighed. "I'll show you the door. Just—get them in there." Backing up, I raised my hands and exhaled slowly. My spark ignited, the arcing energy appeared.

"Fascinating." The woman, Clairee, said quietly.

Blocking them out, I lowered my hands to the where the barrier should be, and the sparks started flying. "This is directly in front of the door." I said, clenching my teeth, hoping that Romulus hurried, because I couldn't do this indefinitely.

"Okay, move out of my way." Romulus said beside me.

Dropping my hands, I didn't stop to see if he could. I rushed into the house and down the hall. Stopping at the barrier I looked into the bedroom. Leone lay on the mattress. "Leone. We're back. The mage is helping them get in." He didn't move. I bit my lip and debated if I should cross the barrier. I ran through it and into the room. Dropping down, I saw Leone was holding my phone, and leaned down to take it out of his hand. He didn't even move when I did.

"Leone?" Michael bellowed inside the house.

"In here." I got up and hurried into the hall.

Purple sparks flew as Michael hit the barrier. "Romulus, get this down." He growled. Two more brothers tried with the same results.

"Hurry." I said and moved so they could see their brother on the mattress.

"You have to feed him, Bethany."

The level of panic in Michael's voice made my heart beat pick up. "He doesn't want to... cave in." I said hurriedly referring to his addiction. "I-I don't know how." I told him, looking back to Leone who hadn't even responded to his brother.

"Bethany," the twin with the goatee said calmly, "go, kneel over him. Lean close so your neck is close to him. He'll do the rest." He nodded to encourage me.

I looked at Leone and then back to the faces standing impatiently behind Romulus. I nodded and went to the mattress and dropped to my knees. I was really going to do this. Let someone with fangs bite me. I nudged him gently, "Leone. You have to feed." No response. "Please." I was scared and freaking out, but more than that I knew if he didn't I could never live with myself knowing I was the reason he was like this. Leaning over him, I got close and pulled my hair to one side. "Leone, come on." I whispered next to his ear. "Your family is here. They can't get through the barrier, I'm all that's on the menu." I leaned closer and pressed my neck against his mouth and held my breath.

When I was about to get up and go try blasting the barrier again, his large hand grabbed the back of my head. I squeaked out a weird noise as I felt fangs biting into me. I waited for the pain, there was no pain. It was actually like trying pot for the first time, that floating feeling you got. Not that I did that more than once, but still, it wasn't all that bad.

As I was floating, voices came crashing through the buzz in my head. "Leone, release her."

It was Michael and then the hands on me registered. Leone wasn't stopping.

"Leone, brother. Let her go." That was Victor.

Hands on my shoulders pulled and then there were hands on my waist moving me aside. I sat there on the floor, my head spinning and blinked a few times. Someone lifted me under my arms, so I was standing. At least I think I was standing.

"Beloved, she's bleeding. Can you seal this?" Goatee twin whispered from somewhere near my head.

"Don't get any ideas from this, your majesty." A woman said beside my ear.

"You are all I can handle, duchess."

I tried to push away deciding this many people too close was breaking all personal space boundaries and I stumbled back several steps only to be caught before I hit the floor. "She needs some juice or something. Someone look in the kitchen."

It was Michael and he was holding me in his arms like a tiny child. I looked from his concerned blue eyes and then turned to see how Leone was. He was on his knees now, a few brothers around him guarding over him. I'd done it, he was okay. "He's okay." I said aloud, at least I think it was out loud.

"Yes." Michael said and then knelt to set me on the floor carefully, so I was leaning against the wall. He hovered waiting to see if I was going to stay upright.

"Get away from her." Leone snarled like a mad animal.

Wide-eyed I looked to see him pushing through his brothers and coming toward me, and them trying to block him and failing. I smirked at him. "Leo," I motioned in the air, "that whole fang thing wasn't as bad as I thought it would be." I snorted and then covered my mouth.

"She's wasted." The blonde woman said as she stepped between the stumbling giant and me. "Leone, stop. No one is hurting her, you've made her very stoned."

He stopped and looked at me over her head and then down at her. "I didn't..." he looked at me again, a pained look on his face. "Fuck." He spat and turned, pacing to the other side of the room.

"I'm okay." I put up my hand and flicked it toward him. The giant with the haunting eyes and black hair knelt in front of me and held a glass to my mouth. "You have very pretty hair," I told him before I took a sip. Swallowing, I looked around the room. "You guys are much cooler than that sicko crew of Davis'—if you weren't holding my best friend as a prisoner, I might like you." I nodded and took another sip.

I was in the kitchen, nursing the oddest hangover I'd ever had in my life and trying to figure out what they were all arguing about.

Leone came stomping into the small space and then froze and looked at me. "I'm sorry, I was too out of it to keep the eufori in check." I must have looked confused. "An inhibitor, so it doesn't hurt." He explained.

I waved it off. "Making it not hurt worked for me." I glanced to the others walking in behind him. "So, what now?" My nerves were strung tighter than they had ever been.

He continued to stand there looking at me, his expressions changing from pain to concern and a few other emotions. Turning his head, he looked at Michael. "I think she'll help."

I cringed and looked around at the tall bodies. I debated if I should stand on the chair to even the playing field a bit. "If she is me," I glanced to Leone, "I think we can all agree bad shit happens when I agree to *help* others." I shook my head. "All I wanted was my friend back and instead I helped a group of lunatics."

Leone knelt down on the other side of the table, so we were closer to the same height. "Hear us out first, then you can decide, please?"

I gnawed on my bottom lip and stared at his deep brown eyes. When they weren't shooting daggers at me, they sucked me in. "Fine. I'll listen." I held up my hand, "then you have to do what you said you would and take me to see Erin."

His jaw clenched, but he nodded. "I will." He stood up and sat on the edge of the table and looked at his hovering brothers.

Romulus came in. "I need someone to call Ellis and ask if they buried any markers around the house." He looked stressed, "or I can't bring it down."

"Don't." Michael said.

The mage frowned. "Don't bring it down?"

Nodding slowly, Michael crossed his arms over his chest. "We're going to lay a trap for Davis and company. Let them think Leone is still locked behind that barrier."

Romulus sighed. "I don't know if I can replace it with something they'll think is theirs." He looked to the small woman I now knew was a witch. "Can you help create an illusion that they'll buy?"

She nodded slowly. "I think we can manage it. How much time do we have?"

Everyone looked at me. I opened my mouth and then closed it. "They just told me they'd call after they contacted you."

One twin turned to the other. "They're probably unable to get through our guards in the lockdown to reach us." The other one with the goatee nodded. "Let's make it easier for them."

Michael leaned on the table and gave me a serious look. "Can you contact them? Inquire as to why it's taking so long?"

I heaved a sigh of relief. If that's the help they wanted, easy, I had no problem with that. "Sure. No guarantees Davis will tell me, but I'll try."

They all stood looking at me.

"Oh," I grabbed my phone, "you mean *now*." I cringed, "sorry, brain is a little groggy still." I smirked at the big guy with eyes the same as Leone's. "If you guys could like sell that on the streets you'd be..." I stopped and rolled my eyes at what I'd just said. With shaking hands, I scrolled and found Davis' number. "Do you want it on speaker?" I hovered my finger over the send button. Leone nodded. "Okay." I pushed it and set the phone on the table in front of me.

Davis answered. "Bethany, is there a problem?"

I snorted and looked at the giants all staring at me. "Yeah there's a problem, Davis. You said *two* days—we're getting really close to four days. What the hell?"

There were other voices in the background. "We hit a snag in getting the message to the royals..."

"Are you serious? They don't even know yet?" I shook my head, staring at the phone. "Fix it, Davis, there isn't shit to do here. You could have at least picked a place with a t.v. and I've been wearing the same clothes for days now..."

"How is Leone? Any problems?"

I looked up to see angry eyes looking down at me. "He's pissed and the furniture in his room is—trashed."

Davis chuckled and the aura in the small kitchen darkened, almost visibly.

"Seriously, just walk up to someone and say something like, I have news of Leone..." I glanced at the guard I'd said that to myself.

"It's not so cut and dry, Miss Finley." I cringed, he reminded me of a teacher I once had. I didn't like them either. "We have someone on the inside, it will mean we lose that person, but the message will be delivered to the royals today."

"Awesome. So, we get Erin back, when? Tomorrow?" I stood up and picked up the phone. The amount of large bodies closing in around the table was starting to freak me out.

"That is the plan. I will call you in the morning and let you know when we'll be over for the exchange."

"I will be here."

He laughed. "Where else would you be." The line went dead.

I set the phone on the counter and turned around to see all eyes on me. "You guys need to all step back." I motioned with my hands.

"They still have someone inside." Leone turned to look at Victor.

He glanced to the one they called Crissy, "That's impossible. She would have known when she saw the aura."

I shrugged. "Maybe they called in sick," I offered, "I do." I frowned remembering I didn't have a job now. "Did."

Michael sat on the edge of the table, his back to me. "We didn't check for absences, just announced a meeting."

"So we could have missed one?" Leone said thoughtfully.

"It is possible." The one with the long hair said.

I went to the fridge and opened it. Whatever they were figuring out, had nothing to do with me, and now that my head wasn't mush I needed food. Picking up the last yogurt, I straightened and grabbed a spoon. Going back to where I had been leaning, I noticed that Leone's eyes tracked every move I made. Was he even listening to what his brothers were saying? I wasn't sure. All I knew was they had until I finished this yogurt to talk, and then I was going to see Erin.

They were all moving closer to the table again. Motioning with the yogurt in my hand I started for the door. "I'm going out to get some air, you are sucking all the oxygen out of this room."

The guard blocked my path then glanced to the twin without the goatee. He inclined his head and the guard stepped out of my way.

I rushed out the door to see two more guards standing there. I pointed to the tree. "I'll be right there." I smirked when they gave me a hard look, "seriously, where else would I go?" He made some kind of grunt in acknowledgment and stepped out of my way.

I was sitting by the tree stabbing my spoon into the empty container, trying to work up the courage to demand Leone take me to see Erin. The short time I'd been out here, the reality of what I'd done had sunk in. How did you fix something like this?

I looked up to see Michael walking over. He stopped a few feet from me and squatted down. "It's not over yet."

I gave him a stupefied look. Did he think I was that naïve? "I got that."

"Leone has filled in some of the blanks, with your involvement," he gave me hard look, "you should know that it's a toss-up among us as to whether you're punished or not." He watched me glance to the blades on his back and smirked. "We're not sadists."

"Good to know." I huffed out a breath. "I'm pretty sure Davis and his crew are."

He inclined his head. "They are." Looking at the ground for a moment, I could see his indecision by the clenching of his jaw. His blue eyes connected with mine again. "It took a great deal of courage for you to come and find us."

I looked at my legs. "I've never walked that much in my life." I shrugged, "but when I mess up, I own it."

The expression in his eyes lightened. "Thank you." It was barely audible. "Shortly, my brothers are going to descend upon us. I will try to keep you from being harmed."

I scowled, "yeah well, I'm not without some defenses." I held up my palm so the sparks were moving over it.

"Fair enough." He stood up.

A moment later large bodies started filing out of the house and headed in our direction. I set the container down and stood up. Several stayed by the house, and I finally figured out that the ones walking with great strides were all brothers of Leone.

I glanced around. At least I wasn't trapped in a small space with them.

Victor stopped, leaving about four feet between us. "You're going to help us set a trap."

It wasn't a question. I looked at him then to Michael. "Isn't that what I just did on the phone?"

"It is, but it isn't," the goatee said, "all that call really accomplished was we heard Davis, and have a rough timeline so we can get everyone sorted out, and set up something that will most definitely…"

I held up my hand, sparks and lights swirling it, "stop talking or that little beard goes up in smoke. Just cut to the end."

The tall woman beside him laughed quietly. He frowned and looked at her.

"You're supposed to defend me." He said in a hushed tone.

She nodded, "I know, but really, Chase, how many of us would love to be able to stop you from talking?"

There were a few snickers. Chase motioned a hand to his twin and then crossed his arms.

The twin inclined his head to me. "I'm Troy, by the way." He glanced to Victor briefly, "we're going to need you to be present when Davis comes to arrange the trade…"

"Wait," Leone stepped over and placed himself between them and me, "we didn't discuss that." He looked at me, his expression hard, "we're not using her as bait." He motioned to the space around us, "what if things go sideways?"

Several of them started talking as once and he argued back. Shaking my head, I moved around Michael's large body and touched Leone's arm to get his attention. He stopped and looked down at me.

"It's fine. I'm the reason this whole mess is happening, I'll help." My heart thudded in my chest when his eyes changed to red while he looked down at me, his expression was either pained or angry, I wasn't sure.

He looked at my hand. "Marcus and Willis are to blame, not you." He growled low, "all you wanted to do was to help a friend."

Pulling my hand away, I looked up at him, trying to decide how I felt about those red eyes now. Yep, they still freaked me out. "Wow, you're more forgiving then I am. After what I did to you." I stepped back and looked to Michael. "I'll do it."

Leone made some guttural sound and stomped away. He stopped with his back to us and stood there looking out into the open fields.

I glanced around at everyone giving me a strange look. "So," I shrugged, "what-what are we doing exactly?" At least I'd learned to ask questions.

I watched as they talked, went in the house a few times with Clairee, the witch, and the greasy mage. So far no one told me the plan, so I waited. Michael and the one I'd called Tarzan, Rafael was his name, were talking to Leone out of hearing range. I don't know what they were talking about, but Leone was waving his hands around and all three, kept looking at me every few seconds. I decided I preferred feeling invisible as I had for most of my life.

They all started walking toward me, I glanced behind me hoping there was someone else waiting, and that's where they were really going. There wasn't. Wrapping my arms around my waist, so I wouldn't go with my gut reaction and toss energy at them, I waited.

Leone stopped in front of me, a look of indecision on his face. "I'll take you to see the witch."

I gave him a look of surprise, I'd honestly thought that had been postponed. Guilt hit me again, despite what I'd done and everything that had happened, he was keeping his word. I nodded. "Thank you."

He took a deep breath and exhaled slowly, like he was trying to build up courage. Hesitantly he stepped closer and touched my shoulder and then dropped his hand away and stepped back shaking his head. "I can't. I can't." He muttered.

Michael put his hand on Leone's shoulder. "It's okay, I'll take her back. We'll meet you there."

Rafael nodded and patted Leone on the back. "Baby steps brother, you got this."

Leone exhaled loudly and nodded. "I'll meet you there." He looked at me and then just vanished.

Like there one second and then gone. Just gone. "Uh…" I looked to Michael and then to where Leone had been standing.

He actually smirked at me. "You'll get used to it." Stepping in front of me, he grasped my elbow. "Close your eyes and take a deep breath."

I did—neither. I'm looking at a tree one moment and the next there was a big steel door with my stomach trying to jump out my throat. I dropped to my knees and tried to breathe through the nausea. "What the hell," I was shaking, "Hollywood is so full of shit," I swallowed the rising bile down, "you never see Captain Kirk tossing his cookies."

A strong hand rested on my shoulder. "Just take a few deep breaths." Michael said.

I listened this time and it got better, but still this transporting thing sucked. "Okay," I whispered after a few breaths. "I got it." I slowed my breathing further and then raised my head testing if the room still spun. Meeting Michael's amused blue eyes, I scowled. "Seriously, what the hell, Michael."

He actually smirked at me. "It gets better."

I snorted, "Can't get any worse." With shaky legs, I got to my feet and stood there assessing if it was over. I still felt off but was going to make it. I looked at Leone, whose expression said his own personal demons were riding him hard. "You okay, big guy?"

He gave me a surprised look and then nodded and opened the door. "Let's get this over with."

I followed him in, Michael right on my heels.

"We're going to be listening." He said quietly behind me.

I nodded. "Fine." Leone came to an abrupt stop, I almost walked into him. "So, magic won't work, right?"

Michael nodded. "Not in her cell."

"Good." I shrugged, "our disagreements can get nasty and it will stop me from sending energy into her brain in hopes of jump-starting her sense again." Leone did something with the little pad and suddenly I could see Erin. She looked awful, to put it mildly. Her hair was matted and sticking up everywhere, where normally there wasn't a hair out of place. She was ghostly white with dark circles around her eyes. "Is she okay?"

Michael crossed his arms and studied her. "She refused to eat for a few days. We think she had a blood bond with Marcus when she first came in…"

"What?" I looked at my palms and then clasped my hands together. "Like bond…"

He shook his head, "no that's blood brother pact, they had a blood bond…" he huffed out a breath, "I'll explain it later."

I looked from him back to her. "Okay." Turning, I looked up at Leone. "Thanks." He gave me a curious look. "For keeping your word, that's pretty rare."

He inclined his head but didn't speak.

I looked over the wall. "How do I get in?" Michael pointed, so I went and stood where he said. The wall opened, so I stepped in quickly. I heard it close but didn't turn to look. Erin turned and looked at me. Her eyes went wide, and she jumped off the bed.

"They got you too?" She rushed over and hugged me.

I hugged her as tight as I could. I never thought I'd see her again. Leaning back, I looked up at her, she looked like she hadn't slept since she'd been taken. "Are you okay?" I asked.

She rolled her eyes. "I suppose." Her hands dropped, and she frowned down at me. "I don't think we're getting out of here."

I gave her a 'duh' look. "You tried to kill people, Erin."

She opened her mouth and then closed it and paced the other way, a whole four feet until she came to a wall. "You don't understand."

"Really, then explain." I stood with my hands on my hips and glared at her, wishing I could use my magic and give her a little jolt. "Because you didn't end up here for no reason."

She turned, her expression one of pain. "They're forcing people to stay, and they can't leave."

I raised my eyebrows. "Who?"

"The royal family." She rushed forward and grabbed my hands. "Have you seen them? Evil." She leaned down. "The one, Arius, he can get inside your head and make you do things." She sounded crazed.

What I did to Leone floated to the surface of my mind. "Well, sometimes you have to do things." I said quickly.

She dropped her hands and stepped back, crossing her arms over her chest she glared at me. "You don't understand. Marcus explained…"

"Marcus," I got in her face, "is a lunatic." Her expression changed to anger. My eyes popped wide open. "Tell me you and he haven't…" I glared at her.

"What? No. It's not like that. He's ancient." She shook her head. "He's a brilliant mentor, showed me so much…"

"He's a brilliant maniac." I almost shouted at her. "Do you have *any* idea what he's been trying to do? Like really, aside from the flashy crap he's dazzled you with?" I flung my arms up and spun in a circle, wishing there was more space to pace. "He's hurting people, Erin, and I don't mean a slap kind of hurt, his crew are holding people against their will, making them do things…" I had to stop, some of the things Leone had told me that first night still made me want to throw up.

"Where are you getting this information from?" She gave me a hard look. Waving me off, she glanced around at the walls. "Can you access your magic? We need to get out of here and find Marcus." She pulled on the red cuff on her wrist. "I think my magic is blocked by this, I can't get it off."

I dropped my hands, my heart sinking as they fell. "No. I can't." This wasn't my friend. This wasn't the girl I'd gone through so many things with, that I thought for the rest of our lives nothing could shake what we had. "There is no way out, Erin."

She looked at me and shook her head. "We have to *try*, they need us to free the others. I have to get Marcus out." She tapped her head. "I can't hear him anymore, but I know what he needs me to do." With jerky movements, she started to run her hands along the wall.

I looked at the wall I knew Leone and Michael were standing behind, my eyes tearing up, I shook my head. I turned back to her. "Erin…" she stopped moving her hands and looked at me, I blew out a breath.

Before I could say more the wall changed and we could see Michael and Leone on the other side. Leone held the staff that Marcus had given her.

"My staff." She rushed over to the glass and stared at it. "They have my staff. If we can get it. I can get all of us out of here. They won't be able to stop me. I *will* make them pay."

I looked from her to Leone, he wasn't watching Erin at all, his eyes were on me. There was a pained look on his face. I didn't know if it was for himself or for me as I realized all he'd told me about my friend was true.

I wiped a tear off my cheek and looked back to Erin. She stood there staring at the staff like a mother would a child.

"I'll try to come back and see you soon." I nodded as I stepped back to where I knew the door was.

"You can't leave…" she whispered, "You have to help me. Marcus needs…"

The door against my back moved and I stepped backward and stopped. When it slid back over, I could still see the shocked look on her face. I didn't know if she could see me, but I put my hand against the glass and held it there. Another tear rolled down my cheek.

I felt a hand on my shoulder and glanced to see Leone standing there. "What has he done to her?"

"The same he's done to many." He said. "We're still trying to piece together how so many believe them unfailingly—we're pretty sure it's a strong glamour, or magical at least."

His hand fell away. I stood there a moment more, willing myself to not be upset. So many that would otherwise still be innocent if it weren't for Marcus and his lies. Shaking my head, I forced the tears back. "Let's go get the bastards." I said and turned and nodded at both men. "You can lock me up later, right now I just want to see them stopped."

Michael turned to give Leone and odd look.

Leone was looking down at me with so much pain in his eyes I almost started crying again. "Hey, big guy. Snap out of it, we have a trap to plan." I nodded again when he blinked and looked like he actually saw me this time.

Turning, he walked back down the hall.

Chapter Five

Once again, I found myself in the too small kitchen surrounded by too many large bodies. I'd been listening to the plan, but hadn't caught all the details. I was getting details this time. I held up my hand. "Okay, so they come over and then what?"

"You're asking a lot of questions." The big brown-eyed one said.

I pointed at him. "Look," I tried to remember his name.

"Quinton." He supplied.

I gave an abrupt nod. "Quinton," I waved my hand around in a very exaggerated way, "this whole," I wanted to say mess, "situation is *because* I didn't ask questions. I just stupidly took lunatics at their word and did it." I pointed at him again. "I'm getting details this time." I lowered my hand and looked around, no one seemed to object. I paused on Leone, who stood leaning against the wall with his arms crossed, and hadn't said a word in quite a while. His brown eyes moved over me, but he said nothing. I looked at Michael. "Then what?'

He nodded slowly, "we'll be cloaked, so only you and Leone will be visible..."

"Cloaked?" I stopped him.

"Yes." Clairee stepped forward and moved her hand down over the nearest body, Arius. He vanished from my sight.

I shoved by Michael, my eyes wide as Arius came back when she did it again. "So is that like a chant spell thing, or is the power in your hand?"

She gave me a small smile, "mostly a spell." She looked at my hands. "Yours isn't a spell?"

I shook my head and held up my hand, sparks moved over it. "No. I think it, and there it is."

"Fascinating." She took my hand and turned it over and looked at it. Then looked back at me. "What you did to Leone's," she hesitantly glanced at him, "mind. How did you do that? We couldn't break it or find a trace."

I huffed out a breath. "Not easily. I'll tell you that much." I lifted my hand then shook my head. "I can't explain how I do it, it takes more focus than just thinking," I rolled my eyes. "Like *a lot* more focus. I think I lost ten pounds with the energy I used up…"

"As much as all of this intrigues me," Victor said with a haughty tone, "perhaps we can *share* later and get back to the plan?"

I felt all eyes on me. "Sorry." Nodding I looked back to Michael. "Is everyone going to be… cloaked outside or in here?"

He looked to Victor and then Clairee.

She thought for a moment. "I could do one, maybe two inside, but if more than one mage comes with Davis, they could sense them."

I looked around at all the men. "What about one hiding in the shower, cloaked?" I shrugged, "that's at least one close at hand."

Victor nodded and looked to Clairee.

"Yes, I can hide one for sure." She paused and glanced around and then zeroed in on Chase. He nodded, looking quite pleased she'd selected him.

His twin, Troy, shook his head and then Chase held up his hand. "Your skill will be better outside, brother, if they bring others you can get inside their heads," he shrugged, "or cut them off, I'm not particular on how you disable them."

Troy smirked. "It will be my pleasure."

A chill went down my spine at their tones.

"Bethany is transported out as soon as they arrive." Leone said in a quiet tone.

I spun and looked at him. "What? Hell no, I'm helping."

He gave me a hard look and started to say something, I held up my hand and then focused on the cup on the counter, flicking my hand down and open, the cup shattered in a flash of red sparks. I looked back to him. "I'm staying."

I could see his jaw clenching as his eyes held mine. He looked to Michael and then gave a slight nod.

"Fire without flames!" Crissy said loudly.

I turned and looked at her, she looked so happy.

"I'll be damned." Quinton grinned, "So it is."

All eyes were on me again and I had no idea what was going on. I connected with the tall woman, Chase's wife I think, Alona, she smiled at me.

"You get used to it."

I snorted. "So everyone keeps telling me, about everything."

"I'm hungry." Rafael said out of the blue. "I say we leave Romulus and a few guards here to do his thing and go back and eat."

There were several nods of agreement and then everyone looked at me, again, no idea why.

"I'm…" I was going to say I'd stay right here, when Leone grabbed my elbow.

"Coming with us." His tone left no room for argument.

I was handled like a suitcase and gently shoved toward Michael. When I turned to give Leone a piece of my mind, he walked out the door and vanished as soon as he cleared the barrier.

Michael's expression was almost apologetic, but there was something else, too. He guided me out the door and then after a few feet stopped and looked down at me. "This time, close your eyes and take a deep breath."

"Crap." I squeezed my eyes shut and sucked in a breath as he pulled me against his chest.

Despite his preparation tips, my stomach completely bottomed out and then bounced back up to stop in my throat. I squatted down and moaned. "That," I lifted a hand, not even knowing if Michael still stood there, "is much cooler in theory."

Someone held a cup of something near my face, just the aroma helped. I looked up to see Leone offering it to me. With shaking legs, I stood slowly and took the cup, holding it under my nose and inhaling. He stepped back and a sweet, red-headed lady stood there smiling at me. She motioned. and I saw a chair beside me, and sat down quickly.

When my stomach was back down where it belonged, I looked up to see I was sitting at the biggest table I'd ever seen in my life. The little red-haired lady came out with a tray and then set it down. There were several other trays spread out already. Michael was sitting on my left side, six, I counted, chairs away from me and Leone on the right, just as many chairs away. There were a lot of chairs. They sat there looking at each other. Not speaking, but facial expressions kept changing like they were.

As the others started to file in, I was invisible. They all sat and as the woman brought more food out, started eating. The three women glanced at me, looks ranging from curiosity to sympathy.

The twins came in one after the other. Troy held up his hand. "We've gotten the message. Noon tomorrow. Also have a chambermaid in the cells." I watched as he set the vial of blood on the table in front of Leone.

Leone picked it up and then he glared down the table at me.

"It wasn't me." I offered.

"I know." He said in a low lethal tone and set it back down on the table.

The woman was back and headed in my direction.

She smiled, a real smile. "Can I get you something, love?"

I shook my head. "I'm good."

"You need to eat." Leone stated.

"I'm…"

"You will eat, to keep up your strength." He enunciated each word slowly and then looked at the woman. "She'll have some fruit, Mitz."

Mitz nodded and turned back to the kitchen.

I scowled at him.

He glared back at me. "You're eating because after we have, you're going to prove your little sparks can defend you if needed." He looked to Michael. "If she's staying in the house, we don't have time to babysit her."

Everyone gave Leone an odd look, then turned and looked at me slowly.

"Guess you're coming to practice, sparky." Chase said with an amused look.

I didn't reply. I was too busy trying not to blast half the stuff off the table. Between each bite, Leone looked down to me. Each time the expression in his eyes was different.

I did eat some of the fruit Mitz had brought, all while trying to decide if these men were this size because of the vast amount of food they were shoveling in, or if the amount of food was needed because of their size. Whichever it was, I had honestly not seen this much food at once in my life.

"We should get her a change of clothes." The blonde suggested.

"We can't, Daxx, she mentioned to Davis she had no other clothes." Michael said between bites.

Daxx looked down at me. "She can change back tomorrow." She waved her fork around. "I dare any one of you to walk half of Alterealm for three days and stay in the same clothes."

Many paused and looked at me.

"We'll show her the closet before practice," Alona said and smiled down the table at me.

The closet was ten times the size of the closet I slept in at home. Inside it were stores worth of clothes, in every size and color. I stood there trying to decide what to pick.

Alona came in and held out a plastic bag. "Just put your clothes in this and you can put them back on tomorrow."

I took the bag. "Thanks." I couldn't help notice the ink on her arm. A woman of her class and grace with a sleeve tattoo was unusual.

She sighed. "I can feel the gauntlet of emotions your feeling, and let me just say, from one who not long ago was in your position," she waved her hand around, "well, not exactly the circumstance you are, but new to all of this." She took a deep breath. "It does honestly get better."

I looked at her for a moment. "We're in another realm."

She smirked. "Yes, it is hard to grasp at first."

I gave her a wide-eyed look.

"If we don't get there soon, the guys are going to come looking and we don't want that." Daxx came walking in.

"They can wait." Alona said. "Bethany deserves a few moments to freshen up, at least."

Daxx also had a sleeve tattoo, I was going to ask but was interrupted.

"Victor is going to be upset with me." Crissy said coming in, adjusting the fingerless gloves on her hands. "He told me not to get too close, but I don't see any bad around you." She looked at the air above my head.

I glanced up and then looked at her. "Oh, bad seems to find me, everywhere." Now I was beyond curious, Crissy, who I swear was a schoolgirl also had a tattoo on her arm. I frowned, come to think of it their husbands did as well. Maybe it was some weird marriage thing over here.

She nodded. "But you have the flower and flameless fire, so it's okay." She smiled. "It's okay."

Giving Alona and Daxx a quick look, they both nodded. "If you say so." I pointed to the clothes. "Does it matter what I pick?"

Daxx shook her head. "No. We've already taken what we want."

Still holding the plastic bag, I went over and looked at the jeans closest. "So whose is it?"

"No ones." Crissy said and then walked out.

"We'll come back in a few minutes to get you." Alona pointed across the room. "There's a bathroom in there."

After a quick sponge bath and change, I felt ten times better. Until I opened the door and Leone stood in the hall.

He didn't say a word, just motioned down the hall.

I started walking.

"You left me a knife." He said quietly.

I shrugged. "I didn't know if I was going to get lost, I wanted you to have something to defend yourself if Davis came back before I found help."

He was quiet for a minute. "I'm sorry if I was rough when I..." he exhaled slowly, "fed from you."

"It was fine." Not really, but it hadn't been at all what I'd thought. "Sorry if I messed up your sobriety count, but it was kind of an emergency."

He made an odd noise in the back of his throat. "Yes, thirty plus years and I'm back to day one again."

I stopped, he kept walking for a few steps then turned to see I wasn't following. "Excuse me?" I had to have heard him wrong. "Thirty years." I looked him up and down, he looked to be around my age, just twenty-six.

He sighed, "When I was explaining the differences between our realms, I may have left out a few things."

I nodded, "differences, yeah fangs, changing eyes... teleporting, that's some pretty big differences."

He nodded slowly, "we live longer too."

"Like, what are we talking here to a hundred, hundred and ten?" I could tell by his expression I wasn't even close. "Older?" He inclined his head slightly. "How old are you?"

"Two hundred."

I mouthed the number and then just stood there for a moment. "You're serious?" He nodded. Daxx came around the corner before I could say anything else.

"Thought maybe you got lost." She stopped and looked from Leone to me. "What's up?"

"She's just found out how old I am." He said quietly, still looking at me for a reaction.

"Oh." She laughed, "Yeah, he's just a baby." He turned and gave her a blank look. "What? Troy's words, but it's the truth and you know it."

"I'll see you at the practice room." He inclined his head and then walked around the corner.

Daxx came over. "It's all weirdness from start to finish, I get it, but it's pretty awesome once it all sinks in."

I looked at her, like really looked at her. "You're not two hundred or something?"

She shook her head. "I was a perfectly normal twenty-something human until I mated with Troy," She held up her tattooed arm, "now I'll live longer. No one explains how much longer though."

I closed my eyes and then looked at her again. "All of this is," I waved my hand around, not knowing what to say.

She sighed, "Yeah, it is." She motioned to the direction Leone had gone. "Come on, beating on the guys always makes it better."

We stepped into the 'practice room' I stopped and gaped at the wall of weapons. "Did a military bunker go out of business?"

Daxx laughed, "I know. Isn't it awesome? Three hundred ways to beat someone." She headed over to the others.

I stood there thinking that she and I didn't quite connect in that conversation. Everyone turned and looked at me. Yeah this is a bad idea, I thought. Sighing, I walked over. At least none of them were in head to toe leather and armed with swords longer then my body. That was good, right?

I stopped so there was at least ten feet between me and the nearest giant. Something caught my attention in the corner of my eye. Turning, I watched Crissy going up the rope as fast as most would climb stairs. No one else seemed concerned, so I left it at that.

A few of the men held poles, I didn't see any real pointy weapons though, so that was good too.

Leone stepped out from behind a few of them, his hard expression was back. Gone was the soft-spoken guy in the hallway. Maybe he had a split personality. He motioned for me to come closer.

"Let's see how your sparks are going to save your ass if they bring backup." His tone was low and even.

I gaped at him, he'd watched me try to blast through the barrier. How could he not know how much force they could have? He had been drugged up then though, I sighed and then shrugged. "What do you want me to hit?"

He gave me a cold look. "You think this is target practice? They're not going to be offering you options, Bethany. This is life or death, make no mistake about that."

I walked closer. "You watched me try to break the barrier, you know this isn't pretty sparkles."

He sent me a look, "show me." He motioned to his own body.

"You want me to hit you?" I shook my head. "I don't want to hurt you."

He sneered at me, "that didn't stop you from fucking around in my head…"

I stepped close enough, so I was in his face, or at least below it, "I did nothing to endanger you. When you needed to focus, I muted my voice, so you could focus." I growled at him.

He leaned down so our faces were much closer, his eyes were turning red. "Show. Me."

"Maybe we should…" Michael stepped up, both Leone and I glared at him. Raising his hands, he backed away again.

I snapped back to glare at Leone. "Okay cupcake, you asked for it."

I turned around and walked a few feet back. I stood there, trying to calm down a bit.

Daxx leaned closer to Troy. "Does this look familiar?"

"Eerily so." He nodded and leaned down to kiss the top her head.

"Now." Leone barked. "They're not going to let you meditate on it."

Eyes huge, I flipped my hands forward and my fire whacked him in the chest.

He stepped back a foot and then sneered at me. "Is that all you've got?"

I raised my hands above my head, making sure all could see the arc of bright energy flowing between my hands. Gritting my teeth, I sent it at him, he was knocked back, but caught his balance again. Baring my teeth at him I flung all I had.

Michael stepped in front of him and then went flying back when it connected.

Covering my mouth, I stumbled forward. "I'm sorry. Shit." I fell to my knees beside him. "Are you okay?" I looked up and glared at Leone. "Happy now, jerk?"

He crossed his arms and stood there snarling at me.

"I thought I'd be on fire." Michael said still lying flat on his back, "but it's cold." He touched his chest where I'd hit him. Giving his brother a blank look, "I think she'll manage to hold her own if they come at her."

Leone sighed and his whole demeanor changed. Holding his hand out to Michael, he pulled him to his feet. "Stupid move, brother, stepping in the way."

Michael rubbed his chest. "I thought maybe you weren't noticing the anger pouring off her. We just got you back, I didn't want you hurt."

I got up slowly and stumbled back a step. Rafael caught me by my arm. I offered him a meek smile. "Thanks. Using it has a price."

"I have cookies." Crissy called and then dropped down by a cable to land in front of me. "Cookies will help." She nodded and pointed to her backpack.

Someone started clapping. I turned to see Chase looking very amused.

"That was a showstopper, sparky." He turned and held up his pole. "Who can I beat today?"

Quinton laughed and waved his. "Let's see you try, brother."

I looked at Rafael.

"They won't really."

He motioned to Crissy's backpack. "Let's get you something to drink and a cookie."

I nodded and was glad for his hand to keep me on my feet. I'd used a lot more than I'd intended, which always happened when I let emotions override my control. Leone stood near the wall of Daxx's beating tools, holding a large wooden sword. Michael was beside him talking, but I don't think Leone was listening. His demeanor was changing again.

"Is he all right?" I asked quietly.

Rafael looked over to Leone, not needing clarification. He sighed. "He will be. We all knew what it meant to have you feed him, but there was no time to wait."

I stopped and looked at him. "I'm sorry."

Rafael smiled down at me. "Just don't call me Tarzan again."

I laughed.

A screech like a wounded animal echoed through the large room. Jolting, I turned to see Leone charging at Chase. Moving fast, Chase spun and blocked the large sword. Leone turned on Quinton and swung at him. That brother also blocked it.

Rafael leaned down, "he'll burn off the frustration then be the chill Leone again." He walked to the wall and grabbed a long sword.

I nodded, not taking my eyes off the brothers that were jumping in to allow their sibling to work through his issues.

Crissy appeared next to me and held out a cookie and bottle of water. I took them and nodded my thanks, then looked back to the men. I sat, eating the cookie, trying not to let the emotions threatening to overtake me in.

"If you're not used to being in a family environment, you're in for some difficult moments of adjustment."

I looked to see Alona sitting next to me. "It's ah…" I looked back to the men. Quinton stood off to the side now, leaning on his pole. His eyes followed Leone's every move.

"It's called unconditional love." She said quietly.

"I feel responsible." I whispered.

"You're not." She leaned closer. "I'm an empath, by the way, so I feel the turmoil inside you."

Daxx came over and sat down. "I can't compete with that."

We all watched Michael back away shaking his head. There were now three brothers having to rest.

Daxx leaned over and looked at me. "You can stop this." She tilted her head. "At least I think you have that power."

"Oh, hmm." Alona said looking at her.

I raised my eyes. "I think I'm the cause of it."

Daxx smirked. "Exactly."

Shaking my head, I turned to watch. Leone's swing connected with Chase's pole with such an impact, Chase hit the mat. Leone didn't even stop to see if he was all right, just spun and went for the next closest body. The look on his face was pain. Pure heart-wrenching pain. "How do I stop it?"

Daxx looked from me to the wall. "Do you have any weapons skill?"

I shook my head. "My hands are my weapon."

She gave me a careful look. "Can you use that again so soon?"

I took a deep breath, "probably not much, but maybe enough to stop him from killing one of his own brothers."

Alona nodded. "I think she should try."

Sighing, I stood up, pausing to see if I was steady enough. Looking down at my hands, I checked all was functional. With a slight nod, "wish me luck," I whispered and walked toward the commotion on the mat.

Leone was down to two brothers now. Arius and Victor were trying all they could to keep up with his anger. I waited until his back was to me and then sent enough fire to hit his back. He spun around, swinging. I'd gotten his attention.

"Are you finished bashing your brothers around?"

Arius and Victor stopped and stood there, staying out of it. They were both panting, trying to catch their breath.

"I'm not hurting anyone." Leone said, as breathless as his siblings.

"Not physically." I motioned to my body. "It's my fault, take it out on me." I held my hands up, hoping I had enough if he took me up on it.

He cocked his head to the side and stared at me, his chest rising and falling rapidly. "You know I won't."

I raised one eyebrow. "Do I? You have every right to."

Taking a ragged breath, he dropped the sword to the mat, but continued to stand there and stare me down. Spinning on his heel he stomped the other way and went out the door on the far side.

Michael dropped his weapon and gave me a quick nod, then ran after him.

I exhaled the breath I'd been holding and my shoulders slumped forward. "I'm sorry," I said to no one in particular.

Victor looked at me. "Intriguing." With that he held out his hand to Crissy. She ran over and they walked out.

My head was spinning, so I sat right where I was. Rafael came over and sat beside me. "Thank you." He huffed out a breath. "As soon as I catch my breath, we'll go get you some juice or whatever you require."

I just wanted to curl up and pretend it was a month ago, and none of this was real. I shrugged, defeated. "Sure."

Chapter Six

I sat on a bed that was bigger than my half room in my apartment. On the table beside the bed was a stash of drinks, bars and snacks. I wondered if anyone would be offended if I packed those to take with me when I went home.

Home. Did I still have one? And what was I doing without Erin? I had no job, no way to pay rent.

All this quiet was bad for my internal morale. Didn't these people watch television? I hadn't seen one on either side.

When someone knocked on the door, I almost ran to answer it. Anything to get me out of my head was good right now. I opened it to see Michael standing there. I opened it further and then turned to walk back to the stand by the couch. Yes, this bedroom was big enough there was a couch and chairs. I couldn't even think about the tub, it was like a small swimming pool. These people did nothing in small measures.

I watched him as he walked in, trying to figure out what the expression on his face meant. "Is Leone okay?"

He kind of nodded and shrugged at the same time. "It will take some time."

I clasped my hands together in front of me. "If I could roll back time, I would."

Tucking his hands in his pockets, he didn't even acknowledge I'd spoke. "I came to see if you were all right after the workout."

I snorted. Using magic was like a workout. "I'm good now, thanks."

His blue eyes searched my face. "Tomorrow isn't going to be easy."

"Why break the pattern of my life and do something the easy way?"

He did smirk at that. "I know a lot has been dumped on you the past few days." He inclined his head like he was trying to decide what to say. "I'm not entirely sure we're on the same side in all aspects, but I did want you to know that I am here if you have questions."

I stood there trying to figure out what that meant. How weren't we on the same side? I swallowed. "What's your," I waved my hand, "job here?"

"I uphold the law." He stated it simply.

"And Leone is the enforcer of… the law?"

He nodded.

My stomach tightened. I had this horrible feeling I was going to end up in my own personal glass cube again after I helped them trap Davis and his creepy crew. I swallowed the lump in my throat. "I don't have any questions. Well, I have about a million, but none that I need answers just yet."

Michael continued to stand there and look at me. "Leone is…"

"Standing right here."

We both turned to see Leone standing in the open door.

Michael gave me a brief nod and turned to walk to the door. He stopped in front of him. "Do you want me to stay?"

Leone glanced to me over Michael's shoulder and shook his head. "I'm in control."

Michael turned to me. "I'll see you in the morning." He went past his brother.

I hugged my arms around my waist, almost wishing for the barrier to make things simpler. "Sorry about earlier."

He walked in a few feet and then stopped and crossed his arms. "I think that's my line." He tapped his head. "I'm a bit of mess, in case you missed that."

I shook my head. "No, I got it." I wanted to offer him something. "Uh, after spending some time in there, I'd like to tell you that it's not as bad up there as you think." I sighed. "Or it wasn't until I messed it up today."

The strain of the silence had my heart beating, then he spoke again.

"How much did you see, then," He motioned to his head. "When you were whispering to me constantly?" His jaw was clenched.

I stood there, not sure if I should answer or change the subject. "It's not like I was browsing through your memories." I leaned against the back of the couch. "It took a great deal of energy, to keep the connection, so I really only felt your immediate thoughts." I smirked. "Like wanting me to shut up and go away."

He almost smiled, then sobered immediately. "I'd been wondering."

"If I could see everything, I would have known you were ten feet tall and had fangs," I motioned to the air, "and all this other realm stuff and would have run the other way, fast."

"Six foot five-ish." He said unamused.

I rolled my eyes, "well from my elevation of a whole five feet, I'm seeing ten." I was having trouble thinking of how to keep him from exploding again. I couldn't take seeing that pain on his face, knowing it was more my fault than anyone. "I have an odd question."

"Which is?" He dropped his arms, like he was expecting something that would be hard to handle.

"Don't you guys watch t.v.?" I lifted my hands. "I haven't seen one."

His mouth twitched. "We do. Can you handle a six foot t.v screen?"

My eyes widened, I put my hand on my chest, then gaped at him. "Did you say six feet? Oh my god, is this heaven?" I looked around.

He laughed. "Come on, I'll show you."

I nodded, then held up a hand and ran to the bed and grabbed a few of the food items. "Okay, now I'm ready."

I stood in the middle of the room, not caring if I was blocking a small portion of the large screen Michael was trying to watch. Surrounding the room full of huge couches and chairs were rows and rows of movies. Like every movie ever made, I was sure. I wiped my chin and looked at Leone, "did I get all the drool?" I rushed over to the nearest wall and ran my hand across the titles. "I've found my zen," I whispered and kept looking. Glancing over my shoulder, I smiled at him, "Can I just sleep in here? Actually, I volunteer to live in this room and keep it clean and…" I frowned, "and… I don't know but I'll do it." Turning I leaned back against the movies and looked at him. "Is this like the family room or does all of Alterealm watch t.v here?"

He sat on the back of a large couch. "Family, a few of the guards." He shrugged, "sometimes it is decades between uprisings and crises."

I held both hands over my chest and gave him a pleading look. "I vow to serve and protect…" I turned and ran my hands over the movies, "every single title on these shelves… forever and ever."

Michael laughed. "I take it your favorite sport involves a remote control?"

I turned and grinned at him. "Yes."

He raised one eyebrow. "T.V. pause." He said evenly.

The movie that had been playing paused. I stumbled toward the screen. "Oh my god. T.V. play." It started playing and I squealed like a schoolgirl. "T.V. rewind." It did. "T.V. play." It started playing. I spun around to see Arius standing there smiling. "Can I stay?" I looked from Michael to Leone. "You don't understand my t.v is like," I held up my hands in front of my face about a foot apart, "fifteen inches. One of you could probably span the whole screen with one hand."

Still smiling, Michael looked around at Arius, "Were you looking for me?"

Arius nodded, "yeah, need to go over a few," his eyes flicked to me briefly then back to his brother, "things with you."

Michael got up. "I was just trying to unwind a bit." He rolled his shoulder, "a little tense after earlier."

Leone looked guilty.

Arius shrugged. "We're all out of shape, Leone, thanks for the hard work out."

I snorted. "I don't want to see you guys *in* shape."

Michael glanced to Leone. "You good?"

Leone nodded. "Yeah, I think I'm through the crisis for the moment."

Glancing to me, Michael inclined his head to me and followed Arius out of the room. I cleared my throat. "Do you need to be in on planning or a meeting or…"

Leone shook his head. "No. My part tomorrow is pretty simple, just act pissed off when Davis shows up." He shrugged, "won't even have to act." He motioned to the t.v. "Did you want to watch something?"

I nodded. "Anything." I sat down on the nearest large chair, that was bigger than my bed. "The television is my spirit animal."

Leone chuckled. "If I get up and leave, don't take offense. I don't usually allow myself to be near…"

"Female humans?" I'd remembered our talk when he was trapped.

"Yeah."

"No offense will be taken." I turned and looked at the screen, actually had to slump down to look *up* at the screen. I watched out of the corner of my eye, he sat on the couch on the other side of the room, facing me not the screen. "T.V., play." I grinned as it did.

I tried to focus on the screen, usually when there was something on the magic box, I was enthralled, and nothing else got through. After several scenes, I couldn't even concentrate on the dialogue with Leone still watching me. "You know, you'd probably relax more if you looked at the screen and not me." I said while looking at him.

"I find you far more fascinating than what's playing."

I looked at him. "Me?"

He nodded. "Yeah. I don't know what to make of you."

What is someone supposed to say to that?

Leaning forward, he studied me. "I know you're a fierce, loyal friend or you wouldn't be in this situation." He shrugged, "I wouldn't be in this situation. But I don't know anything else about you." He looked at my hands, "magic skills aside."

I turned so I was facing him. "There is nothing special about me." Sighing I looked at my hands, "magic is it. I grew up a street rat and learned to get by, that's my life in summary."

"Street rat?"

I nodded, "yes, finding places to live because you really have no home to go to."

"You were in the system?"

"Foster system, yeah, but I didn't stay in it long."

He clenched his jaw a few times. "I've heard that from a few others recently as well." He motioned around. "I don't understand a life like that. As the second youngest of so many…" He snorted, "I've, at times, had too much family."

"From what I've seen, how can that be a bad thing?" I pulled my legs up and sat crossed legged, watching him.

He leaned back. "It has its moments. Try having your first girlfriend with seven brothers interfering all the time. Or worse, not aging along with seven brothers so the girl you're infatuated with is like 'oh your brother Chase is soo hot'." He rolled his eyes.

"It's true." Chase said from the door.

Leone rolled his head and looked at his brother. "Figures you'd walk in."

"My timing is always impeccable." Chase grinned and hugged Alona against his side. "We're going to try to sleep for a few hours." He looked at him for a moment, concern on his face. "Are you good?"

Leone exhaled loudly.

I sat forward. "I've promised not to bite him or keep him out too late."

"Ah, very good, sparky. We'll see you tomorrow."

I waited until they left and then looked at Leone. "He's going to always call me that isn't he?"

Leone nodded. "Yeah."

"Great." I sighed. "I'm tired. This has been a day, and then some."

Leone stood up, "I'll show you back to the room."

I looked at the t.v longingly.

He smiled. "Too many are in and out of this room to get any sleep."

"OK. Fine, lead the way."

The walk back was completely silent. The thought of what would happen to me after tomorrow kept rolling around my mind. I didn't think any of them would just use me that way—then again, I'd used Leone so all bets were off.

When we reached the door, he opened it and then stood there. I looked into the room and then up at him. "It's huge. My bed is in a closet at home." I pointed to the actual closet. "That closet is bigger than where I sleep."

He blinked, "I don't," he frowned, "I can't picture a room that small."

I looked down at his feet and back to his face, "you probably wouldn't fit, so that's a good thing."

The silence was back. His brown eyes moved over my face, I held my breath, not knowing what to expect or do. Should I just walk in and close the door, did I wait until he said good night? We were the epitome of awkward right now.

His expression changed, but before I could figure out to what, he lowered his head and kissed my mouth softly.

Straightening again, he frowned. "I'm not..." He nodded. "Good night, Bethany." With that he walked down the hall with long strides.

I released the breath I'd been holding and went into the room. That was—I didn't know what that was. Shaking my head, I kicked off my shoes as I walked and headed for the swimming pool in the bathroom. Some soaking and thinking was required to work that out.

Chapter Seven

I paced back and forth in the small kitchen. I couldn't remember a time when I was this nervous, or was it fear?

"Are you trying to build up the momentum to blow us up?" Chase asked leaning in the doorway.

I blew out a shaky breath. "I don't think I'm actually combustible."

"Good thing," he smirked. "We have an hour, so try not to exhaust yourself before then." He walked out the door.

I sat down at the table and was trying to settle down when Leone walked in. I hadn't seen him since the night before. He was dressed in black leather from neck to boots with swords and other deadly blades strapped to him. He gave me an abrupt nod, then walked to the bedroom.

I gnawed on my lip with indecision, then got up and followed him. He stood looking out the window. He seemed bigger today, as if that were possible.

Turning he looked at me.

I motioned to him, "Won't they notice your weapons and outfit?"

He shook his head. "Clairee will make them see what we want."

I opened my mouth and then closed it. I couldn't wrap my head around that.

"How are you doing today?" He asked quietly.

I lifted my hands and then dropped them. "Nervous."

He moved over so we only stood a foot apart. "What I said yesterday," he looked distressed, "when I said we couldn't babysit you." He sighed. "We-I will not let anything happen to you."

I stared at him. Wondering why, after what I'd put him through, he'd care what happened to me.

He lifted his hand toward me, then dropped it. "Look, I'm going to be—unpredictable for a while," he blew out a nervous breath, "let's just say you're my kryptonite."

I smirked at his reference.

"But," he continued, "Even when I'm growling, I'm going to protect you. Even if it's from me." He nodded, like he needed to agree with his own words.

I pointed to the kitchen. "I can stay out of—" I motioned between us, "whatever distance you need me to be if it helps."

Closing his eyes, he inhaled slowly. "It does, but it doesn't." Moving he came closer, touching my chin I looked up into his red eyes. "I can still taste you," he whispered, "so even when I can't smell your essence. You're there inside me."

A shiver traveled down my spine. When I could breathe again I'd figure out what that meant. Good or a warning.

"Now," he said barely audible, then leaned down and kissed me lightly. "Get away from me."

Backing up, I held his eyes as I stepped into the hall. Turning, I walked right into Michael's chest. He caught me and gave me a concerned look. "I'm okay." I said breathlessly. He looked over my head to Leone. I couldn't turn and look at him. I had my own internal war going on right now.

Michael walked past me and went into the bedroom. "Did you feed this morning?"

"Yes." Leone said quietly. "Tasted like ass."

I stood there, my back to them still, but smirked. He didn't like biting someone else. I frowned, that shouldn't please me. Great, I was broken too. In my defense though, the last week had been full of surprises.

"You think too hard and your head may explode." Chase said. I just looked at him. "Bethany?"

I shook my head, "yeah, I'm good. Just need some fresh air."

He motioned for me to go by him. "Don't go too far."

"Ah, I've already walked these fields, once was enough, thanks." I almost jumped outside, trying to give myself some distance. I paced away from the house and stood there taking deep breaths. A minute later, I turned and made my next stupid move of the day and looked to the bedroom window. Leone stood there, his eyes on me. I could see Michael and Chase behind him, he nodded and said something, but he didn't look away from me the whole time.

My phone ringing snapped me out of the daze. I looked at it and then to Leone as I answered it.

"Bethany, are they there yet?"

It was Davis. "There where? I thought no one can see the house?" Looking at Leone, I pointed to my phone, my eyes wide.

"They can't, but they may send out patrols to try to find him."

"I was just staring at the empty fields. I don't see anyone, or anything for that matter."

"Good. We'll be there soon to move him."

Michael and Leone came out the door. I put the phone on speaker. "Move him where? How? Maybe you don't remember the last time you tried to *move* him." I reminded him as I was giving Leone a panicked look.

"I think he'll be more cooperative when he learns we're taking him home."

"You're taking him home?"

"No."

I frowned, "But you just said…"

"It was figure of speech. We're going to set the meeting at an undisclosed location. They won't know until I tell them."

"Okay, so you're coming to get him now?"

"In about a half hour. Which is earlier than we said for a reason."

"Smart." I rolled my eyes at Michael. "Okay, see you shortly."

The call disconnected.

Michael took out his phone and texted something, then gently took my elbow and stared steering me to the door. "Go inside."

I looked over my shoulder at Leone, he'd been right, he didn't have to act at looking angry.

Chase met me at the door and almost pulled me inside. He held out a device similar to the one Davis had given me. "Put it on." He popped it open. "That button transports you out of here to a room in our royal chambers." He leaned down and looked in my eyes making sure I was listening. "If things get messy, use it."

I nodded and took it from him. Leone came in with Clairee right behind him. He glanced to my wrist and gave Chase a quick look, then walked into the bedroom.

Romulus came running in the door. "My king, get in the bathroom," he said motioning down the hall. "Clairee and I have a lot of things to do."

Chase waved his hand. "I'm going."

My King? I watched him walk out. Why hadn't my brain associated that earlier, a royal family usually meant a king. Wow, so Alona was a queen. Huh, things are never normal here. Snapping out of it I tried not to have a panic attack and sat down at the table. Then I changed my mind and jumped up and opened the fridge, grabbing a bottle of water. Someone once told me if you needed a moment to stall, take a sip of water while thinking. That may come in handy when they got here.

Clairee and Romulus came out. "We'll be behind the house." She told me with a small smile. They went outside, closing the door.

I stood and leaned to watch them both stopping outside the door and waving their hands around. I was glad I only had one part to remember.

I sat back down and lifted my hands, making sure I could feel my magic. I couldn't hear a sound inside or outside the house. It was probably the scariest non-sound I'd ever heard. The silence. If there had of been a real clock here, the ticking would have echoed.

If felt like hours before the door opened and Davis walked in, Baldy was right behind him. I threw my hands in the air. "About time. I'm going out of my mind here." That wasn't a lie.

I looked behind him. "Two of you are going to move him?"

Davis gave me a blank look. "No. We brought others."

I got up and looked out the window. I made a point of using my hand to count. "Twelve." I shrugged, "I guess twelve of you can handle one man." I said it loud for Leone and Chase's benefit.

Davis stood at the hall entrance. "How's he been?"

"Come and find out for yourself, Davis." Leone growled from the bedroom.

Davis smirked and went into the hall. He stopped where the barrier was. "Hello, enforcer." He said with a sneer. "I have good news."

"Nothing you could say to me would be good." Leone said, now standing in the bedroom doorway.

"We're going to meet your kings and trade you."

Kings? More than one?

"Trade me for what?" Leone glared at him.

"Marcus and his witch." Davis said with a smile.

I cringed when he said it that way.

"Bullshit." Leone spat out. "My brothers would never negotiate with you."

"It seems you under-estimate your value." Davis put his hands on his hips. "Are you going to cooperate, or do we have to drug you then tie you up like some kind of animal?"

Leone growled low, his eyes now red. "Try it." He backed into the bedroom.

Davis sighed and pulled a syringe out of his pocket. "Go get a few of the men." He said to the bald one, and then walked toward the bedroom.

Before the man could reach the door, I sent a shot of energy at him, hitting him in the back. He spun around and looked at me. As I raised my hand again, Chase appeared and slugged him in the face. Baldy fell to the floor.

Alona appeared beside him and looked down at the man. "Hello, Lou." She opened the door and Daxx bolted in.

"Got him." He vanished with a pop sound when she held a small box over him.

I raised my eyebrows and was going to ask, when there was a sound of breaking glass in the bedroom. Daxx stepped out the door.

"They went through the window."

We rushed outside.

I know my jaw dropped when I saw the brothers fighting the men Davis had brought. I looked around and found Leone. Davis was cheating and using magic. Leone stumbled back. I ran in their direction, raising my hands I flung as much as I could at Davis. He fell back, then scrambled to his feet and held a hand toward me and his other toward Leone.

Something was pushing against me, I couldn't take a step. Gritting my teeth, I raised both hands above my head, letting the arc build. I made a sound that was between a banshee cry and a howl as I hurled all the energy I could gather at him. He tumbled backwards, his feet flying over his head for a second roll. I dropped to my knees, but kept my hand pointing at him. I didn't have anything left but hoped the thought that I might would deter him.

Leone rushed toward him and pinned him on his face with one foot. He couldn't move.

"I've got him, brother." Victor said rushing over. He had a vanishing box thing, too. Davis disappeared.

Dropping my hands, I fell forward and barely stopped my face from meeting the grass. I tried to shift so I was sitting, and ended up leaning on my elbow to keep my face off the ground. I could hear the others, the sounds of fighting and metal clanging, but I didn't have the energy to look.

"Bethany?" Leone was beside me.

"Never been that strong before," I whispered. My head started to spin, my eyes blurring. "Might pass out." I informed him. Someone picked me up in their arms.

"Take her inside, we have the last few." Michael said from beside me.

I knew we were walking but couldn't lift my head.

"What does she need?" That was Alona.

"Juice, she always goes for juice." Leone was the one carrying me.

I felt him sit down, with me cradled in his arms. I just wanted to go to sleep.

"You poor men. You keep finding us complicated women." Alona said getting closer.

"Nonsense beloved, what fun would easy be?" Chase was here too. "You good, brother?"

Leone shifted, "yeah I used his body to break the glass."

Chase chuckled.

"We'll be right outside if you need us, Leone." I felt a woman's touch on my face.

"Thanks." Leone answered.

He shifted me in his arms, "come on, you need to take a drink, Bethany. My turn to revive you." He placed something cold against my lips. "Don't make me kiss an incapacitated woman to get her attention."

I couldn't help but smirk. "So tired," I whispered.

"I know, just drink. It will get better, I promise."

I opened my mouth and swallowed a few sips, it took a lot of effort to get that far.

"We're going to have to find a way to make this stop happening to you."

I could hear the worry in his tone, his heart was beating fast in his chest. It dawned on me I was a lot closer than he would normally want me to be. I took another drink, hoping it helped restore some control of my arms. "Just put me down." I said as loudly as I could manage, which wasn't above a whisper. "I know you don't want to be close to me."

Leone laughed softly, I could feel it rumble through his chest against my ear.

"What we want isn't always our choice."

I took another drink. I could have stayed in his arms forever. I felt safe—which was probably the exact opposite of what I should be feeling in the arms of a man with fangs.

"How's she doing?" Michael said from the direction of the door.

"She's pretty out of it."

"We're going back now."

Leone shifted me a bit. "She wouldn't cope with transporting right now."

"Okay, I'll be right outside."

Leone made an annoyed noise. "Do you guys really think I'm that fucking weak? That I can't control myself when she's almost unconscious in my arms?"

There was a long silence.

"I'll see you at home." Michael said quietly.

I heard the door close and tried to lift my heavy head.

"I won't hurt you." Leone said in a shaky voice. "Drink some more, you're shaking."

I must have drunk the whole bottle before I was able to open my eyes completely.

"There you are." Leone smiled. "Thank you, before I forget. I'm glad you didn't use that much power on me in the practice room when I was being an ass. My brothers would never have let me live it down," he gave me a serious look, "for a thousand years."

"I've been wondering what the downfall to a long life was."

He smirked. "Finding something that keeps it interesting is the downfall." He gave me an exaggerated look. "I don't know how Victor has not lost his mind in five hundred years," he chuckled, "well, he has Crissy now, so that should keep it interesting."

"Might be a little too interesting, she's—something." I finished.

He grinned. "She has visions. Hundreds a day. I don't know how she does it."

"That explains why she just blurts things out." He offered more juice, I took a drink. "So, Chase is a king." It wasn't a question. "I heard kings, plural, so I'm guessing Troy?"

He nodded, "yeah. I'll try to explain the history of Alterealm when you're up to it."

"I think I can sit up now."

Something went through his eyes, but he continued to hold me, looking at me with a sadness.

My heart skipped a few beats. I was scared the next words out of his mouth would be that he was locking me in a cube, now that they had Davis.

"I'm trying to decide," His brow furrowed, and he looked away from me.

Panic filled me, but just as fast a peace came over me. I owned up to my own mistakes, always. I reached up and touched his jaw. I deserved whatever his family decided after what I'd done. Red eyes looked back to mine. I didn't know why, but they didn't scare me this time. "I'm sorry for what I've done to you, Leone."

"Don't be." There was pain in his voice.

I could see his fangs when he spoke. I swallowed, both nervous and scared.

"I want to feed from you." He said with a strained voice.

I was about to tell him he could when he looked at my mouth.

"I want another taste almost too much." He palmed the back of my head and lifted me closer.

When his mouth brushed over my own, I touched his jaw again, encouraging him to kiss me again.

"This is a bad idea." He whispered against my lips.

"Probably," I answered breathlessly.

Gripping the back of my head, he brought my face closer and covered my mouth with his. It started as a slow exploratory kiss, a sampling, then deepened into much more.

Like a hesitant virgin, that I hadn't been in years, I dipped my tongue into his mouth, touching it against his fangs. A shiver ran through me and ignited my whole body.

He shifted me in his lap, so he could deepen the kiss further still. With a low sound from his throat, he pulled his mouth away and rested his forehead on mine.

We were both out of breath.

"I don't know what I want more right now." He said, his breath brushing against my lips. He inhaled deeply. "And because I don't know, we need to go back and not be alone right now."

I couldn't find fault in his logic at all. I was feeling the same way. The fact I was even thinking of his fangs biting into me again with such anticipation, almost frightened me. I looked at his mouth and with a move I couldn't have anticipated, put my finger in and touched a fang as he panted.

He moved and sucked in a ragged breath. "You're not helping."

"I'm—of two minds as well, Leone. I don't know what I want."

He made a sound in the back of his throat and brought our mouths together again. It wasn't a gentle exploration this time. It was heat and hunger. A claiming.

"Oh my goodness. I am so sorry."

We jerked out heads apart and turned to see Clairee in the door, her hand over her mouth.

"I didn't—" she motioned outside, "we're removing the spells."

Leone cleared his throat and stood up. "Hold on." He said quietly.

I was about to ask why, then my stomach plummeted. "Oh crap." I moaned as the bile rose. "Put me down." I didn't want to throw up on him. How sexy would that be?

Gently he squatted down. I rolled out of his arms and landed on my hands and knees.

With a soft touch, he rubbed his hand across my shoulder. "Sorry. I didn't want to have to deal with Romulus walking in behind her."

I took deep breaths and tried to wait out the nausea. "That's fine."

He sat beside me.

As cooling off heated situations went, that was better than a cold shower, I thought.

I pushed up to my knees, continuing to inhale slowly though my nose and blowing out through my mouth.

He brushed the hair out of my face.

I opened my eyes to see the worry in his brown ones. "I think I might live."

Leone offered a weak smile. "You're very pale."

I gave him a 'duh' look. "Redhead, pale skin goes with the package."

Giving me back the same look, he rubbed a hand over his own hair. "I've noticed." He frowned. "Seriously you need to eat." Getting up, he scooped me into his arms and carried me to the bed. Setting me down on it, he straightened up. "I'll get Mitz to bring you some tea and fruit."

"What happens now?" He just looked at me. "Now that you have Davis." I frowned, "I didn't see the other mage, was he outside?"

He cocked his head, "what other mage?"

"There was another one the day they got you, Herman."

He pulled his phone out and tapped the screen. "Arius, yeah we're back. Did we get another mage today? Herman?"

His look was somber. "Beth says the day they got me, there were two mages." He shook his head. "Get Clairee and

Romulus away from there in case they come looking." He nodded and then looked at me, his eyes moving over me. "She needs time to recover. No. Her room," he lifted a hand, "the one with *the* closet."

Hanging up the phone, he sighed. "A few of the others will be here in a moment." He dialed again. "Mitz, can you bring some tea and…" he smirked, "yeah we are." He shook his head. "I am fine, thanks." He tucked the phone in his back pocket and then started undoing straps and taking off weapons. Pausing, he motioned to the table. "Drink some juice."

I blinked and turned to pick up a bottle. I'd been too busy ogling him to remember my own health.

By the time he was out of weapons, Arius came walking in. "No mage named Herman. Just foot soldiers, Lou and Davis."

Leone crossed his arms, his jaw tense. "Is this ever going to end?"

"We're getting there, brother, don't despair." Stopping by the bed, he gave me a concerned look. "Still shaky?"

I nodded, then glanced to Leone briefly. The heated moments in the kitchen hadn't helped, but there was no need to share that.

"I should talk to Clairee and see if they can make her a brew or something to prevent that." Arius looked at Leone.

"I was already thinking that." He answered.

Arius looked back to me. "That move on Davis. It made your show in the practice room look like little sparklers." He winked at me.

I smirked, not even understanding how he had time to notice while fighting. "I've never used that much force before."

"Someone needed to film that." Chase said as he came through the door. "Seeing Davis literally go head over heels was a show stopper."

Mitz came through the doorway carrying a tray. "I'll have a kettle brought to your room with this tea blend, love. It takes time for a body to adjust going from side to side so often." She set it down with a smile.

"Thank you." I said already reaching for the cup.

Turning, Mitz looked up at Leone and patted his chest lovingly before she walked out.

"What's this about another mage?" Quinton came in scowling.

Leone turned and leaned back against the wall. "Bethany says there's another, Herman."

Chase looked from one brother to the other. "Isn't that the mage Ellis was with over here?"

Arius nodded. "At least we know what the house was for now."

"Yeah, to trap me." Leone straightened and shook his head. "Timeline doesn't fit."

"Fit what?" Quinton asked while he perused the snacks on my table.

Leone pointed to me. "She was in my head when Ellis was there, why didn't he see her?"

"Because I wasn't there," I took a sip of the tea. "I didn't get brought over to the house until the night before I…they—"

Leone gave me a hard look. "Where were you before that?"

"On my side of—" I waved my hand, "not in Alterealm. Which is why it was so hard for me, I was trying to stay connected to someone in another *realm*."

Arius looked at Leone.

Leone sat down on the edge of the bed. "Do you know where you were on your side while you were doing that?"

I nodded.

"Were there others there?" Chase asked putting one knee on the bed.

I nodded again. "A few dozen, sometimes more, people came and went."

"All men?" Quinton asked as he sat on the end of the bed.

I thought for a moment. "I don't think there were any females, other than myself. I stayed in my room unless I was hungry though."

Chase looked at Arius.

"Way ahead of you." Arius pulled out his phone and hit a button. "Victor, we need everyone at…the girl's room, now." He nodded. "Yeah that one." He hung up. "We need to give this room a name." he said looking at Leone. "Found mates are in and out so briefly."

"We have other things to worry about than naming a damn room." Leone snapped and got up.

"Tell me we're going to kick some ass." Daxx came in with Troy right behind her.

Arius nodded to them and headed for the door.

"Where are you going?" Chase called out.

"To visit Davis. He can buy us some time to get a plan in place before they notice he hasn't returned with Marcus."

Troy and Chase exchanged a look. I decided I didn't need to know, it looked that serious.

Chapter Eight

"I don't like it." Leone growled, his face inches from Victor's.

I didn't know the eldest brother well, but I recognized shock on his face. I'd witnessed enough interactions to know that when he spoke, the others listened without argument. "It's the only way in." He motioned to the window of graffiti covered boards. "There are too many variables to rushing in the front door."

I stood near the back of the crowd. We were standing inside the abandoned storefront across from the condemned building Davis and his bunch of morons stayed at. Where I had stayed. All the brothers, eight guards and us four women stood there waiting for this disagreement to play out. The difference of opinion was about whether I was walking in the front door and working my way to second floor to open a window, so they could gain access. No one had asked my thoughts on the matter. At this point, I just wanted to do something. It was starting to get dark and standing here wasn't going to get it done.

I looked at my phone, checking the battery. Alona and Daxx had installed some app that would let any here listen to what I was saying. The plan—that Leone wasn't liking, involved him and a few others coming in from the second floor after I opened the window. Clairee and two other witches were on the roof—they could cloak and protect any innocents nearby. I needed to learn more about their magic. As plans went, I thought it was solid.

A few more brothers decided to get in on the discussion. I glance to Daxx standing beside me, she rolled her eyes. Sighing, I hopped down off the crates we stood on, to make seeing over the giants was easier, and pushed my way through the bodies to get to where the action was.

When I reached them, I touched Michael's arm, he looked down at me then stepped out of the way.

"Tick tock." Chase murmured when I moved by him.

I nodded and pushed between Victor and Leone. "Leone."

He looked down at me, his face may as well have been sculpted in stone, he wasn't in the mood to negotiate.

"I have to go in. Maybe I can get numbers for you—give you an idea of what you're up against."

Leone shook his head.

Placing my hand on his chest I gave him a pleading look. "Let me do this. I'll go up, open the window and then stay out of the way." It was the least I could do. I could never make up for what I did to him, but I could help others from being harmed.

The nerve in his jaw twitched as he considered what I said. "You don't use your magic." He gave me a hard look. "If you collapse again, anything could happen before I get to you."

I nodded quickly. "Okay." I bit my lip, "unless it's to save my ass..."

Grabbing my arm, he held it up. "Then you use this."

I looked at the device and nodded. "I will." When he released my arm, I turned to leave. He grasped my elbow and guided me to a corner by the door.

Turning me to face him, he leaned down and lightly held my chin. His eyes held mine. "When this is done," he was close enough I could feel his breath on my mouth, "we have to talk."

I stood there. That hadn't been what I'd expected to hear. I nodded. I'd known, sooner or later, he would be taking me to a cell. I hoped though, that maybe one of his brothers could, and not him. "Be careful." I whispered and then pushed past him into the alley at the side of the building.

I pulled out my phone and took the app off mute, clicked to turn off the speaker and tucked it in my pocket again. I looked at the door wondering if Leone was on the other side. I shook my head. As things went in my life, this situation with him would be the usual. Complicated. Wrong. Hopeless. "Here we go," I said for the ears listening through my phone.

I was halfway across when I saw Leone and the kings running to the building. The fire escape was broken in many places, but Leone swung up, climbing like it was no challenge at all. His brothers weren't far behind him. Jolting back to focus, I looked at the door in front of me.

I crossed quickly and opened it, before I could change my mind. Closing it behind me, I turned and checked to see if anyone was lurking in the hall. "Third door on the left is the kitchen." I said softly. "All of the rooms on the right are where others bunk in." I started walking down the hall, listening. "Many voices present." Reaching the end, I went out into the large room that may have once been a lobby. There were a few sitting around. "End of hall, lobby and stairs."

Moving silently, I headed for the stairs. I made it halfway.

"Where have you been?"

I turned and looked at the mage. "Herman." I made a sound of annoyance and motioned to my clothes. "Went home, grabbed *clean* clothes. Thanks for leaving me stuck over there for four days without any, by the way." I looked around. "Is Davis back yet?"

He shook his head. "No. They had to lay low for a few hours until the guards stopped searching."

"But Erin is with him?" I swallowed the lump in my throat.

"And Marcus." He nodded.

"That is awesome. Yes." I could only fake enthusiasm so much. I turned and looked around. "Where is everyone? Shouldn't they all be here to greet Marcus when he returns?"

His face lit up. "You're right. We need to gather everyone."

I pointed at him. "Yes. You grab everyone here and I'll go check upstairs." I started walking.

"No one is allowed up there, the floor is not safe." He called after me.

I glanced over my shoulder, "Sure, because we *all* listen to what we're told."

He laughed. "Right."

I didn't look to see if he watched. "Most should be in the lobby." I said to my listeners. Hurrying up the stairs, I paused when I reached the top. In the low light it was hard to make out the missing sections of the floor.

"Flooring of the second floor, sketchy." I said quietly and started working my way to the window.

When I reached it, I unlocked it and tried it. Years of neglect had sealed it shut. Leone helped from the outside and slid it open.

He came through, his eyes appraising me quickly.

"Watch the floor." I whispered.

He kissed me on the forehead. "Stay here."

I nodded and turned to watch the twins come in.

"Good job, sparky." Chase moved by me.

"Stay safe," Troy said as he followed his brothers.

I looked out the window at the fire escape and thought it was pure luck it hadn't fallen off the building when they'd climbed it. Across the alley I could see a guard with Alona and Crissy—probably to deal with any running out of the building.

The sounds of fighting registered. I moved back to the stairs. I couldn't just stand here and not know if everyone was safe. I stood at the top and gasped at the scene below. Each brother was a force to be reckoned with. It was like a dance without music, I thought briefly.

Arius had his weapon out but was chasing down those not fighting. He'd catch them, hold onto them and look at them for a moment, then the person would walk and stand by the wall. Okay, never letting Arius touch me, or was it his eyes? Probably best to avoid both.

I turned to see Leone kick a man almost as large as him in the chest, he stepped back, then swung a large sword at Leone again. The clang of swords meeting was deafening. I'd been in his head when he fought, and it was methodical and calm, but to *see* it happening, my heart was racing.

"Why aren't you helping, witch?"

With my eyes wide, I turned to see Herman coming up the stairs. He glanced over his shoulder at the commotion below.

"We should bail." He said and then nodded.

When I didn't respond, he paused and gave me an odd look.

"It was you. You led them here." He raised his hands.

"Shit." I hissed and lifted my own. Something pushed me back before I could hit him. Looking behind, I saw no floor boards. I quickly side stepped so I wasn't being shoved into the center of the room.

He was at the top of the stairs now, his hands waving.

"Crap. Back off asshole." I raised both hands and let the arc build. Flicking one hand down I smacked him, hoping he'd fall down the stairs. I needed to buy myself time to use the device. He was pushed back a few feet, but not far enough. "Anyone listening? Going to use the device. Angry mage on the second floor."

I backed toward the window, keeping my hands out, hoping the show of sparks would deter him from following me. I got one foot out the window when he flung his hands up. A strong force hit me hard enough I was shoved out the window. My head cracked off the wooden frame of it. "Oww, shit."

Before I could open the device, another blast hit me. Two things registered at once, the sound of metal giving way and I was free falling to the ground. I clutched my head.

"Bethany!" Someone yelled.

Then I felt nothing. I heard nothing.

Suddenly, I felt too much, and the voices were everywhere.

I couldn't move. Why couldn't I move?

"Bethany. Don't try to move."

It sounded like Clairee, which made no sense she was on the roof. I was not on the roof.

"Alona, get back, you're going to pick up her pain." Clairee again.

I could hear sobbing but didn't know who it was.

"Where's the mage?" That was Michael.

"Victor is pulling Leone off him, or what's left of him." Arius was here too.

"Bethany!"

Leone.

"I tried to slow her fall, but I couldn't cast fast enough." Clairee sounded so upset.

"Beth, don't try to move." Leone's voice was right beside my head. "Clairee, can you do anything?"

"I'm not qualified, Leone. Quinton went for the doctor."

"Beth, stay with us." Leone sounded so upset.

My head was so foggy. The pain radiating from my leg was excruciating.

"Raf went to highjack an ambulance." Michael again. "We can't try to port with her like this."

"Brother, you can't give her blood until the bones are set." Victor was here now.

"Her head is bleeding," Leone said in a painful tone. "Where is the doctor?"

I tried to open my eyes, move my hand. Something, anything. It was like I was disconnected from my own body.

"Don't move, Beth, we're right here. You're going to be fine." Leone's voice broke as he whispered to me.

"Quinton's back." Clairee's voice moved further away.

I could hear sirens, they were getting louder.

"Clairee, you have to cloak that ambulance." Michael was moving away as well.

"Bethany, you stay with me. Stay with me. I'm right here."

Leone's voice.

I tried to focus on his voice.

I couldn't get my eyes to open and I wasn't sure I wanted to. My head throbbed, which was tolerable compared to the pain in my shoulder and entire right leg.

"She's coming to, try to give her blood now."

"Beth." Leone sounded like he was right beside me.

"Before you do that," Chase's voice, "you'll have a blood bond afterward. You healed the incision on her head."

My head? Blood bond. Wait, wasn't that the bad thing Erin had done with Marcus? Or was that a blood pact? Why couldn't I think?

"I don't care. I'll help her manage the pain." Leone again. "I can't move her. I'm afraid to touch her." He sounded upset again.

"Use your wrist, Leone. Closer to heart is better, but until she can be moved, wrist is better than none." Michael's voice was patient and understanding. "Doctor said to do it as soon as possible. There's a lot of healing to be done."

I tried again to open my eyes.

"Don't try to move." Leone was beside me again. "I need you to swallow, Beth." He whispered next to my ear.

I felt something touch my mouth. I tried to do as he asked, but I couldn't focus.

"A bit more." A shaking hand touched my cheek. "Rest."

"Go get cleaned up." Michael said sounding irritated. "Leone, look at me. You're covered in blood, you need to feed. Go. We won't leave her alone."

"I won't be long."

I tried to stay here, I tried to listen, it was hard. The voices blended, the words I heard didn't register. I couldn't think.

"… what are the chances?"

"We're lucky she's alive…"

"I'll stay. Everyone go get cleaned up."

The voices faded until there was nothing but silence.

Moaning brought me to the surface again. The moaning was my own. There wasn't a part of my body that didn't hurt.

"She's in so much pain." Daxx was here.

"Doctor wouldn't give her anything, said he didn't know how she'd react with the head injury, and something about possible allergies." Michael.

I tried to open my eyes. The pain from the light almost made me cry out again.

"Pull the blinds, it's too bright in here." Leone's voice, I'd been hearing it off and on. "You need more blood, it will speed up the healing."

When he put it that way, I wasn't going to object. My mouth was so dry I wasn't sure if swallowing would work, but I'd try.

"We'll go heat some soup. Maybe we can get some in this time." Daxx's voice faded.

"Beth, you have to take this. Please. It will help."

I felt my head lift, which caused it to spin. Pain shot through my shoulder, like someone stabbed me.

"Try, just a bit."

Warmth pressed against my mouth. I opened it and could feel it on my tongue. It was tasteless, but warm.

"That's it."

Just a few swallows and I was exhausted. I felt my head being lowered. I managed to open my eyes slightly, just enough to see the outline of Leone's form beside me. "Leone." The pain was making me feel sick.

"I'm right here."

"Did she take some?" Michael was back.

"More than the last time." Leone answered.

"That's good. Here's some broth."

I tried to move my hand to reach out to him, the pain shot through me. I moaned.

"I don't know how she's doing it. I'd be screaming like wounded animal." Leone said.

I felt his touch against my cheek. "Leone."

"I'm here." His breath was against my cheek.

"Eufori." I said. Hoping I had the right word because more talking wasn't going to happen.

"Did she…" Daxx was on the other side of me.

"She wants me to bite her?" Leone sounded hesitant.

"She wants you to dull the pain." Michael told him.

Points for Michael.

"I don't…"

"You can't feed off her, she's too weak, but the eufori will act as a pain killer, or the very least she'll be too stoned to care."

"Michael—I-I want to help her, but I don't… can I do that? Not feed but still—" Leone sounded frantic. He wasn't beside me now.

"It can be done." Michael sounded distant.

"I don't know if I can do it."

"Don't look at me. No fangs." Daxx's voice again.

"I would do anything for you, brother, but I'm not naïve enough to do that and feel your blade in my back." Michael's tone was hard.

"I know it has to be me or no one." Leone was beside me again. "Daxx, can you ask Troy to come here?" His voice was shaking.

"Yeah, I'll call him."

I tried to lift my hand in his direction and cried out when pain shot through me.

"Tell him *now*, Daxx." Leone growled. "Beth," I could feel his breath against my cheek, "I'm going to help, just hang on." I felt his lips touch my mouth. "Hope I'm strong enough for you, kryptonite."

"What's going on?" Troy was here.

"Doctor won't give her anything for the pain." Michael explained.

"Did you threaten to break his legs? He might reconsider." Troy didn't sound amused.

"He says with the head injury and unknown allergies it's not worth the risk." Daxx said quietly.

"Okay, what do you need from me?"

"You and Michael need to hold onto me." Leone's voice was rough. "Beth wants me to use eufori to dull the pain."

"Ah," Troy made a strange sound, "and I suppose one of us doing it instead of you isn't an option?" He hissed out a breath. "I thought as much." I could hear movement. "How do you want to do this?"

"Each take one of my hands?" Leone's voice was near me again. "Rip my arms out of the sockets if you have to, but don't let me feed off her."

"I believe in you, brother." Troy said sounding confident.

Leone snorted. "No. You don't. None of you do when it comes to that." I felt a soft touch moving the hair from my neck.

"Whenever you're ready, Leone." Michael's voice was strained. "Try not to crush our hands, please."

I could feel his hot breath against my throat. His breathing was uneven as he licked where he intended to bite. "You have to get better." He whispered and then I felt his fangs pierce my skin.

I knew it was working when the pain started to fall away. I felt completely detached now, but the endless throbbing was leaving.

"Leone, that's enough." Michael sounded loud.

I felt the cool air on my throat where he'd been.

"Let me heal the marks." He hissed out a breath and the warmth was back for a second. "Okay, let go." His breath was on my face. I felt him kiss my forehead. "Rest." He was out of breath.

"It's working, she's much more relaxed now." Daxx was on the other side of me.

"Yeah." Leone's voice was uneven. "I have to go feed. I'll be right back."

"Go with him so he doesn't rip someone's throat out." Troy sounded shaken.

"I've got him." Michael's voice faded.

There was silence. No pain now, and silence.

Chapter Nine

"I don't care where he is. It's been three days. Tell him to get here and check on her. *Now.*" Leone wasn't happy about something.

"Leone, she's improving. We knew it wasn't going to happen overnight." Rafael was here.

"I know, but it's been three days. She's opened her eyes for maybe five minutes total, never talks. I just keep biting her and drugging her." Leone was very agitated. "Fuck, she's going to be an addict before this is over."

"The fact that you can even do that is nothing short of a miracle, and you know it." Rafael said sounding closer.

"It scares the hell out of me each time I do it." Leone whispered. "You know what I went through, how bad it was." He sighed loudly. "I almost went insane when I was confined and going through withdrawal."

Rafael made an odd noise. "Yeah, I do, it was my face that took the beating when I tried to keep you company."

"Yeah. Wasn't just you, brother." Leone sounded further away now.

"I never had the nerve to ask—then or in the time since, but was it," Rafael paused, "was it…"

Leone made a scoffing sound. "It wasn't sexual, Raf." He sighed again, "It was just... I don't know, the scent from women appealed ten times more than from males."

"I'd say that's a good thing, but I know it's not in this case." Rafael's voice was flat.

"What am I going to do? What if I'm not strong enough to do what I technically have no choice but to do?" Leone sounded so tense.

"I don't know, brother. All of this is so far out of my scope of knowledge." Rafael said quietly. "Have you talked to Victor?"

"Briefly." Leone sounded like he was moving away. "He says it's entirely up to me. Which is no help whatsoever."

Even through the pain and fog in my head, I felt like I was eavesdropping. It wasn't like I could just get up and leave the room. I tried to lick my lips, my mouth was too dry. "Drink?"

"Beth." There was a clunk and then Leone was beside me. "Let me lift your head."

I felt my head move and then something touched my mouth. A straw. It took a lot of energy, but the reward of cool water was worth it. "Thank you." I felt my head lower back to the pillow. I opened my eyes slowly. It wasn't too bright. The first thing that registered was Leone's handsome face over mine. "Hey."

He smiled. "Hey."

I had no idea where I was. I could see the reflection of lights off the large shiny window. "Where am I?"

"Alona's apartment. We can't transport you back until you heal more."

I moved just my eyes and looked at the window, then around to the other side of the room. There were no cracks in the wall, no chipped paint, or stains on the ceiling. "Nice neighborhood?"

Rafael snorted. "The best money can buy."

"I thought Alona was a queen in Alterealm?"

Leone knelt on the floor beside me. "She is, but this is home base for her."

"I live in a closet."

He grinned. "I remember."

"I ache—everywhere."

Rafael moved and stood where I could see him. "You did jump out a second story window." He raised his eyebrows, "the landing didn't go well."

"I didn't jump." I licked my lips, "that idiot shoved me—with magic. Did we get them all? Did we get Herman?"

"We got them." Leone nodded.

Rafael cleared his throat. "Herman didn't make it."

I glanced to Leone to see the lethal look in his eyes. "So, I can't even say you should see the other guy. Crap."

Leone smirked. "Can I get you anything?"

"I don't know. My back is numb. Have I moved at all?"

He shook his head. "We can help you sit up a little."

"Please."

Leone looked at Rafael, who was giving him an odd look at the same time. "Just let us figure out how without hurting you."

I frowned, "how bad is it?"

Leone motioned for his brother to move to the other side of the bed. "Ah, you cracked your head…"

"That explains the throbbing."

"You messed up your shoulder and right arm…" Leone placed his hands under my back carefully.

"But saved your head more damage by holding it." Rafael added as he did the same on the other side of me.

They started to lift and slide me toward the top of the bed, both watching my face. I bit my lip and tried not to make a sound. It hurt, everywhere. "Stop for second." They immediately froze. I breathed slowly.

"Your right leg was shattered," Leone said with pain etched on his face, "but as far as they can tell no nerves were severed."

I looked at him, "will I walk again?"

They looked at each other over my face.

"That's what I'm here to find out." An older man came into the room. "Stop dallying and prop her up. Doing it slowly hurts more."

Leone and Rafael both looked at me. I closed my eyes, bracing for it. "Do it." I whispered. I went from flat to barely propped up, and decided no bending was good. I couldn't stop the sound of pain that came out of my mouth when they lowered me and my body adjusted. Blowing out a few breaths, I looked at the Doctor. "My whole back hurts, is that a good sign?"

He bobbed his head, not telling me one way or the other. "The bruising is extensive, not to mention a few cracked ribs, but pain is good in this case. It's no pain that is worrisome."

Still trying to breathe through it, I gave him an exaggerated smile. "Then I'm the picture of health right now." I clenched my jaw together and tried to adjust my head on the pillow, which brought more pain down through my shoulder.

"I wrapped your leg, arm and shoulder in a light, temporary casting. A longer, permanent one shouldn't be required with the blood healing speeding up your recovery. Without it, you would be months in recovery." He flipped the blanket off by my feet.

I looked down to see only my toes sticking out on my right foot.

"Coloring is good." He glanced at me. "Close your eyes." I did. He stabbed the one of my toes and I jumped, then cried out as pain flew through my body from the movement.

Leone growled and stepped toward the doctor.

"Brother, let him do his tests." Michael stood in the door.

Rafael walked around the bed and stood between Leone and the doctor.

"Full feeling is a very good sign. The damage was so extensive, I wasn't sure." He stopped talking and went around the bed, completely avoiding where Leone stood.

"Can you move the fingers on your right hand?" He flipped the cover down.

I looked down to see my right arm bent and wrapped flat against my body. It took a lot of concentration to focus through the pain and numbness to get my fingers to move. Which turned out to be the slightest jerking motion.

"That's good." He moved back to the end of the bed and then looked to the worried brothers watching. "I need her leg supported, so we can shift her onto her left side for a moment. I have to check her back."

As much as I wanted to know, I knew this was going to suck. Moving half a foot up the bed had been excruciating.

"Use a pillow to keep her leg from jarring." The doctor instructed them.

I watched Michael take one from the top of the bed and go down to my leg. Rafael moved around to the edge of the bed. Leone climbed on the bed and propped himself up beside me.

"I'll try to help you block some of the pain." He said softly.

I had no idea how he could do that, but I'd take it.

"On three." The doctor nodded.

 Rafael put his hands under my back.

"One."

Michael placed the pillow over my left leg and nodded.

"Two."

Leone placed his hand on my hip and slid closer. I felt a presence in my head, it was calming, soothing.

"Three."

Despite all best intentions and gentleness, I cried out as my stiff, battered body was rolled onto my side. Biting my lip, I breathed fast through my nose.

"Slow breaths."

I opened my eyes to see Leone right in front of my face.

"Give her a moment to adjust." Michael said in a tense tone.

I tried to inhale slowly. "So..." I exhaled, "I've decided," I winced as I tried to relax and let some of the tension go, "I don't like mages." I blew out a slow breath again. "Do it doc, this is as good as it's going to get." I watched the pain on Leone's face as he looked over me to Rafael. I wanted to turn my head and ask why, but I wasn't moving anything.

"Bruising is still developing, so it looks much worse than it is." The doctor said leaning down.

"Yeah? And how bad does it look?" I asked in a tight voice.

"You don't want to know." Rafael told me in a hushed tone.

"I have some concern about this area," he must have been showing Rafael, because Leone was resting his forehead against mine, his eyes on mine. "I think we should wrap her ribs, until it shows more improvement."

I winced at the idea. I didn't know how they were going to do that, but it the very idea of it hurt.

Giving Leone a wary look, Michael turned. "Leave what is required, we'll take care of it."

I didn't know why they didn't just let the doctor do it, but if they had some plan to move me enough to do it without pain, then I was all for it. Doctors weren't always gentle in their execution.

"I'm sorry, but I'm going to have to test for feeling down your spine..."

My eyes widened. Leone's darkened.

"Brace her so she doesn't jar anything."

I clenched my jaw and waited while Leone moved closer and held my hip. Rafael put his hand near my neck and held me still. I didn't even know if Michael was doing anything, I was too focused on how much this was going to hurt.

"Just tell me when you feel it." The doctor sounded like he was sitting on the floor.

"Okay." I held Leone's look. I felt a pressure near my shoulder blades. "Felt that."

"Good, good."

Another poke, and I was guessing was on top of a bruise. "Sure felt that one."

"And where am I trying now?"

I winced, "lower back."

"Good." The doctor stood up. "Let's leave her on her side for now, to relieve the pressure off her back."

"I'll go and get some more pillows." Rafael said quickly.

"Thanks." Leone said in a hushed way, still looking at me.

"I'm seeing remarkable things here. The road to recovery is going to be longer then I'm sure you would like, but you are recovering." He cleared his throat. "Michael told me you've been using eufori to manage the pain, I don't have any issues with this. Pain medication blocks the pain receptors and you could do more damage not being able to feel everything. The aid of eufori is allowing your muscles and circulation to relax which in turn is helping the healing process." There was a pause. "I don't suggest getting up just yet, but possibly by tomorrow or the next day we can remove the catheter and get you upright…"

My brain paused on catheter, why hadn't I realized that. Oh, wait, probably because everything hurt *but* there.

"Plenty of broths and liquids—and blood several times a day. I will check in tomorrow."

I looked to see the doctor standing at the end of the bed as if he were waiting to be dismissed.

"Thank you, doctor." Michael moved into my line of vision as he walked the doctor out the door.

Rafael came in, arms full of pillows. "Let's make you a pillow bubble." He grinned.

Michael came back in. "Mitz is coming over with Daxx to help wrap her ribs first."

Leone lifted his head and looked at his brother. "Has Mitz ever been over to this side?"

"Not that I know of." Michael looked serious.

"Me either." Rafael added as he placed a pillow behind my legs.

"Nonsense." Mitz stepped into the doorway, "your mother and I… well, never mind." She touched her head. "Whoa, head's a bit light. I'd forgotten the rush."

I looked at her. "Sadist."

She smiled and came in. "Oh, I had my time to feel like my insides were coming out."

Daxx walked in carrying a bowl on a tray, with other items.

Mitz looked to Michael and Rafael, "You men, out. Out. Now." She leaned over the bed and touched Leone on the shoulder. "Give her a little something to dull it love, then get out."

Leone looked to his brothers leaving. "I need…"

Mitz made one of those sounds mothers make to say, 'don't be silly', "You're not going to do a thing to harm her." She motioned to the door. "Daxx and I will be right by the door."

Leone looked to her then back to me, I could see the worry in his eyes.

"Would it help if I said bite me?" I tried for a smile, but the pain seemed to radiate through my body like a heartbeat. I tried to move my good hand to reach for him, then realized I was laying on it. I winced.

"Don't try moving around," he said with annoyance, "the doctor just said not yet." He took a deep breath and exhaled in a nervous way. He brushed my hair over my shoulder, "how is it the addict has turned into the drug?" He mused, quietly as he leaned closer. I could feel his breath on my neck, hot against my skin.

"Be my superman." I whispered against his ear.

With a quiet sound in his throat, his fangs bit into me. I inhaled sharply, not from the pain, but the intimate feeling it brought. I could feel each muscle relaxing and must have made a soft sound in appreciation, because he jerked his head up.

Red eyes looked down at me, assessing I was all right. With a ragged breath, he leaned down and licked where his teeth had marked and then rolled away in slow motion.

I felt bereft when his warmth was gone.

"Just thought we'd check in on sparky before bed."

I looked over to see Chase and Alona in the doorway.

Alona smiled. "I've come to help. Chase will help me block my feeling your pain."

Chase hugged her against his side. "Brother?"

Leone made a sound of annoyance. "I'm fine." He sat up. I could see the tension in his body now. "I'll help you lift her, then go feed."

Mitz shook her head. "We'll manage, Leone, she probably doesn't weigh as much as your dinner plate when it's got half a cow on it."

"Oh, not the cows," I said with a calm tone, "they were my only company when I walked half of Alterealm." I smiled. "I thought of trying to ride one…"

Michael was standing in the door. "I've seen your riding skills, it's probably best you didn't try."

Leone glanced from me back to him.

Michael shrugged, "put her on Lucian."

"You put her on my horse? And Lucian let her ride him?" Leone got up off the bed.

"I wouldn't say riding, but he sniffed at her and allowed her on." He shrugged, "she must have carried your scent."

"Michael recognized after ten seconds—it wasn't going to end well." I told him.

"I've come to help. I brought our strongest healing salve." Clairee pushed past Michael and came in. She looked like she was going to cry when she saw me. "I tried to slow your fall, I wasn't fast enough."

I would have shrugged, but figured I'd scream for trying. "It was a pretty fast trip. Thanks for trying."

Mitz walked up to Leone and looked up at him. "Go, feed and freshen up. I left some food in the kitchen here for when you come back." She reached up and touched his cheek softly. Leone hugged her briefly and then looked at me.

"I'll be right back."

After he left, Mitz looked at me with tears in her eyes. "You just have to live through the first fifty years of stupidity," she nodded, "and then your heart fills with so much pride you fear it might burst."

"Fifty years? I think that might be one hundred and fifty when it comes to Raf." Chase said with a grin.

"Raf is standing right behind you." Rafael said, not sounding amused.

"I know. What fun would saying it be if you didn't hear me?" He turned and kissed Alona, "I'll be right outside."

When the door closed, I looked at the four women looking back at me. "This is going to suck." I whispered.

"Yes. You may not know it, but you are so much better than you were the first two days." Clairee said coming around the bed. "Rafael called me and told me how bruised and swollen your back is, this salve will help with that." She leaned over me, so she could see my face. "I can't believe Leone is able to use his eufori and not be tempted to feed. That's... amazing."

"I'm his kryptonite." I mumbled, feeling like my head was floating.

"You are his something, that's for sure." She said quietly. "Now, will it be better to put this on first, before we sit you up to wrap our ribs?"

I made a face, "now. Sitting up is not going to go well."

Alona came over and knelt so I could see her face and not have to turn. "We'll do it as fast as possible." Her brows were drawn together.

"If you can't be this close, it's okay." I told her.

She shook her head. "It's not unbearable, I'll just blubber all over Chase when we go home."

"That will go over well." Daxx quipped as she unwrapped bandages and set them on the bed.

"Oh, thank you for letting me use your apartment." I sighed, "I don't think my place would fit even a few of you." I remembered my rent and having no job. "What are the chances of being up and moving within a week?"

"Too soon to know, love." Mitz was shifting pillows around.

I winced when Clairee touched my back.

"Sorry." She whispered.

My mind was swimming now, from the eufori I hoped. "Can you take a picture of it? The guys won't tell me how bad it is."

All of them paused and glanced to one another.

Daxx nodded, "I got it." She pulled out her phone and went behind me. I heard the sound of her using her camera. She reached over and held it in front of my face.

I looked at it, barely recognizing it was a back, never mind my own. There were scrapes, welts and larger puffy areas. The colors ranged from deep red to almost black. "I almost died." I said feeling hollow. "How didn't I die?" I looked at Alona to see a tear running down her cheek.

"We don't know." She said in a strained voice.

"Beloved?" Chase's voice came through the door.

"I'm fine, Chase." She took a deep breath and looked at me. "It may have been your connection to Leone or the traces of it. You were barely responding that first day."

"We were afraid we'd lose him." Mitz said with sadness.

That brought me back full circle. To what I'd done to him, to this family. I cleared my throat. "I'm probably going to be evicted soon." Not that it mattered when I would be living in a clear cube, I thought. "I'd like to get some of my stuff before they toss it out." Would they let me take anything with me to their prison?

Daxx was in front of me again. "We can pay the rent…"

"No. It's not the same without Erin." I inhaled through Clairee's touch, trying not to wince. "I gave up my job to try to…" I wasn't out of it enough to say kidnap Leone's mind, "get her back." I looked to Alona. "I had no idea the truth of all of it."

She nodded in an understanding way. "Yes, Michael told us about your visit to her."

I sucked in a breath, from both the pain in my heart and my body. "I don't know what Marcus has done to her."

Clairee stood up. "I was discussing it with Rafael, we're going to try a few things, Romulus and I, to see if we can," she gave me a soft look, "find her again."

"You can do that?"

She shrugged, "hopefully."

"I really need to know more about magic. Erin did stuff like you do, but I just—mine is just there."

Clairee smiled, "yours is purer than all of ours. That's very rare, a natural witch and not a learned one."

"Is that good or bad?"

She chuckled, "In my world, that is both coveted and admired."

"Okay, love, we're ready to do this." Mitz stood behind me.

I cringed, "and if I say I'm not?"

"Let's get it over with." Daxx said, giving me a nod.

Closing my eyes, I nodded. "How bad can it be, right?"

It was bad. I almost threw up a few times, only willing my body not to because that would have hurt worse. I broke out in a sweat and they had just laid me back on the stack of pillows when Leone opened the door with such force I thought it would fall off the hinges.

He looked at the women, and then to me and came over to the bed.

My face was wet with tears. "All done." I said completely exhausted.

"I could feel it." He whispered, "I may have broken Rafael's jaw."

Rafael appeared in the door, rubbing his face. "We held him back so you ladies could finish."

Chase came in behind him and zeroed in on Alona. She immediately went and wrapped her arms around him. "I don't think I'm man enough to do that again." He said hugging her tightly.

"It had to be done, loves." Mitz smiled at me, "I think Bethany took it better than all of you did."

"Daxx?" Troy came through the door and went to her quickly. He lifted her chin. "Are you all right?"

She nodded and leaned into him. "I'm not cut out to be a nurse. Breaking bodies I can do, but fixing them, not so much."

Leone was beside me on the bed, his back to everyone in the room, He touched my cheek with a shaky hand and wiped the moisture away. "I don't think any amount of eufori would have blocked that."

I closed my eyes, still trying to settle down. "It did help but sitting up is evil."

Leaning down, he kissed my forehead softly.

"Bethany is going to be evicted from her place soon." Daxx said.

Leone turned to look at her then back to me. "Do you want me to go speak…"

I shook my head. "No, I have no use for it now. With Erin…" I couldn't finish, the pain had made me breathless.

"We'll see how you're doing in the next few days and I can take you there to get your things." He offered.

I nodded. "Okay."

"I'm going to be a raging alcoholic soon if we don't stop all this." Chase said with a smirk.

"Alcohol," I frowned and looked at Leone. Why hadn't I remembered before? Oh, wait … because you tried to fly and have been busy being unconscious. "A bar." I bit my lip, trying to remember. "I think I know another place they use."

I hadn't even realized Michael was in the room again. "Use?"

"Yeah." I glanced at the water on the table. Without asking Leone reached over and got it for me and held it so I could have a drink. "Erin and I went to a bar to meet Marcus." I nodded telling him I was done with the water. "When she was still herself. It's like a biker bar, but I don't think they're bikers." I looked to Chase then Rafael, "they dress almost the same as you do to fight, and they just— some of them gave me the creeps."

Michael looked at Chase for a long moment before looking back to me. "Do you remember where it is?"

I closed my eyes, trying to dig through the fog. Opening them I glanced at Leone, whose expression was as close to murderous as I'd ever seen. "Yeah I think I can point it out on a map." I looked at Michael, "it's outside of the city."

Michael's jaw clenched. He looked at Alona. "Do you have a map here?"

She moved away from Chase. "Yes, we have one on the wall in the office to help with our searching." She left the room.

Michael looked back to me, his eyes flicking from Leone's back to me a few times. I wasn't sure what it meant, but I hoped I'd just bought myself a little more favor in his eyes when it came to my judgement.

Chapter Ten

"You are *not* coming, Leone." Victor's voice carried into the bedroom before he reached it. Crissy sat on the floor with her notebook, even the silent company was better than looking at a window I couldn't get up to look out.

"Victor." Leone followed him into the room and grabbed his arm.

The surprise was very clear in the way his brother turned around slowly to look at him.

Leone stepped closer, so they were eye to eye. "What would you do if it were Crissy?"

Victor's whole posture changed. He glanced to Crissy and then back to his brother. "I...

"Rampaged." Crissy blurted out and then nodded. "Came back with blood on you all the time, showered a lot." She looked at Leone and then smiled and turned her attention back to her notebook.

Victor's jaw tensed, he slowly looked from her back to Leone.

"I'm going." Leone said not allowing for any further argument.

Inclining his head, Victor held out his hand, "Cristy, heart, a moment."

Getting up, she set her notebook down and then took his hand and followed him out.

"I'll give you some space." Alona got up and walked out.

Exhaling slowly, Leone came over and sat on the bed. "Alona and Crissy will stay here with you."

"I'm fairly easy to keep an eye on right now." I looked at my arm and down the bed to my legs.

His eyes moved over my face, concern plain. "Is it any better today?" He rubbed a hand over his short hair. "The pain, it feels so constant to me—through the bond."

I still had trouble getting used to that. "It's bearable." I tilted my head as much as I could without screaming. "You do see the irony, right? You wanted me out of your head so much, now you're voluntarily connected to me."

His brown eyes didn't look amused. "Fate has her own reasons."

"Oh, did she have one for tossing me out a window?" Fate, I had learned was never on my side.

Leone shook his head, "to scare me half to death." He leaned closer and brushed my hair back from my face. "Do you want me to dull it?"

I shook my head. "No, I'm trying to tough it out a bit more today. The foggy head gets to me after a while, but I may change my mind after a few more hours upright."

He nodded. "Okay. I'm getting you a t.v. later, when I get back."

"You know how to get to a woman's heart."

Leone chuckled and leaned closer. "Rest, eat more soup, I'll give you more blood when I return."

"Are my eyes red yet? I think I have as much of your blood as you do. "

He smiled. "No, they're still smoky brown." Brushing a kiss over my lips, he watched my eyes, his breath lingering. "Why can't I stop doing that?"

"Because she's your favorite flavor." Crissy was back.

Leone sat up and looked at her.

She nodded. "I told you that you'd find your favorite flavor." She rolled her eyes and then sat down with her notebook.

Alona came in. "Daxx is transporting the guys over."

Leone gave her an abrupt nod then looked at me. "I'll be back soon."

"Be careful." I said quietly.

He stood up and looked down at me briefly before walking out.

"I hate this part," Alona sighed and sat down in the chair. "Last time we had to go rescue them."

"The waiting is hard." Crissy added, without looking up from her book.

"Can I get you anything, Bethany?" Alona stood up and looked around.

"A new leg would be great, so I can use the bathroom."

Alona gave me a sympathetic look. "If I only I could. I'm going to make tea. Crissy? Would you like some?"

Crissy shook her head without looking up from her notebook. "I'm trying to find pieces."

Alona smiled and walked out.

I looked at Crissy, trying to decide if I should ask, or even if I wanted to know. My thought process was a little clouded with the pain.

"It's okay." She looked up at me. "It's not what you think. The prophecy book—" she nodded, "the one with the leaves, it explains it all."

"Explains what, Crissy?" Alona came back in.

"That it's not what Bethany thinks it is." She put her head back down to her notebook.

I looked at Alona, who shrugged. "If you have any questions about this, other realm stuff, I'm fairly new at it myself, but I can try to answer your questions."

I had so many questions, but only one I needed an answer for. "Does anyone ever get out of the cells once they're put there?"

With a surprised look, Alona studied me for a moment. "Your friend?" She shook her head, "I don't see them releasing her. She did try to kill them." She waved her hand around, "as did my father, but he needs medical help, so it's best he stays there."

"Your father?"

She nodded slowly. "Yes, a torrid story really, let's see—I met my father when I was ninety-eight, for the first time, after thinking he abandoned my mother on this side before I was born. He was working with Marcus and tried to decapitate Daxx."

I know I had a shocked look on my face, but really what else could you feel? "Puts my problems into perspective."

Alona nodded and took a sip of her tea. "Yes."

"What about lesser crimes—where they didn't try to kill anyone?"

"Mmm, I really don't know. Chase has so much to monitor as a king, I suppose if you're curious about the cells and penal system you could ask Arius, it's his job."

"Arius is the—warden?" The same Arius that having him touch or look at you was bad. That was news I didn't need.

"Has it been long yet?" Alona sighed, "It feels like hours. At least Daxx is there to keep an eye on things."

"Hope it's not like the mud pit was—when we had to help her shower to see how bad the cut was so Troy wouldn't lick it with the mud still on." Crissy didn't look up, just muttered as she wrote.

I looked at Alona, who had much the same expression on her face. Neither of us wanted that story clarified.

"What pieces are you working on, Criss?" Alona sat back and stared into her tea.

I suppose she was hoping Crissy talking would fill more time, or she was interested. I was trying not to think about Leone and what they may be facing right now. My situation couldn't get more messed up than it was. How often does someone fall for their target? Target may not be the right word, but I had held his mind captive, that I did know. Now he was all I could think about. Could that be from the blood bond?

"I keep seeing Emil again, which is silly—he's found." She nodded and then looked up. "I'm so glad the flameless fire and daisy is solved." Her face became animated. "And the cows too." Her expression sobered as fast as it had become excited. "There's nothing connected to Emil, so I'm missing pieces. Unless the girl is part of it, but I don't see how." She bit her lip, "herbs, I think it's herbs—I don't know why I'm seeing them though. Clocks, broken clocks…" She looked at me quickly and then to Alona, "can I go bounce the ball in the office?"

Alona nodded, "Yes if it helps you sort it, go ahead."

"Okay." She jumped up and reached into her pocket. "I'll be right down the hall if you need me."

After she ran out, I looked at Alona. "Leone told me about her visions."

Sipping her tea, she raised her eyebrows. "I don't know how she copes at all." Standing, she smiled at me. "I was instructed to make you broth and to force you to eat it," she smirked, "please don't make me force you."

I sighed, "What I wouldn't do for a cheeseburger right now."

"I'll tell Mitz you need cheeseburger flavored broth—I have no idea if that's possible, but with Mitz, I suspect nothing is unobtainable. I'll be right back."

I was starting to like these people. I paused, thinking they're far more than people, despite fangs and all. Each one as uniquely weird as I was. I'd tried to make it up to them, but I didn't know if it would be enough. I wondered if the women would come and visit me. Chances of queens and a princess stopping by the prison though—probably not.

Feeling overwhelmed, I just wanted to cry. What I'd done to Leone, to his family, was unforgiveable, I knew this. I wanted it to be different. I had to think of another location. I had to. Each lunatic I gave them helped my chances.

Completely forgetting about the restrictions, I dropped my head back against the pillow and cried out when the pain radiated down my neck all the way to my hand.

"Bethany..." Alona came running in.

I waved her away with my good hand. "I'm an idiot...forgot...and moved." The tears started to fall, I had no control over them. "Such an idiot." I babbled. "I've made such a mess of everything." I looked up to see my feelings reflected in her face. "And now I've upset you because you're an empath." I cried even harder.

Alona sat on the bed and grasped my hand. "I'm really no help, am I?" Why ever did they leave me here?" She was crying too.

"It's not your fault I'm a mess. If there's a way to screw something up, I'll find it." I sobbed harder. "I held Leone captive, in his mind, in person and to complicate it even more I've fallen for a man that can't be near me." The tears were free falling now. Alona was balling as hard as I was.

"Oh no! No, no, no" Crissy came in. "No, let's not cry. I'll cry. Victor gets very upset when I'm upset." A tear rolled down her face. She rushed over and fell to her knees and rested her head in Alona's lap.

"*What* in the name of the gods is going on?" Chase stumbled into the room, out of breath, covered in blood.

"Oh Chase. My carpet." Alona sobbed.

"Scorch the carpet." He dropped blood covered swords onto the white carpet and went to Alona, pulling her into his arms.

Crissy continued to hug Alona's legs and cry.

"It's all my fault." I choked.

"What the hell happened?" Leone charged into the room, leaving bloody boot prints.

Alona started crying harder.

There was blood on his face, reminding me of the stupid things I'd done. "It's all my fault. I'm to blame."

He fell to his knees beside me, touching my face softly. "Calm down, breathe slowly. Your ribs..."

I pulled his head down, not caring about the blood and clutched it against my shoulder that didn't hurt. I started crying harder.

"Chase?" Leone tried to turn to look at him. "What happened?"

Alona motioned to me, then Crissy, then her carpet and started crying uncontrollably.

Victor barged in. "My heart, what is it?" He scooped her up into his arms, holding her so tenderly.

The very sight of it made me mourn more for what I almost cost this family. I started gasping and crying, which set off both of the other women even more.

"What is going on?" Daxx stood in the door, pointing one of her long blades at everyone. Her hand was shaking. "Which one of you bastards made them cry? I will stick this in you…" Her eyes were tearing up.

Troy rushed in and carefully took the blade from her. "It's the family bond, you're still getting used to it…"

"Do something, Troy. Be a king and order this to stop." She looked so distressed.

He pulled her into his arms. "Chase, maybe taking the *empath* out of the room of ramped up emotions would be a good start." His tone was hushed and even.

Chase stood up and picked Alona up into his arms and walked out of the room.

"Victor," Troy said in the same soothing tone.

"We'll be at home if needed." They both vanished.

"Okay, okay." Daxx huffed out a breath. "That's better." She nodded, looking at Leone and motioned to me. "Is she all right?"

Leone gave her a lost look.

"Uh, Bethany are you okay? Pain?"

I shook my head. "I'm fine." I hiccupped.

"Okay." Daxx looked up at Troy. "You find out what *that* was and fix it. We can't have that happening."

He nodded and pulled her back into his arms. "Yes, dearest, I will. Let's go home."

I watched them both vanish.

Leone leaned back and looked at me. "What happened? I felt your pain and then… then—is it too much? I was afraid it would take its toll without something to dull it." He wiped the dampness from my cheeks.

I looked at the blood on him, now worried I'd distracted him when he shouldn't have been. "Are you hurt?" My bottom lip quivered, the tears still threatening to fall.

He shook his and looked down. "It's not mine." Sighing, he reached into his pocket and pulled out his phone. "Yeah." Giving me a brief glance, he stood up beside the bed. "How many from Alterealm?" His brows drew together. "Yeah they were trained." He rubbed the back of his neck as he walked around the bed, pausing he looked down at Chase's weapons on the floor. Glancing back to me, he shook his head. "I'll grab a shower here and come over to get caught up when you or Raf can come here." He nodded. "Yeah, I think she was just overwhelmed and it got to Alona… and Crissy." He smirked, "let's hope not." Hanging up, he tossed the phone on the bed and looked down at his clothes. "I'm going to go wash this off, then I'll give you more blood," his eyes assessed me as he spoke, "and make you more comfortable."

I bit my lip and nodded as slightly as I could without jarring anything. "I'll be here."

Standing there for a moment more, he gave me an abrupt nod and walked out.

Focusing on breathing slowly, to ease the ache from my ribs, I closed my eyes for a few minutes. Opening them, I looked at the weapons and blood on the carpet and felt guilt. One more thing because of me. The fact that the men had rushed here when they felt their women's upset was not lost on me. I didn't understand quite how Daxx knew what was happening, but that too was incredible. That kind of caring didn't exist in this world. Every person was out for themselves, and didn't give a crap who they hurt to get what they wanted.

The last thought brought me full circle, right back to where it started…

"You keep thinking that hard and you'll give *me* a headache.

I looked up to see Leone standing there—in just his black pants. Weapons, shirt and boots gone. "Either my brain is slower or that was the fastest shower in history."

He gave me a half smirk and tapped his head. "The vortex of emotions you were going through started to feel a little heavy."

I frowned, "How can you be tapped into me like that and I don't feel it? And why don't you drop from exhaustion because of it?"

Crossing his arms over his chest, his very 'oh my' muscular chest, he leaned against the doorframe.

"I don't get tired because I'm not actively doing anything, just monitoring. If I were to block out the pain, or help you feel calm through those never-ending swirling emotions of yours," he shrugged, "I'd tire or need to feed more often."

"I'm jealous." Staying in your mind almost turned me into a vegetable a few times.

"This isn't magic, this is a connection through blood. If we take enough of each others', it's stronger and goes both ways."

"So, the guys rushing back here, was a blood bond?"

He cocked his head, "Mmm, yes plus mating bond." He paused at my curious look, then motioned to his arm, "the tattoos. They're mates." His expressions grew serious. "It's hard to explain, but they're completely connected."

"By tattoos?" I was having a hard time getting this and that alone annoyed me.

"They're not normal tattoos. They didn't go *get* them done—the mark appears, on its own."

"Oh." Really, what could I say to tattoos that appear by themselves? "How did Daxx know we were upset then?"

Moving from the door, he came over and sat on the corner of the bed. I found my eyes following each move he made. When he sat, there was no 'relaxed' stomach posture. The muscles were still tight."

"Our family…"

I quickly looked back to his face.

"Well, my brothers and I—I don't know if it goes back further. We have a mental link," he frowned, "it's so much harder to put into words."

"You can talk to each other in your heads? Without magic or a spell…"

He shook his head. "More feelings. I don't know how it works exactly, but we can sense what each other feels and know which one of us is feeling it. Not all feelings, we have to… project it. Sometimes we project it when we don't intend to though. Chase and Troy have mastered nagging us through the family bond. It's quite annoying at times."

I heaved out a breath, feeling pieces were finally fitting together. "So, that's why Herman and Davis warded the house. So your family couldn't use it to find you."

His jaw clenched briefly. "Yeah. I knew as soon as I tried to port out of there that they blocked everything."

I leaned my head into the pillow, feeling tired and confused. "This is all so complex." I smirked. "Who knew anything like all of this was possible."

"It's carefully guarded for a reason. What do you think would happen over here if people saw eyes changing colors and fangs?"

I snorted, "Mayhem. Then they'd do what they always do when someone is different. Kill them."

He inclined his head. "Yes. We're not new. Alterealm has been monitoring this side since time began. An irregularity that allowed those not for here to cross over has always been around. We've always monitored both sides— kept the balance."

"Marcus, Davis—all of them, that's what they're trying to really do isn't it? Trying to make it so all can come from your realm and be here."

He nodded. "It is and there are so many that shouldn't be over here, many that would take advantage of innocent humans in so many ways."

A pained looked was on his face. I closed my eyes, unable to look at him right now. "And I was helping them…"

He touched my hand. "You were trying to get a friend out."

Opening my eyes, I looked at him, guilt riding me hard.

"What would you have done if you'd gotten Erin back?"

I gave him a 'duh' look, "locked her up for the rest of her life so she wasn't anywhere near any of them ever again."

His eyes searched mine. I wasn't sure what he was looking for, but it felt like it was an important moment. I hoped he saw some sort of redemption. The long silent made me tense and that just hurt.

"The blood bond…exchange, can both of us do it?"

He gave me a surprised look. "You do not want to be in my head right now. It's a mess."

I grinned. "Yeah and mine is complete serenity and balance."

That made him smile. "We have a slight one from when I—" his eyes moved to my neck, "heal the punctures from my fangs."

"I don't feel anything."

"You're looking for something noticeable, it's less obvious."

"Not like some annoying chick whispering in your head day and night."

Crossing his arms over his chest, his dark eyes moved over my face. "Exactly."

I scowled, trying to focus, see if there was a small trace of this connection I could feel. I sighed. "I can't feel it."

Leone got up. "It's probably drowned out by the pain you're in. Why didn't you say something about how bad it's getting?"

"I was trying to distract myself from it by talking to you." I moved my head like I was shrugging, without moving any other part of my body. "I like talking to you."

He looked surprised again. "We can still talk after some blood and we dull the pain a bit."

I rolled my eyes, "Yeah I'm so intellectual on eufori."

He chuckled. "It's not meant to be performance enhancing or stimulating. It's to keep your body relaxed so you can heal."

I pouted. "I'm over it. This laying here and healing is boring."

"Do you want to lay on your side for a while?"

"Oh can I? That wall is ten times more exciting to look at then the ceiling and window."

Grinning, he crawled on the bed. "Blood, eufori—then if you eat the broth still sitting in the kitchen, I'll get your t.v."

I scowled at him. "Are you bribing me?"

He smirked. "Is it working?"

I closed my eyes and whispered, "Yes."

"Okay, let's get you on your side. Maybe tomorrow you can sit up completely."

"I don't even know if my body remembers how to bend."

He shifted the pillows around so there was one to rest my leg on. "It's only been a few days."

"That's not what you said when you were yelling about the doctor."

He paused, "you heard that?"

I nodded.

He stopped and knelt there. "I just—I feel guilty that you're not in a hospital with more care. I'm the one that wanted you here, so we could use blood to heal you faster."

"I thank you for that. From the sounds of it, I'd be weeks in the hospital before I even came out of it." I couldn't help by stare at his chest and abdomen, not to mention his arms. I didn't even know arms could be toned like that.

He cleared his throat.

My eyes shifted back to his like a guilty child caught doing something they shouldn't be.

"I'd like to get in a few times tonight—with the blood. I really think you'll feel better by tomorrow, at least enough to move around a bit."

I nodded. "Let's try it."

"We'll get you on your side first. It's easier for both of us." He lay down and reached a hand to my lower back. "The closer to the heart the blood is, the better."

I gave him a small nod, bracing myself for the pain I knew was coming.

"Hey," his breath brushed over my face, "look at me, we'll do this slow and easy."

I looked up at him. "That's good, I don't think I'm up to fast anything right now."

His mouth quirked, like he wanted to smile, but didn't. His eyes showed the strain he was feeling, just being close to me.

I felt the pressure on my hip as he started to pull me toward him. "Bet you never thought in a million years you'd be this close to a female human again."

He glanced to me briefly, "maybe a thousand. I figured if I could resist that long, I'd be okay."

"Sorry about that—for being human." I grit my teeth as sore muscles started to shift.

His mouth was beside my ear, as he reached to shift my upper body. "Don't be sorry for that. It's what makes you who you are." Sitting up, he leaned down to gently lift my leg to follow the rest of me. "I like who you are." He said so quietly I wasn't sure he'd actually said it.

"At least one of us does—" My breath left my body when he moved me completely onto my side as every injury and bruise settled into the new position at once.

"Breath through it, don't tense. Shit," He swore softly, "I should have given you the eufori first." He sighed, "I was afraid…"

"To do that first and be tempted by staying close to me after?" I inhaled through my nose. "I'm good." I huffed out, cringing.

"Liar." He said in a flat tone.

As the pain subsided, I opened my eyes and looked at his concerned ones. "At least I'm alive. I hear that was questionable at first."

"When I looked out that window and saw—your broken body on the ground below…" The muscles in his neck tightened visibly. "I lost it. I've never been so—enraged." He let out a slow breath, "Victor had to pull me off Herman…"

"I think I heard that. It's very fuzzy, but I could hear you when you reached me. I don't know why, but it was what I needed to hang on…"

Dark eyes met mine. I could see the emotions flashing through them. He leaned down and kissed my mouth softly. Moving back, he shifted so he was up on the bed further. My eyes went wide when he reached and pulled a knife from his pocket. Tossing the case for it aside, he looked down at me. "I heal quickly, so I may have to cut it open again."

It, I realized was his own chest. How had I not been coherent enough the past few days to know this.

He smirked at my expression, "did you think I had a tap I just turned on and off?"

"I—I am really out of it. I mean how else did I think *blood* healing would work?" I sighed, "I feel dumb now."

"Don't. Heads are not meant for high impact. The fact you are able to think is a miracle."

I lifted my chin slowly and looked up at him. "I think you are the miracle."

The muscle in his jaw twitched, but he didn't speak, just placed the blade against his pec and sliced it across it.

I gasped and watched the blood run down his chest.

With a gentle touch, he cupped the back of my head and adjusted his body, so my lips were a breath away from his skin.

With my tongue I licked the blood trail off and then placed my mouth over the incision. I expected that metallic taste blood usually had, but instead it was almost sweet, not at all what I'd figured it should taste like.

"Stop playing with your tongue, Beth, before it closes." His voice was rough.

Closing my lips over it, I sucked gently, trying to take in as much as I could so he wouldn't cut himself again.

When it sealed, he leaned back and cut into his skin again without comment. I didn't waste time this round. I was completely lost as to why he wanted me to get better so desperately. After what I'd done to him.

"Stop thinking." He said softly.

The cut healed closed again, I smiled against his chest. "I'm a thinker."

Holding me gently, he slid down again so I didn't have to look up. "You need to give the thinking a rest, for now. It seems to cause emotional waves."

I sighed, "I don't have much else to do right now."

"I'll remedy that shortly, with a t.v." Shifting, he kissed my mouth softly. "Let's dull the pain a bit."

I wanted to reach and touch his face, but the arm I could move was trapped half under my body. "In case someone needs to point this out, you don't have to have your brothers hold you now when you do that."

I watched Leone's eyes swirl as they started to go red. "It would be safer for you if they did."

"Do you want to feed from me again?'

He gave me a blank look. "No—yes—no. You're too weak." His red eyes moved over my face. "I'm too weak."

"What if I connect with your mind while you do, my way? Talk you through it?"

He shook his head. "No magic. Clairee is going to help you when you heal, but it takes too much out of you," he shook his head, "and you don't have much to give right now."

I knew he was right, but I wanted to help him. He was helping me survive, since I fell—even after what I'd done. If I could help him beat his fear of his addiction—

"There's that thinking again."

I rested my forehead against his. "You're helping me heal, with the pain—even getting me help with my magic. I just want to give something back, help you." I opened my eyes and looked into somber red ones, "after what I did…"

"You saved my ass with Davis at the house."

"No, I meant…"

He kissed me before I could finish. "Stop talking." Inhaling slowly, he brushed his lips over mine again and then moved my hair from my neck.

Instead of biting me, he nuzzled my neck, taking his time.

"Is it hard to do this without feeding?" I felt his tongue brush over my pulse.

"Yes. It's the hardest thing I've ever done in my life."

"I think you're the strongest person I know."

His fangs pierced my skin and I closed my eyes. I knew what came next, knew the pain would fade, just enough to breathe easier and to relax. "Leone," I inhaled slowly, "thank you." I whispered.

Lifting his head, he fought to catch his breath for a moment, then licked over the wound he'd left. "You always say my name the same way as you did in my head. No one says it the way you do."

I leaned my head against his, his breath still tickled my throat. "Am I saying it wrong?"

"You aren't, it just sounds, different. It's how I knew when you spoke my name out loud the first time, you'd been the woman haunting me."

"I didn't want to haunt you." My whole body felt looser, the pain was there but not unbearable.

"You did." He inhaled deeply again, "you do." Lifting his head, his eyes still red held mine. Lowering his mouth to mine, he kissed me softly, lingering long enough to take my breath away.

When he lifted his head, I looked at his mouth. Those fangs that had scared me the first time, meant something entirely different now.

"You need to stop looking at me like that."

My eyes went back to his. "Like what?"

"Like you *want* me to take a bite out of you. I need very little encouragement."

I gave him a small smile. "I'm just curious. Your fangs, they scared me that first time, which I think you meant to do, but now," I sighed, "they mean something else." I rolled my eyes, "I want to run my finger over them, but I can't move either hand currently. Kiss me again."

He made a soft sound in the back of his throat, I thought he was going to say no, then he leaned down and took my mouth gently. Using my tongue, I did what I'd want to do with my finger, running it slowly over his fangs. He growled softly and pulled his head back, closing his eyes, a look of pain on his face. His breathing was uneven, mine wasn't much better.

"Brother."

Chapter Eleven

Eyes wide, I turned to see Michael in the door. He looked like he'd barely just finished dressing after a shower, his dark hair still glistening with water.

Leone inhaled slowly and then opened his eyes and looked at me. "I'll be back shortly."

I nodded carefully.

Leone got up and then picked Chase's weapons off the floor, and walked out without another word.

I waited a moment and then looked to see Michael staring at the stained carpet. "He called you here, didn't he?"

His blue eyes flicked to mine. "Yes." Crossing his arms, he watched me. "He's pushing all the boundaries."

"He's succeeding. I know how hard it is for him to be near me." My head felt strange this time.

"To a certain degree he is, succeeding. After decades of watching him struggle it is heartwarming to see him do this, but even he has his limits."

"I know." My stomach felt off too. I frowned, "I don't feel right."

Michael straightened, "too much eufori?"

Closing my eyes, I tried to assess what was wrong. "No. Less, I stopped him earlier than normal." Opening my eyes, I tried to figure out why I felt off.

"How did you do that? Was he too rough?" He came to the side of the bed and knelt, so I could see him easily.

"No, he's always gentle. I spoke to him and he stopped."

Michael gave me an odd look. "How much blood did he give you?"

"Uh, he cut his chest twice." I didn't know how much. "Will too much make me feel strange?"

He shook his head, "not normally, no." His eyes moved over my face, then paused on my neck. "How much of yours did he take?"

"He closed the punctures, so I guess however much that is."

Reaching over, he touched my forehead. "No fever. What do you feel?"

"My head is swimming. I know I'm not brilliant after the eufori, but I can usually hold a thought." I moved my eyes looking around as I tried to figure out what my stomach was feeling. "My stomach is tense, like when you have a bad feeling in the pit of your stomach."

"Sounds like you may be feeling a trace of what Leone is feeling right now." He looked at my neck again. "He must have ingested enough for a bond."

"Should you go check on him?"

Shaking his head, he stood up. "I'll know if he needs me."

"That's something other families could use, that connection." He continued to look at me as if he was trying to see through me, into all those hidden spaces you try to hide the things you don't want to share with the world.

"If it is a bond, it should settle in a few minutes. After Leone feeds, he'll settle down."

He just stood there, giving me that strange look. "Why is Leone helping me?"

Cocking his head, his pale eyes locked on my face. "Helping you heal?"

I would have shaken my head, but in my current position if wasn't easy to manage. My stomach seemed to be settling.

"Helping me everything. Heal, control the pain—he's even set up some sort of magical training with Clairee—why?"

"I'll let him explain the finer details. In all honesty though, any one of my brothers would help you heal. I would if Leone was unable to..."

"Be near the human girl." I sighed.

"Yes." His eyes moved over me slowly. "We owe you a debt, as odd as that may seem. If it weren't you in that house with Leone, they would have found someone else. That someone probably wouldn't have come and found us. You placed yourself in harm's way by doing that, despite your crimes and involvement, you stood before us adamantly demanding that we hear you and listen. That is to be commended."

I couldn't think of anything to say to that, which was probably best. I was in enough trouble already. If he was feeling grateful, I'd take it, because I knew somewhere in all the fog in my head that once that feeling wore off, I was in a lot of trouble.

"Are you feeling better?"

"Yeah, a bit I think." I smirked, "heads fuzzy but that's normal after—"

Giving me and abrupt nod, he went back over to the far side of the room near the door and leaned against the wall. I wondered if he always came off this way, or if he just didn't want to be in the same room as me. My mind wouldn't let me not ask, it was just part of my nature and I needed to know, even though I didn't want to. Stupid brain. Taking a deep breath, I exhaled slowly. "So, what happens after I heal?"

He raised an eyebrow. "Victor and I were just discussing that earlier."

My stomach tensed, did I want to hear what I'd feared? Was it better to just keep pretending that life was going to be fun and fluffy after I recovered? "And?" I'd never been a coward or avoided reality.

Leone walked in. Somewhere in the short time he'd been gone, he'd stopped to get dressed in jeans and a black t-shirt. "And what?"

Michael straightened away from the door. "She wanted to know what happens after she's healed."

Leone tensed and glanced to me briefly. "There will be plenty of time to talk about that." He motioned down the hall. "Everyone will be here shortly."

Michael gave him a hard look. "What's going on?"

Leone shrugged, "Emil called and he's meeting us here, something's up." He looked at me for a moment. "Think you can handle the discomfort if I carry you to the couch?"

"To get out of this room, I'll handle it." I didn't know why I needed to be included, but I'd take it.

"I'll go get the couch set up." He came over, grabbed a few pillows, and then hurried out the door.

Michael turned his head slowly and looked at me. "He hasn't left you unattended since you fell."

I didn't have time to process that.

Leone came back in, "Give me a hand, grab some more pillows when I pick her up." He came over and knelt on the edge of the bed behind me. "All at once, or onto your back first?"

I squeezed my eyes shut. "Let's go for it."

"Okay, scream if I hit anything that's too painful."

I didn't answer, trying to focus on breathing evenly, hoping this wasn't going to suck as much as I thought it might. I was allowed my delusions, I had fallen out of a building. I could feel the heat of his body close in on me, then his hands as he carefully placed them underneath me.

"Get her leg when I lift." He said in a rough voice.

I heard Michael move closer, but kept my eyes closed. I was about to tell him to get it over with when the whole world spun as I was lifted. My ribs and shoulder screamed. Clamping my jaw tight, I didn't want to make a sound. Breathing fast through my nose, I refused to so much a moan in pain, for fear he'd put me back in the bed. My leg didn't hurt nearly as much, and I guessed it was probably because it had been lifted at the same time.

"Got it?" Leone asked.

My head started to feel light as we went down the hallway. I kept my eyes closed. A wave a nausea washed over me.

Leone made a sound of exasperation. I felt a presence in my head and then the pain was so faint I could breathe again. I opened my eyes just as he lowered me to the couch. The expression on his face was one of complete concentration.

"You can't hold it for too long, Leone." Michael said softly, as he propped pillows around my leg.

"I know." Leone answered.

"I'll get more pillows." Michael walked out quickly.

I watched as he tucked the bag, still attached to my body under the blanket. With my arm free, I reached and touched his arm, so he'd look at me. His dark eyes flicked to my face. "Thank you."

The hard look softened. "I can't do it for long, but once we get you comfortable, I'll gradually release my hold on it."

I nodded, unable to say anything. There was a sheen of sweat on his brow now. "You can now."

Michael came back out and handed him more pillows. His eyes moving over me slowly and then to his brother. He didn't have to speak, I could see the worry in his eyes.

"Leone," I squeezed his arm, "do it now before they get here so I don't upset Alona again."

His eyebrows went up, but he dropped to his knees beside me and took my hand. "Lean back, close your eyes, breathe slow..."

I did as instructed and willed my muscles to relax. I could feel him gradually letting it go. It wasn't nearly as intense as it had been when he lifted me. I squeezed his hand hard, shaking a little bit. My back complained, but not as much as my ribs. Blowing out slow breaths, I kept my eyes closed. "Thanks for the short break."

"Just rest until the others come. They were grabbing food." He kissed my forehead and was gone.

I didn't open my eyes, just focused on keeping the pain at bay. I was out of that room, so I didn't want to do anything that would make Leone take me back there. Hushed whispers made me open them. The room was just as white as the bedroom carpet used to be. Leone and Michael stood on the other side of an island that separated the kitchen from the room I was in.

Leone stood, gripping the edge of the counter, his arm muscles tight. He had his head down, so I couldn't see his face. Michael was leaning against it, his back to me. Whatever he was saying Leone kept shaking his head.

"Hey, superman," He looked across the room at me, his eyes were red. "What's is it?"

He gave Michael a hard look before shaking his head. "It's nothing."

I just continued to look at him, hoping my 'that's bullshit' look was translating from this distance.

Chase appeared by the door before we could stare each other down.

"Thought I'd come and see if it's under control here before Alona arrives…" He stopped and looked at me, then to Leone and Michael. Going over he stood across from Leone, who had still been looking at me. "Is it your turn for a meltdown?"

Shaking his head, Leone looked at him. "I'm…"

"Don't say fine—", Chase waved a hand up and down his own body, "emotion feeder, dear brother, in case you've forgotten." He put his hands on his hips. "Even without that fabulous feature, the red eyes and vibrating muscles give away your lie. Didn't you feed before coming back?"

Leone exhaled loudly. "Yes."

"He blocked all Bethany's pain while he carried her out here." Michael said quietly.

Chase glanced at me and winked, "how chivalrous." Turning back to Leone, he flicked his hand toward him. "Go feed and grab some food, then come back."

Leone glanced over to me.

"She'll be fine. We won't leave her alone."

Walking by him, Leone came over to me. I could see he was shaking.

"It's like I said that in my head to myself, and not aloud." Chase mused. "He's doing the exact opposite of what he should be."

Michael made a grunt of agreement.

Ignoring them, he knelt beside me and reached out a shaking hand to touch my cheek. His eyes were still red. "Is it bad? The pain?" He took a ragged breath. "I had to…"

Grasping the hand against my face, I squeezed it. "I'm good." I rolled my eyes, "or as good as I can be right now. Go do what you have to do."

Turning his head, he kissed my palm. "I will. You need to eat."

"I'm sure one of those giants over there can push a button on the microwave. Go on, superman."

He smirked briefly. "I'll be back shortly."

I nodded slowly, still afraid to move much. "I will be right here in this very expensive, tastefully decorated apartment."

Standing up, he glanced to his brothers and then vanished.

"Well." Chase pulled his phone out. "I'll let the women know it's safe to come over." He pointed to the bowl on the counter. "Michael figure out how to heat that. Leone is liable to break off arms if we don't get it for her." He snorted and walked down the hall.

I hadn't even gotten through half the bowl of broth before Alona's apartment started to fill with Leone's family. Which was okay, it was an excuse to stop eating the bland liquid. Not to mention just getting that spoon to my mouth was exhausting.

Leone had come back looking better, but still seemed tense. He'd also arrived holding a t.v., which he carried to the bedroom. It took me a minute to focus on anything but the fact he'd brought one twice the size of my own. He stood leaning against the wall now, watching.

Alona stayed as far from me as possible, and I couldn't blame her for that.

Several of the males arrived carrying large plates of food. Which took me back to wondering just how often they ate.

Emil, I had concluded with some help from every person here, was another brother. One that was born on this side but wasn't found for three hundred years. Three. Hundred. Years. I was still trying to wrap my head around that. While waiting for him to arrive, they bantered back and forth—even when the topic was serious, they kept a light tone to the conversation.

Daxx came over and gave me a quick assessing look. "It's nice to see you almost sitting up."

I smirked, "it's as upright as my back wanted me to go."

She stood there looking slightly uncomfortable. Glancing at Leone briefly, she smiled at me and then went and sat on the step between the kitchen and sunken room I was in.

A buzzer sounded, making Chase and Alona go to the door. She did something on a pad and then turned and looked Michael up and down. "I'm going to go out on a limb and say Emil's other son looks like you."

Michael and Rafael went over and looked at what I'd figured to be a monitor.

"He's a better-looking version of you." Rafael said with a smile.

Michael elbowed him for it.

When the door opened the Arius and Michael look-alikes walked in. If the one that looked like Arius was the father, the other must be this son. They were both giant size, and I wasn't surprised anymore to see people that size, really.

Alona was introducing everyone around the room. She paused when she looked at me. I lifted my good hand.

"Broken human, here. Hi."

Emil raised an eyebrow.

I sighed, "Tried a backflip out of a building. I don't how my execution was, but the landing was a total fail."

The other one, Abraham his name was, came over and squatted down and held out his hand. "Abe."

I took his hand cautiously and shook it with as little movement as possible. "Bethany."

He smiled.

There was a low growl coming from the other side of the room. I looked around Abe to see a red-eyed Leone.

Rafael and Quinton stepped in front of him and put their hands on his chest.

Michael came over quickly and put a hand on Abraham's shoulder, "come sit so your father can explain why we're all here." He glanced at Leone as they moved back toward the island.

Chase had an odd grin on his face. "This day is just drama." He laughed and looked at Leone. "Go sit over there." He pointed to me.

Leone, pushed through his two brothers and came over and sat on the floor next to me, leaning against the couch.

"Okay." Chase looked back to Emil, "what's going on?"

Emil rubbed the back of his neck and heaved a sigh. "I—we," he motioned to his son, "can't find Rena."

I glanced to Alona and she mouthed 'daughter'.

"When I got back and Dad explained what's been going on, I decided I'd go check in with her." He shook his head. "Her place is empty."

"It's not like her to not get in touch if she's going away."

"Oh," Crissy jumped up from the chair she'd actually been sitting in. "Does she have white hair?" She looked from one to the other.

Emil frowned, "her hair is very light yes, she takes after her mother."

Crissy looked to Victor, "It's not good when I see her, she's not happy."   Victor moved around the counter and rubbed his hand down her back.

"It will be all right, heart."

She nodded and leaned into him.

"You saw her?" Abraham frowned.

Crissy nodded and tapped her head, "in here."

Emil cleared his throat, "I explained her visions."

Shaking his head, Abe looked at his father. "I know you explained, but it's…." he waved his hand around at everyone in the room, "a little much to swallow in one try."

I snorted, "I'm with you there."

Leone exhaled slowly. "When did you last speak to her?"

Emil glanced to his son briefly. "A month? I was waiting for Abe to return from his trip to go see her and explain—" he sighed, "all of you, this."

"If Ellis finds out, he won't stay hidden." Abe said, with a serious expression that was almost identical to Michael's.

Chase looked from him to his brother, then from Arius to Emil. "Now I understand what all of you saw when you looked at Troy and I."

Victor rolled just his eyes toward Chase.

"Sorry," Chase took a deep breath. "Ellis has to stay put. We've already got enough bodies to keep out of harm's way." His eyes moved over Alona as he spoke.

Michael nodded. "I agree. The women we know they want too much, but men—anything goes."

"What do you mean?" Emil crossed his arms over his chest and stared at Michael.

Clearing his throat, he glanced to Victor, who gave a slight nod. "We've recently found out they're trying to—" he looked uncomfortable, "increase their numbers through…"

"Breeding." Daxx said with a loathsome tone to her voice.

"Excuse me?" If I could have jumped up, I would have.

Leone got up to sit awkwardly on the edge of the couch and took my hand. "Alona had a meeting with Davis and a few of those in charge." He looked around to Chase.

"Women born to this side can give birth with an Alterealm…partner." Chase said in a low tone. "Full blooded Alterealm women can't unless it's with their mate."

Abe turned and gave his father a wide-eyed look.

Emil shrugged. "I couldn't explain what I don't yet understand."

"Speaking of which, I received a message from the guard we have on the inside. She's on the island. It's as we feared and populated with mostly women."

"Wait—reverse." I gave Victor a wide-eyed look, "island?" I rested my head against my hand, then winced from the sudden movement.

"What is it?" Leone took my hand gently.

I huffed out a breath. "Erin and I were supposed to go to an island after she helped Marcus. I refused to go anywhere without her—which is how I ended up…"

He nodded, so I didn't have to finish.

"Where is this island?" Abraham suddenly sounded like the rest of the giants, his tone not allowing for anything but an answer.

"We can't get on it—yet." Quinton answered.

"Why?" Emil looked at Chase.

"It's warded with warning systems." Arius moved from by the door and leaned on the counter. "We're hoping that Kinsley can find a way to get us on it, but we're nowhere near a solid plan yet."

I frowned. "You sent a woman there? Maybe I just missed something, which happens lately, but isn't that…"

"She's very well trained and knew the risks." Victor interrupted.

"As soon as I find Rena, I'm going to help dismantle this madness." Emil said, looking more concerned than he had when he arrived.

Troy nodded, "do you know other locations she uses?"

Rubbing his hand over his forehead in slow motion, Emil was quiet for a moment. Lowering his hand, he glanced to Abraham. "We know most, I believe."

"I'd start with those. Maybe something happened, and she had to move on without time to give you notice." Troy looked from one to the other.

Abe shrugged, "It's happened before." He shook his head. "I'd like to say the last two hundred or so years had been without mishap, but I'd be lying."

Two hundred years? I was beginning to think I was about the age of a fetus, or younger compared to them all here.

Victor straightened away from Crissy, his eyes moved to Emil's arm. He wore a device like the one I'd had. He looked at Rafael. "Go get two more devices, for Abraham and his sister, when they find her."

Rafael set the sandwich down he'd been about to eat. "Be right back." He vanished.

Abraham shook his head, "that..." he turned and looked at his father, "I just..."

Emil smirked. "I know." Nodding slowly, he looked from Chase to Troy. "We'll split up and check her other locations. Cover more ground in half the time."

"Keep us updated." Troy looked to Abe, "be very careful if you're approached by anyone you don't know. They're getting desperate enough to try anything."

"I can look after myself." Abe answered, crossing his arms over his chest.

"Oh yes, you're related right down to the finer details of your ego." Alona said in a sarcastic tone.

Chase grinned, then winked at her. "You love it and you know it." She actually blushed.

"So we don't get to go kick some ass?" Daxx sighed.

Quinton lifted his hands and looked at her, "we *just* took out twenty guys the size of mountains, an hour ago."

Daxx shrugged, "I feel like we have them on the run now. Have to keep the pressure on." She gave me a curious look, "do you know any other places?"

I looked down at my hand in Leone's, "I've been trying to remember if there were any other places Erin and I were..." I sighed, "It's really foggy, but I'll keep trying."

"Don't rush it, sparky, your head has had a rough week." Chase gave me an abrupt nod.

"I was thinking," Alona gave Chase a hesitant glance, "with Lou out of the picture..."

"No." Chase said quickly.

"Absolutely not." Arius added.

Victor turned and looked at her. "We don't know who was on the other end of those cameras."

She slumped her shoulders, "right. How absent of me to not remember."

"Cameras?" I looked from one to the other.

Leone's thumb rubbed over the top of my hand. "There were cameras in an apartment where a few women were being held..."

I jolted, then winced. "Held? By?"

He sighed and looked over to Michael.

Before he could answer, Rafael reappeared and held out two devices in this hand. "Keep them out of sight, anyone on team bad will recognize them."

Emil took them and put one in his pocket and held out the other to Abraham. "Push the button and you'll find yourself in another realm."

Abe took is and turned it over in his hand. "That's the part where I'll want to throw up, right?"

Emil nodded. "Yes, although my system seems to be adjusting to it."

"You suck." I said. He gave me a startled look. "My stomach threatens to move out every time."

Emil grinned, then looked at Leone and the smile faded. "It wasn't pleasant at first, I agree. I go see Ellis every day now, though so I think it's finally getting better."

"Michael, make sure both have all our numbers, in case they need us." Troy looked concerned.

"Should we use bonds?" Arius asked. "Emil may be part of the family connection and not know it, but a blood bond would help us find either of them if something happens."

Troy raised an eyebrow and looked to his twin, before both turned to Emil.

Emil opened his mouth, then closed it and frowned. "I had thought I was too old for new things."

His son looked up from the device on his wrist. "I need more details, before I agree to something involving blood."

Arius motioned down the hall. The two men walked out of sight, followed by Michael and Arius.

I turned to Leone, he was looking down at the floor beside the couch, his brows drawn. I gave a little tug on the hand he still held. Jerking his head up, he looked at me. Cocking one eyebrow I asked him what was up without advertising it to everyone in the room.

He gave a brief shake of his head, his eyes moving over my face.

When he looked at me that way it gave me goosebumps. I looked at his mouth. He gave my hand a squeeze and got up. Going to the counter, he looked at the plates of food sitting on it. Michael's eyes tracked his movement as much as I did.

I exhaled slowly, I'd really messed that man up.

His head came up and he looked at me, a cautious expression on his face. I smirked, understanding he was telling me no thinking. Looking back down to the plate, he picked up a sandwich. "Quint, Raf, I need you to go check on Beth's apartment."

Chase's head snapped to him. "Is there a problem?"

Leone shrugged, "they found Daxx's, knew about Crissy—" he motioned to the air around him, "this place is fort Knox, a fly can't even land, but I'd like to be sure." He took a bite and chewed it quickly then swallowed. "She's going to be evicted any day now and before I take her there—"

Chase nodded and looked to the other two. "Go check it out."

They all turned to look at me. I hesitantly looked between them, then the realized why. "Oh, I guess an address would help."

Daxx held up a hand. "Let me get the map, I'll drop them off as close as I can." She went down the hall.

I watched Leone eat, thinking there was so much more to all of this I wasn't aware of. "I'm hoping to try standing tomorrow." Several shocked expressions turned my way. "If I don't get a shower or bath of some sort soon, you all are going to need a hazmat suit to visit."

"Standing might be pushing it." Leone said between bites, "maybe we can manage a bath of sorts though."

Rafael frowned. "Don't push it." He shrugged, "we can get you a little motorized scooter to move around in here."

"Oh yes, Alona would love wheel marks all over her carpets." I rolled my eyes.

Alona held up a hand, "don't mention the carpet yet. I can't even force myself to go see if it's as bad as I think it is."

Daxx came back with a map looking flushed, she glanced to Troy briefly, before he raised an eyebrow and smirked at her. It took my slow brain a moment to catch up, then realized she'd probably walked in on the blood bond process. I paused, glad that I wasn't the only one with a fascination with the whole biting thing.

She came over to me and knelt, putting the map on my lap.

I looked at it and pointed.

"Could be a worse neighborhood."

I nodded, "yeah the tweakers are minimal in that area, the gang however is a different matter."

Chase turned to Alona, "see you could have things like that to be upset about."

She sighed, "I suppose."

Leone looked around at everyone. "Beth needs to rest."

After a few surprised looks at his bluntness, several looked at me and agreed. Just like that, everyone agreed to leave.

Chapter Twelve

I had no idea what time of day or night it was. The curtains in Alona's room were so dark, they blocked out all the light. After the apartment had emptied, Leone and Michael had gotten me back to the bed. The doctor had popped in, literally, for a few minutes and agreed I was improving rapidly. According to my body, that was questionable. Leone had woken me a few times for blood, then I'd find myself lying there with Michael lurking in the doorway while Leone went to feed.

"You don't like me much, do you?" I whispered into the darkness toward his outline in the door.

"My personal feelings in all this are irrelevant, but I don't dislike you as much as you think."

I stared at his silhouette, "your life skill is answering without saying anything."

He made a sound of amusement. "Occupational habit."

Leone came up behind him. "Thanks."

"Call if you need me." Then he was gone.

"Unconditional love." I mused quietly.

"What's that?" He asked laying down on the far side of the bed.

"Something Alona mentioned when you were trying to kill your brothers that day."

He yawned. "Wasn't trying to kill them, just needed to…"

"Rage."

Propped on up his elbow he looked at me. "Something like that." He looked at the t.v. still playing. "Still want it left on?"

I smiled. "Yes. I'm used to having noise to sleep. This apartment is totally soundproof I think."

He put his head on the pillow. "Most likely. Rest."

My head started to feel fuzzy. The effect of the eufori doing its job nicely, still. I closed my eyes, determined to get up whenever it was daytime again.

Opening my eyes, the first thing I saw was Michael in the doorway, and I could see him, so it must have been daytime—or he'd turned on a light. Leone was laying much closer than he had been when I'd gone to sleep. I could feel the heat from his body.

Michael moved to turn off the t.v.

"Leave it," Leone said in a groggy voice, "she doesn't think as much when it's on."

Michael grinned and tucked his hands in his pockets. "I brought you some food."

Leone lifted his head and looked at him. "Awesome, I'm starving."

"I brought some porridge for you."

I looked at him. "Really? I'm allowed to eat again?"

He nodded, "doctor said you could."

"Wow, how sad is it that oatmeal sounds exciting?" I looked from Michael to Leone, they both had a strange look on their face. "You guys doing your mind thing?"

Michael's eyebrow went up.

Leone lay back down and rubbed his hand over his face.

"So what's going on that you don't want me to know, is going on?" I kept looking from one to the other and then paused, and repeated the motions again, only more exaggerated. It didn't hurt as much today. "I can move my head." I whispered, hoping it lasted.

Sitting up, Leone looked down at me. "What about your hand?"

We both looked down at my hand as I straightened the fingers and then squeezed them.

"Still hurts, but not enough to want to scream though." I frowned, "so what *is* going on?"

He sighed and moved to the edge of the bed. "Raf and Quint came back last night when you were sleeping."

"From checking my apartment?" I debated for a second on trying to sit up then decided against it.

"Yeah. It's been trashed." He stood up and stretched.

I paused and watched *that*, then it sunk in. "Trashed?"

Michael crossed his arms and leaned against the doorframe. "There wasn't much left intact, but they did bring back anything that wasn't destroyed."

Leone turned around and looked down at me, his eyes assessing me carefully.

"Why didn't you tell me?"

"I wanted you to rest, because I know you're going to get up today, no matter how much it hurts." He shrugged, "there was nothing you could do about it then."

I blew out a slow breath. "What good is it to wreck my place? Did they think I'd leave a detailed map of where I was?" I cocked my head, "who did it though? The only ones I worked with, you guys got."

Leone stiffened and looked to Michael, "that's a really good question."

"Do you mind company for breakfast?" Michael pulled out his phone, "I'd like Victor and Troy's input."

Leone shrugged. I shook my head. "If you add tea and juice and maybe some toast, I'm game." I grinned. "I'm hungry."

Michael chuckled and walked out of the room, phone to his ear.

Leone came around the bed and squatted down. "Don't push yourself moving. We'll get the doctor here to check your leg beforehand." He leaned forward and kissed my mouth softly, "I will figure out how to manage a bath for you."

I sighed. "Fine, I'll wait." I rolled my eyes at him.

He smirked. "Thank you." His eyes moved over my face for a second, then he straightened. "I'll go get your food."

A few hours later I'd been checked by a doctor, attended to by a nurse and magically scanned by Clairee and the greasy Romulus guy. Popular consensus was they may be using some sort of magical tracer to keep track of those helping team bad, and being a female increased the likeliness of that.

"Nothing?" Leone stood in the corner, his mood dark and serious.

Clairee shook her head, "nothing we can find. Not even a trace."

I looked from her to him, then to Daxx who stood there scowling in the corner. "What about tech tracking?" She looked at me. "It's simple, small, magic won't find it." I looked at Leone, "is there a way to scan for that?"

Clairee threw up her hands, "I don't have a spell for *that*."

Pulling out his phone, Leone tapped the screen. "Arius, get in touch with Elder—" he waved a hand, "the science one. Yes. Find out if they have something we can use to scan for chips or trackers." He shook his head, "not magic, modern technology." He enunciated it clearly. "Yeah. Hope not." He hung up and then turned to look at Troy. "If there is one and it has led them here…"

"Shit." Troy sighed. "Chase will be out for blood—more so than normal."

Daxx looked from one to the other. "I don't want to give up home base."

Troy pulled her against his shoulder. "I know. Let's see if it is fact first, before we wake them."

My chest felt heavy with guilt, again. I'd caused so many problems.

Leone moved over to the bed and looked around at the others in the room. "Let me know when Arius gets here."

Clairee nodded and walked out.

Troy's eyebrows went up, he looked down at Daxx. "We've been dismissed."

She laughed, "Or he'd like a few minutes with Bethany without all of us staring at them."

He pulled her toward the door, "I'm sure that's what it is. I don't think I like being dismissed."

The door closed.

Sitting down on the bed, he gave me a stern look. "Stop. None of this is your fault."

I scowled at him, I'd figure out later how he knew what I was thinking. "It is though. If I hadn't helped them—hadn't done what I did to you, then we wouldn't be here in this situation, we wouldn't..."

"Have gotten Davis and the others working in that group." He picked up my hand. "Or those at that bar."

I closed my eyes, knowing all that to be true as well. Opening them, I looked at him. His dark eyes. "What I did to you—I have to live with that for the rest of my life. The pain I caused you, I can't take that away."

He shifted and moved over to lay beside me, looking down at me with so many emotions flashing through his eyes. "There's some good in this. Some I'm struggling with." His eyes moved to my mouth. "We still need to talk, but not until you're well." With a brief smile, he looked back to my eyes and held them with his.

I wasn't sure what the look meant. "I..."

He shook his head to stop me. "No thinking." Leaning down, he kissed me softly and then lingered just above my mouth. "I want to be here when Arius arrives, so kissing you right now is not a good idea." Lifting his head, he smiled at me. "How about we take that cast off your arm and see how it is?"

My eyes widened. "Really?"

He nodded. "The doctor saying your skin looks good, means nothing to me. I need concrete proof that you're healing, inside."

I opened my mouth, then shut it and nodded.

Getting up, he walked around the bed and sat on the edge. He gently grasped the outer edges of the hardened cast then looked at me. "Ready?"

"Yes." I braced myself for pain. Then was completely distracted when he was able to pull it apart like it was paper. It crumbled, pieces falling all over me and the bed, but I didn't care. He carefully removed it all the way up my arm and then stood to pull the pieces over my shoulder open.

Brushing it all aside, he raised his eyebrows. "Go slow. A little at a time."

I puffed out a few breaths, nervous that it wasn't going to be healed enough. I flexed my wrist back and forth. Stiff muscles complained. Putting my other hand on my shoulder, I slowly lifted my arm. Moving in slow motion I was able to lift it about six inches before I felt a stabbing pain in my shoulder. I sucked in a breath. "It's sore, but nothing like it was."

He sat back down and ran his hand gently up my arm, in a gentle massage. "It's going to take some time yet." His eyes flicked to my face for a moment then back to his hand. "Considering the way it looked when you fell—it's healed a lot. Maybe a sling for a few more days, so you don't forget and try too much."

I nodded. "Yeah. Think we can try me sitting up?"

He smirked, "you're going to push it aren't you?"

I shrugged carefully. "I *am* bathing today." I left out that with the catheter removed, I'd be using the bathroom like a big girl again.

Sighing he stood up. "Let me help from the other side, so you can use your good arm."

I waited for him to go around and get on the other side of the bed.

"If you can't sit up yet, don't force it for a bath. I'll stand holding you under the shower spray, clothes and all, if that's what it takes."

I grinned. "Okay. Let's do it." Inhaling slowly, I waited for him to reach under me to help lift me up on the bed.

Using my good arm caused my ribs to hurt, but it was manageable after the last few days.

When I was sitting up, I was out of breath. He tucked pillows in behind me and then I slowly leaned back.

"You're white as a ghost right now." He frowned. "No bath until you don't look like you're going to pass out."

I nodded, "I'm staying just like this for a while."

I was still struggling with the head rush and catching my breath when the door opened, and Arius walked in.

He paused and looked at the pieces of cast lying all over the bed then smiled. "Break it over his head?"

Leone gave him a blank look. "Did you bring something?"

Arius nodded, "yeah, Elder Arian said it's simple to use. If it lights up there's something under her skin, if not then she's clean." He held up a small device that looked like a hand-held metal detector.

Leone stood up and held out his hand. Turning to look at me, he held it back out to his brother. "I'll help her lean forward, you scan."

Arius nodded and went around the bed.

Troy and Daxx stood in the doorway, watching.

"Breathe." Leone whispered.

I realized I was holding my breath, afraid they'd find something. He ran it over my back, both arms and then Leone leaned me back against the pillows and took it from him. I watched as he slowly ran it over my abdomen and then both legs. No lights came on.

Leaning back on his heels on the bed, he held it out to Arius. "That's good, but back to how they know."

Daxx sighed, sounding relieved. "Did the guys check for cameras?"

Arius looked up from the detector he'd been studying. "You think they'd leave them?"

She shrugged. "I would, but if they did have cameras there, they already know she's with us. I'm sure Raf and Quinton were easy to see."

Leone sat down and pulled one knee up, resting his arm on it as he fidgeted with his hand and looked at the floor. Lifting his hand, he dropped it and turned to Troy. "Can they go back to look, take Tim and a few guards with them? We have to know."

"I'll go see if I can get anything out of Davis or Lou." Arius inclined his head to me briefly. "Good to see you upright."

I smiled.

When he left, I looked at Daxx. "I need a stool our height."

She gave me an odd look.

I waved my hand toward the hall. "So I can sit in the shower without having to bend."

Her eyes went wide with understanding. "I'll find something." She looked at my legs under the covers. "Cast still on?"

I nodded.

"Okay I'll see if I can come up with something to wrap it." She shrugged, "had my fair share of them."

"Don't remind me of the risks you take when hunting." Troy said, pulling her closer to him.

"Can you guys wait a few minutes?" Leone rubbed the back of his neck. "I want to give Beth more blood…"

"We'll be out here, just call if you need us." Troy pulled Daxx back out the door.

Leone started brushing the plaster onto the floor. "I'm going to have to bring a cleaning crew in here to restore Alona's apartment." Getting up, he grabbed the edge of the cover and flipped it up to knock the rest onto the floor.

"It will be good physio once I can move more. To clean this up."

Pausing he looked at the stained carpet. "I think the carpet is a lost cause."

I studied the bloody boot prints. "You might be right."

Climbing back on the bed, he sat beside me, facing me. "More blood, rest and then we'll negotiate about showering."

I smirked, "deal."

With a nod, he pulled his t-shirt off and tossed it beside him. Reaching down, he pulled a blade from under the cuff of his jeans.

"Have you always had to be ready to fight?"

Shifting closer, he paused and looked down at me. "Not always, but being prepared is always necessary. The royal family has many enemies."

I hadn't thought of that. I'd actually forgotten he was a prince. "So, do they call you prince Leone?"

He snorted, "They better not, or they'll find this stuck in them." He wiggled the knife between us. "I use my title, the enforcer." He shrugged, "prince sounds so…"

"Royal?"

"Yeah." Taking a deep breath, his expression grew serious. "This is going to be harder."

I frowned. "What is?"

"You, being upright and not as—broken looking."

I realized he meant being close to me. "Oh." I took a deep breath and exhaled slow, trying to think of how he must feel. I couldn't. "I believe in you."

His brown eyes held mine for a long time. "None of my brothers do." His expression became thoughtful. "I've caused them a lot of grief and worry. When I was going through withdrawal—the first time, I've had a few incidents…"

"They love you, unconditionally." I whispered and touched his jaw, so he'd look at me and see I did believe in him.

He looked at me, his eyes flicking to my mouth for a moment.

"If it makes you feel better, you look at my mouth far more then my neck."

Snorting, he shook his head. "That may be true, but even I don't know which I want more right now." Moving closer, he leaned over me, resting one arm on the other side of me.

The light mood faded as he sliced into his own chest. Reaching out, he cupped the back of my head and lifted me closer as I ran my tongue over the cut. He inhaled sharply when I closed my mouth around it. The rise and fall of his chest made my heart speed up. I knew without looking his eyes would be red, his mouth filled with fangs.

When it sealed, I rested my forehead against his heated skin. Lowering my head back to the pillow, his red eyes moved over my face. Reaching up, I put my finger on his bottom lip so he'd open his mouth. When he did I carefully touched the tip of a fang. He made a soft noise then bit my finger gently.

"I have to go." He whispered.

I nodded, knowing his demons were riding him hard. "I'll be here when you get back."

Looking at my mouth again, he stood up quickly and moved toward the door.

"Go, brother. We're here."

Troy stood to the side so Leone could go by him. Turning, Leone disappeared from my sight.

"It's going to take him some time." Troy said softly.

I looked at this man studying me quietly, this king and brother to the man I tormented. "I didn't expect him to help me…"

Cocking his head to the side he gave me an odd look. "I don't think there's a choice, but he's certainly proven he's stronger than any of us anticipated."

I had no idea what he meant. It must have reflected in my expression, because he smirked.

"He's had much more warning than you in this, he just chose to ignore the prophecy."

"Prophecy? Like prophecy of the future?" I didn't know if it meant something different in their realm.

"Yes." Crossing his arms over his chest, he gave me a serious look. "Then again none of us had seen this situation in any of it."

"Which? Me being human or my helping to kidnap your brother?" I honestly wasn't sure if he'd be for or against me when it came to deciding whether I was going to be locked up.

He smirked, "all of the above. Leone thinks he has a choice in the outcome, but really, he doesn't. Fate doesn't allow for that."

"Troy? Help me get this into the bathroom." Daxx called down the hall.

Looking over his shoulder, he gave me a brief nod and walked out.

I exhaled the breath I'd been holding. I looked at the t.v. and for the first time ever, I didn't feel like watching it. Even if I could get on my feet, where could I go? I had no place to live. I sighed and closed my eyes. I couldn't run anyway, it wasn't in me. Blowing out a steady breath, I tried to think this through.

"Why is it every time I leave, I come back to heavy thoughts and emotions all over the place?"

I opened my eyes to look at Leone. "Was just talking to your brother and trying to figure out what he was talking about."

Leone cocked and eyebrow at me. "What did he say? Troy is usually very easy to understand."

"Something about prophecy and none of you anticipated this situation, and you don't have a choice with the outcome." I hoped he'd laugh and tell me it was nonsense, but instead he blew out a breath in the way you do when you don't want to face the truth, or your about to give someone bad news.

Before he could say anything, Troy came in. "Quinton just called. They went back to the apartment. It was cleaned out. The mess, everything."

Leone looked from me to him. "The landlord?"

Troy shook his head, "Raf went and asked."

"What? Why—why would they do that?" I tried to sit up and then my ribs objected. "There was nothing there connected to them."

Leone rubbed the back his neck. "There is no reason."

I groaned. "As soon as I can get up I'm going to go stab a knife in Marcus' heart." Both men looked at me.

"I'm really starting to like you." Daxx stood beside Troy and nodded. She touched his arm and looked at Leone. "Bathroom is all set when she's up to showering." She smiled at me. "I left some comfortable clothes and a robe in there too."

"Thank you." I gave Leone a pleading look, "I'm hoping to give it a try in a few hours."

He sighed and looked to Troy, who was smirking.

"Michael is out with Victor checking some locations, so if you need anything I'm available."

Leone nodded. "Thanks." He motioned to the carpet. "Maybe see if Mitz has any ideas?"

Troy looked at the carpet with a serious look. "As soon as you bring Bethany over, we'll get someone working on it."

My brain paused on bringing Bethany over. The only reason I could think of that happening was to lock me up.

"I'm not rushing it. Her ribs couldn't handle throwing up right now." Leone gave me a brief appraisal, "yeah, we'll take another day and see how she's doing."

With a nod, Troy patted his shoulder. "We'll see you later."

After they left there was an awkwardness that hadn't been there before. I wanted answers, but was afraid to ask the questions. I wasn't sure, but I think he was in the same place. "You don't have to stay here, if you have other things to do." I looked down at my legs. "I'm not going far."

"I go offer to help anyone and they'll just send me back here. I'm a little distracted." He gave me a gentle look. "Did you want the t.v. on? Maybe take a short nap?"

"I don't know if I can. The idea that those people were in my place, and then cleared it all out like I don't exist creeps me out."

Going around the bed, he sat on the side with my good arm. "You know you're safe here, right?"

"I know. I just…" I couldn't explain it. Feeling like I was being stalked, and worried about being locked away at the same time.

Laying down beside me, he put his head on the same pillow. "I can feel your fear." Gently, he slid me down a bit and put his hand on my hip, so I'd roll into him. It was the first time he wasn't doing all the work for me.

It took me a few tries to get onto my side without jarring anything. Once there, I realized how close we were. Carefully I moved my arm and rested my hand on his chest. It felt right, there was no awkwardness.

"Rest. I'll be right here." He whispered against my hair.

"I don't know why you torture yourself being this close to me." I could feel how fast his heart was pounding beneath my hand.

"Close to you, away from you, I'm still tormented, Beth." His voice was barely a whisper.

When I'd had to find a head to get into, I couldn't have imagined why I'd been able to get into his. "I believe in you, superman." Closing my eyes, I rested my forehead against his chest and focused on the warmth from his body.

"Are you ready?"

I inhaled sharply. "Yes. No." With my arm shaking, I wrapped it tighter around his neck.

"Slowly, don't put any weight on it until we get you standing."

I nodded, afraid to speak. With great care, moving an inch at a time, he straightened up while puling me up with him. Muscles objected as I stood, and they were expected to work again and hold me up. I didn't put any pressure on my damaged leg yet, for fear I'd scream and he'd put me back in the bed.

"I'm going to try to support some of your weight by holding your hips, let me know if my hands hurt there."

I nodded, still too breathless to speak. He moved his hands to my hips and the first thing I thought was his hands were huge, spanning almost all the way around me.

"Okay, keep your arm around my neck and try a bit of weight on your foot." His spoke softly beside my ear. "Don't push it, you only need to balance."

Holding my breath, I let my foot touch the floor and leaned to get some of my weight shifted. There was pain, shooting ones, moving up and down my leg. I gripped his neck harder.

"If it's too much, don't push it." His hands tightened their hold on me. "I'll carry you to the bathroom, then you can get your balance again." Without warning I was scooped up into his arms and we were walking to the bathroom. "I'd rather take a blade to the gut then feel your pain." He said giving me a brief hard look. "I'm such an idiot." He continued, "I should have gotten you out of the building and not just left you there…"

I put my hand over his mouth. "You're blaming yourself for some idiot bouncing me out the window?" I blinked and looked at him again. "It's not your fault. It's not my fault. Trust me, even if I had of been on the ground, something *still* would have happened. A building falling on me, or whatever." I grabbed his chin and jerked his head so he was looking at me. "Not your choice, not your fault. Clear?"

Dark eyes stared at me and I was just about to bark some more when he gave an abrupt nod.

Exhaling I looked to see where we were. "The bathroom is as big as the bedroom." I said feeling completely disarmed now. Then I felt awkward, "uh, do you think Daxx is busy right now."

He gave me an odd look.

I pointed to the toilet, "I'd like to get out of this with some dignity left."

Nodding, he moved to the vanity and lowered me slowly. The counter space was as big as the island in in her kitchen. He set me so my bad leg was on it, then pulled his phone out of his pocket. "Daxx, can you come over for a minute and help Beth in the bathroom?" He nodded and hung up his phone.

"I was just about to pop over anyway," she came walking in holding up a cane with four legs on the bottom, "I know, geriatric, but it's only for a few days to help you keep your balance." She put in on the floor and demonstrated it. "Took a while to find one that's adjustable because I wasn't sure of your height." She looked at Leone then to me and set it down. "First things first." She motioned to the door, "out."

Leone gave me a hesitant look and then walked out.

Closing the door she gave me a wide eyed look. "He's more intense than normal."

I sighed, "Yeah, he thinks it's his fault I fell."

She snorted, "Men." Coming over, she put the cane on the floor and then gave me a nod. "Let's get you up."

I grasped her shoulder with my good hand. "Thank you. I've had to go for an hour and didn't know how to bring it up to Leone."

"I understand. They have this built in need to coddle us." She paused as my good foot hit the floor. "I'll balance you, grab the cane then put your weight on it." I did. "You just have to stand your ground or you're going to be carried around for months, whether you need it or not."

I barely acknowledged as she spoke, I focused on keeping the weight off my leg. I wouldn't be running today, but I was up and moving an inch at a time. I hissed out a breath. "Muscles are not happy their holiday is over."

She laughed, "They can suck it up."

It felt like an hour before I was finally at the toilet.

She motioned to the door. "I'll be right outside. I'll leave it cracked open and inch in case you need me." She looked around the room, "who knows if this room is soundproof as well."

"Thank you, really."

When she stepped out I heaved a sigh of relief. Never again would I take something as simple as walking for granted.

I was debating on calling for backup to get up again, when I heard hushed voices. Struggling more than I'd like, I managed to get to my feet. Or, more accurately to foot and cane and shuffled to the counter to get the robe. Pulling the shirt over my head proved difficult with one arm that wouldn't go up all the way, but I managed, and dropped the shirt to the floor, then pulled on the soft robe. I didn't want to eavesdrop, but I didn't want to interrupt either.

"You don't understand, Daxx…" Leone sounded stressed. "After—I was afraid to be close to any female, even from Alterealm…" His voice was shaky. "I thought that part of me was dead, to be honest. Until I saw Beth." He made a sound of frustration, "How messed up is that? I come to after being drugged, I'm being held captive and the first thought in my fucked up head is how gorgeous she is…"

"Yeah, uh… did—do you want me to call Troy?" Daxx sounded so uncomfortable having this conversation with Leone.

"No. No, I can't have this talk with any of my brothers." He snorted, "Can you imagine how that would go over? Hey, so I thought I was gay—turns out I'm not." He growled his annoyance.

"Yeah, okay, I-I get that." Daxx's voice did not exude that confidence she normally had. "But it's good that, well that—you know now, right?"

"I suppose."

"Okay then…"

"It's great, except that I can't go near her for fear I'll end up killing her by feeding. Look at when you guys found me…"

"That was dire circumstances, your body was starving, you weren't in your right mine."

"You don't get it," his voice was low, "that *is* my headspace when it comes to human essence."

"Oh. Oh. But you're so good around Criss and I now." Her voice faltered.

"You smell like my brothers now, both of you, the mating changed your underlying scent." He explained.

"Weird, but not, all at the same time." Daxx sighed. "I don't think you'll hurt her. I don't." She assured him. "Let's get her well and then…" She cleared her throat, "then there are other matters…"

"Yeah, okay. Thanks."

My heart was beating so fast in my chest, I almost forgot about my leg and let go of the cane. "Daxx…" I called out, being a coward and not wanting to know what the other matters were.

Daxx came in, then smiled. "Yay, for being up." She looked at my leg, then pointed to the plastic on the counter. "I brought that to wrap it in, so you can shower."

"Thank you." The emotion was so close to the surface, I could barely whisper.

"Okay." She nodded and started to open the door, "do you want me to stay and help you shower?"

I shook my head.

"I'll help her." Leone pushed the door open and then stopped when he saw I was standing, shaking arm and all, wearing a white robe.

"Okay." Turning, Daxx gave him a gentle smile. "I'm going home to harass my mate about letting me help with the search.

"Good luck with that." Leone said with a sarcastic tone.

After she left, he came over and without warning lifted me back to the counter. "You're standing there shaking like you're going to collapse."

I went with it. Couldn't tell him it was nerves from what I'd overheard. I glanced to the mirror beside me and then looked up at him. "Can I see my back?"

His brows drew together. "It's still…"

"I know what it looked like, the girls took a picture and showed me."

Heaving a big sigh, he nodded and carefully shifted my leg, so he could turn me on the counter.

Holding the front of the robe, I pulled my arms out with his help. Turning my head, I watched him slowly lower it and undo the wrap that had been supporting my ribs. When my back was exposed, I just sat there. It was yellow and dark brown all over, there were still some scrapes that hadn't healed.

"The bruising took a few days to come out." He said softly. "It's looking a lot better."

I nodded and just sat there looking at it. I knew it was bad, the state I was in after the fall. With my arm, shoulder, leg and ribs… but my back, it painted the whole picture for me again like it had when Daxx had taken a picture of it.

Keeping his hand on my stomach to make sure I didn't slide off, he leaned down behind me. My heart stumbled in my chest when his red eyes met mine in the mirror.

"I don't know if my saliva helps with bruising, but just in case." He licked my back gently.

I sucked in a breath, not because of pain or discomfort, but because it so caring and intimate. I could only handle a moment of it. "Why are you doing this?" I whispered, emotions threatening to overcome me.

He paused and looked at me in the mirror again. "I don't have a choice. I can't see you like this."

I swallowed the lump in my throat. "Stop. Please."

He straightened and looked down at me.

"You told me there is always a choice." I remembered how angry he'd been when he said it to me when he was a captive in that house.

His red eyes moved over my face slowly, "I was wrong." Taking a deep breath, he closed his eyes and exhaled slowly. When he opened them again, brown eyes looked down at me. "Let's get your leg wrapped so you can shower."

Biting my lip so I wouldn't cry, I nodded. I didn't know why I felt like crying, but I did. One moment I was fine, then I wanted to scream, and then, without warning, tears hovered.

"Stop thinking." He said as he worked the plastic up over my foot. "Don't you ever think happy thoughts? It's always so heavy…"

"Like what? Rainbows and puppies?" I watched him as he worked up my leg. "One is pretty colors and the other fluffy and pees everywhere. Is that better?"

He glanced to my face, a slight smirk on his face. "Much. Thank you."

"Bet you'll be happy when you don't have to be connected to me and drown in my *heavy* thoughts."

Securing the plastic around my thigh, he straightened up and looked down at me. "Will I? Be happy?"

I shrugged, "why wouldn't you be? I'm sure there's a list longer than I am tall of things you'd rather be doing."

Shifting my leg, he turned me so I could get up again. I pulled the robe back up and wrapped it around me. When my foot was on the floor, he looked down at me. "No. Not a long list at all." He smirked.

I realized that as I hunched to lean on the cane, I was even shorter and his comment was referencing my lack of height. "Ha ha." I rolled my eyes at him. "How are we doing this?" I looked at the shower door.

"Daxx has a stool in there for you. I'll get you situated on it then you can take as long as you like." He held my hips as I started to move toward it slowly. I wobbled a few times and touched the wrong foot on the floor and tensed. "Slow. It will still be there when you reach it."

Chapter Thirteen

Two days later I stood in the middle of a long hall, leaning on my cane, completely lost. Leone had brought me over yesterday and I hadn't seen much of him since. He'd come and check on me, give me blood, and then was gone again. It wasn't hard to figure out he was distancing himself from me. I sighed, looking back in the direction I'd come from. At least he was waiting until I was recovered before locking me up.

"I recognize that 'which way' look." Michael came walking around a corner. "Where are you trying to be?"

"Practice room." I sighed. "I'm supposed to meet Alona there to help with exercises to loosen up my leg."

He looked at my leg. "Still tight?"

I nodded. "Bending is still really hard."

He rubbed a hand on his jaw. "Considering the damage done, I say you're doing great."

I shrugged. "At least my shoulder is better." I motioned down the hall. "That way to the practice room?"

He shook his head and pointed to the hall he'd come down. "Come on, I'll make sure you get there."

I sighed. "Is there a pocket map or something to these halls?"

He chuckled, "we should hang some 'you are here' signs up."

I grinned. "Yes, you should."

We walked in and both stopped. Alona was on the mat, swirling a nun-chuck in each hand. I held my breath watching as she went through several moves, then one went flying.

"Drat." Turning she noticed us. "I'm glad you weren't closer." Going over she picked it up and shrugged. "I decided I needed to reacquaint myself with these, in case I need to bail out my mate again when he's stupid enough to fight with his body sliced open."

Michael chuckled. "Good luck with that." He motioned to me. "Found her lost in the halls."

She rolled her eyes. "I *still* second guess myself in those halls. We need a phone app for them or something."

Michael sighed, "I'll see if we can come up with something." Walking away from me, he motioned to the weapons in her hand. "Are you able to use those without backlash?"

Alona looked down at them. "For the most part. I don't exactly stand around after I wack someone and ask how do you feel?" She smiled.

He nodded and then glanced over his shoulder at me. "What…"

Crissy came running in the door on the far side. "It's not a broken clock! It's frozen…" she frowned, "stopped." Shaking her head, she grinned. "I have to get to the library." She ran across the large space and out the door we'd come in.

I looked from Michael to Alona. They were both smiling.

"This could get interesting." Michael said quietly. "I'll leave you ladies to it, I need to go see if Leone and Raf had any luck."

I started moving to the mat, slowly.

"Oh?" Alona walked over and hung the chucks back on the wall. "Luck with?"

Michael sighed, "Another possible location." He glanced to me and then back to her. "Troy saw a few landmarks in Lou's head so we've been narrowing it down."

I stopped moving, my mind pausing on the fact that Troy could *see* in someone's head. "What kind of landmarks?"

"Unfortunately, common ones." He sighed and motioned to the door. "Here's hoping they had some luck."

We watched him walk out. I turned to Alona. "I might be able to help."

She gave me a curious glance. "Help how?"

"If I could get in Lou's head," that made me shutter thinking about the sweaty bald guy, "I could get him to lead us to these landmarks Troy saw."

"I thought that was difficult for you to maintain?"

I leaned on the cane and waved my hand around. "It's better than doing nothing. Clairee is going to help me later, to see if we can find a way I can use my magic without it draining me."

Alona stood there, her hands on her hips. "If she can…" she made a hesitant face, "talking the men into letting him out to do this," sigh blew out a loud breath, "that will take some doing." Motioning to the mat, she nodded. "Let's work on getting you in shape, then if Clairee can figure something out to help you—we'll get the other women involved and see if we can *persuade* them.

I was soaked in sweat, lying flat on my back on the mat when the doors banged open and Leone stomped toward me. He was dressed in black from neck to foot, pointy weapons attached all over the place.

"Why are you exhausting yourself? I can feel it." He kept coming.

Shifting so I could get up, I reached for the cane, only to have him smack it across the mat, and bent down to help me up.

Michael and Rafael came running in the door, then stopped abruptly.

When my feet were on the floor, he held my arm and lifted my chin up with his other hand. I placed a hand on his chest to keep my balance.

"You just keep pushing it." His voice was low and vibrating.

Jerking my face out of his grasp, I scowled up at him. "What else am I supposed to do? Lay in bed and look at the ceiling?" I didn't know why he was so angry.

"You don't need to exhaust yourself." His eyes were turning red.

"Leone…" Michael said quietly.

Growling, Leone glanced over his shoulder at his brother.

I looked around his large body and shook my head. "It's okay. He *won't* hurt me." The expression on his brothers' faces said they weren't convinced. Looking up at him, I rubbed my hand across his chest. "What gives, superman?"

His red eyes moved over my face slowly. I could feel the tension draining from him.

"I don't like feeling you this tired. You don't need to push so hard."

I nodded, considering what he said. "I don't like feeling broken." I stared into his eyes. "The helplessness that goes with it." I sighed, "I know you understand that feeling, Leone…" I felt odd having the others watching us. Knowing he could get even angrier, I took a chance and connected with him inside his mind. It took very little effort with him right here where I could touch him. *Leone, I need this.* I said inside his mind.

His jaw tightened, then he blew out a breath and the tension eased. Leaning down, he brushed his lips over mine. "I like how you say my name." He straightened. "Stop using your magic until you're stronger." His eyes were brown again. Looking over his shoulder to where he'd sent the cane flying, he glanced to Rafael.

His brother ran over to it and picked it up, then walked toward us. "You're like a lion tamer, calming the raging beast, sister." He grinned and held out the cane to Leone.

Pulling it from his hand, Leone sighed. "You're an idiot, Raf."

Rafael laughed. "It's part of my charm."

Leone snorted, "If you say so." Setting the cane beside me, he touched my cheek softly. "Don't push it too far, okay?"

I nodded.

"I'll see you at dinner." He backed away a few feet and then turned on his heel and walked with long strides to the door.

After the men had left, Alona cleared her throat. "I need wine after that. Do you like wine?"

Leaning on the cane, I lifted my shoulders carefully. "I don't know, I've never had it before."

Her mouth dropped open. "Oh, well, we'll have to correct that atrocity then." She waved her phone. "It will be a girls only adventure." She grinned. "Gods know, we need it right now."

I lost track of time, and really didn't care. The wine sampling turned into much more. Currently the four of us were in swimsuits in the tub in the room I was staying in. I still couldn't believe we all fit in the tub with room to spare.

Crissy held her dripping phone up and giggled. "Vic is going to be so mad I killed another phone."

Daxx laughed, "at least he replaces them now."

She nodded and set it on the ledge beside the tub.

"I think I might be tipsy." Alona said and then laughed. "I've never had a tub party before."

I raised the glass and toasted the air. "I think I like wine." I looked at it in the glass. "The second one not so much, but this one is…"

Daxx's phone rang, halting all movement. She picked it up. "It's the mate." She chortled and answered it. "Hey, mate." She shook her head, "no, I'm in a tub right now. Hey, how have I never noticed the tub has jets?" Her cheeks darkened. "No, I'm wearing a swimsuit." She rolled her eyes at me, "because I'm not alone." She laughed, "Calm down caveman, I'm with the girls." She reached over and picked up her glass. "In Bethany's room." She smirked. "Maybe a few glasses." She looked at her phone. "I think our girl time is about to get interrupted."

Before any of us could speak, Troy and Chase walked in. They paused, wearing identical expressions as they took in the bottles on the floor beside the tub, and the tray of cheese and crackers Mitz had delivered.

"Unwinding after a hard night, beloved?" Chase smiled at her.

She waved a hand around. "Something like that." Her eyes widened, "Bethany had never tasted wine."

His jaw dropped in an exaggerated way, "and you felt you needed to rectify that."

"Yes. Immediately." She laughed.

Troy shook his head. "This explains why I was picking up such odd sensations."

"Oh," Daxx froze, "crap, I forgot about that."

Crissy giggled.

"Have either of you seen…" Victor came in looking frantic then stopped abruptly.

Crissy lifted up her phone. "My phone drowned, Vic."

"I see. This explains why you're not answering." He looked around, "And why I'm lightheaded."

"I'm sorry," she sighed, "I was only going to taste one, but each glass tasted better and better."

He smirked, "I'm sure it did." He looked to his brothers then back to us. "How did we come to be at a wine tasting in the tub, together?"

I lifted my glass. "That would be my fault. I was sore after the workout, so we decided I should soak." I motioned to the door. "And thanks to the magic closet, we were able to soak together."

"And here I thought you were resting and that's why I couldn't feel the pain." Leone stood in the door. He hadn't been there a second ago.

I looked from him to my leg. "It feels much better." I paused, then laughed, "Actually all of me does."

Chase pouted to his mate. "You could have invited all of us."

Alona looked at us in the tub and shook her head. "I think your being here would put a damper on girl time—not to mention I don't think eight of us would fit."

Troy shrugged. "We could have used the real hot tub."

"We have a hot tub?" Daxx stood, water splashing everywhere, then she wobbled. Troy moved over and scooped her up into his arms. Water dripped down him, but he didn't seem to care. Daxx wrapped her arms around his neck. "I think I'm tanked."

He chuckled. "Yes, you definitely are." He glanced around. "See everyone in an hour for dinner." He walked out, still carrying her.

Alona started to stand, Chase was right there helping her out. "I need to do my hair."

"Mmm." Was his only reply as he picked her up and left the bathroom.

Shaking his head, still smiling, Victor came over and picked up Crissy. She still held her glass and phone.

She looked over his shoulder and giggled. "I had fun. We need to do this again."

After they left, Leone stood leaning against the vanity, his arms crossed over his chest. He looked around the bathroom "I think the mess follows you around."

I chuckled.

"I came to wake you, and try to persuade you to have dinner with us in the dining room."

I frowned, "That's family time, I don't want to intrude"

He raised an eyebrow. "You just had a bathtub party with my sisters in law, I think dinner at the same table will be fine."

"Good point." I set the glass down and tried to figure out how I was getting up.

Sighing, he came over and flipped the toggle to drain the tub, then picked me up in one smooth motion.

"You're going to be soaked now." I wrapped my arms around his neck.

He grinned, "I can change." Moving over to the counter, he set me on it and grabbed a towel, pausing briefly to look at the bikini I was wearing.

I blushed. "That closet out there is like magic, whatever you wish for you'll find in it." I grinned.

Chuckling, he wrapped the towel around me, then picked up another and started to dry my hair for me. I don't know why I sat there and let him, but I did.

"I'm going to miss this." I said without thinking first.

He glanced to me.

I shrugged, "not the broken body part, but," I motioned between us, "this."

Straightening, he patted my neck and shoulders with the towel. "Missing it implies it's going to go away." His hand paused, his dark eyes holding mine. "You want it to stop?"

I shook my head, trying to puzzle out how he came to that conclusion. Thought was more slurred then my words right now. "No. I don't, but..."

Wrapping the towel around my shoulders, he pulled the ends and held them. "You're not going anywhere, Bethany. *Know* that."

Just like that. That fast, my happy drunkenness was gone, and reality was smacking me in the face. It had been the first time he'd said it aloud, what we both knew. I wasn't leaving this place. I took a ragged breath, but couldn't find the words to speak, so I just nodded and stared at the wet marks on his t-shirt.

"Hey," he released the towel and tipped my chin up with a gentle touch. There was pain in his eyes and my breath caught in my throat to see it. "No thinking." He whispered as he bent down and kissed me gently. Lifting his mouth away, his breath caressed over my lips. "You destroy me." He said in a rough voice, then took my mouth with such a force that I could only yield to his demanding kiss.

Grasping my hair, he pulled my head back slowly and looked down at me with red eyes. "You should tell me to get out *now*." His breathing was ragged.

I panted, feeding off the waves of lust pouring from him, "and if I don't want to?" I held his eyes. I didn't know if it was the wine or the desperation I felt inside, but I wanted to give him—something that would place me far apart from everyone else in his life. I wanted him to know he had my trust. That I had faith in his strength. "Leone, feed off me."

He made a wounded sound in his throat. "I can't."

I ran my hands up his chest, ignoring the twinges in my shoulder. "You won't hurt me."

Glancing at my throat he inhaled. "You don't know that."

I touched his chin. "I feel it. I was in your head, you're not going to hurt me." I titled my head to the side, exposing my bare neck to him. "You've cared for me with such compassion, been so gentle. You won't hurt me."

His breathing became uneven, his chest fighting to keep up. Every muscle in his body was so tense he was shaking. Red eyes held mine as he moved closer. "I shouldn't."

"You need to know you can do this. That you're strong enough to do this." I encouraged.

Moving closer, he rubbed his cheek against mine. "You'll have to stop me…"

His hot breath was against my neck. "You won't hurt me."

I felt his lips against my throat. Reaching, I grabbed the back of his head gently and held it. Letting him go at his own pace.

He hissed out a breath and bit into me.

The familiar feeling moved through me as the eufori was released.

With a soft growl, he pulled my hips, so I slid to the edge of the counter. Grasping my hair, he held my head and put his other hand behind me to pull me tight against him.

I moaned when he pushed against my tender back.

He jerked his head up and stumbled back a few feet. His hand over his mouth. Panting he looked at me with panic in his eyes. "I'm sorry." He growled and then spun around and hit the door with such a force I heard the wood crack.

"Leone…" I was too lightheaded from the wine, eufori, or probably both, to get off the counter without falling on my face. "Leone…"

He turned and looked at me, rage on his face. "I should be locked in a fucking cage." He growled.

I shook my head. "No it's not…"

Michael and Quinton came running in.

Leone growled a low warning when the stepped between us.

I held up my hand. "It's okay. It's not what you think. He hugged me and hurt my back."

Quinton looked like he was ready to fight if needed.

Michael looked at my neck, concern etched on his face.

I put my hand up and touched the stickiness, then looked at my hand. I was still bleeding. Holding my hand over it, I looked Leone. "Leone…look at me."

His red eyes zeroed in on me.

"I'm okay." I said softly. "It was my back, not you." He looked at my hand. I gave him a slight nod. "You need to close it."

He heaved a breath and looked to Michael.

"I'm here." He nodded at his brother.

"You won't hurt me, Leone." I whispered.

With hesitant steps, he moved in my direction. I held out my hand, not taking my eyes off his. His large hand engulfed mine and he stepped closer. With my hand still holding my neck, I moved my head to the side.

"Leone," I whispered in his mind. "I'm not your kryptonite."

With a shaking hand, he held my head and leaned down. I moved my hand. With careful movements, his tongue brushed over my skin a few times. After three or four more swipes, he kissed my neck and straightened. Resting his forehead against mine for a moment, he fought to catch his breath.

I looked into those red eyes, so many emotions were visible I wanted to cry.

Moving away quickly, he shoved past his brothers and left.

Quinton sighed loudly and slumped his shoulders in relief.

I wrapped the towel around me, trying to figure out what next.

"Did he feed off you?" Michael asked.

I nodded. "Yes. I told him to."

Michael's face filled with shock. "Why? Why would you do that to him?"

"Because," I glanced to see the same wide-eyed look on Quinton's face. "I wanted him to know he's stronger than all of you think he is."

Both stared at me for a long awkward moment. Michael inclined his head. "I suggest you wear more than a towel to dinner." He pointed to the door. "Turn right, first left, third door." He turned and walked out.

Quinton jolted and went over to the tub and grabbed my cane. He set it in front of me and then rushed out the door.

Sighing, I leaned back and then winced and sat up again. "Why does it feel like I'm a guest at the last supper?"

Looking at the cane, I eased down off the counter. Glancing around at the bottles on the floor, then the broken door, I shook my head. "I'm a menace." Turning I hobbled out to the magic closet to find clothes.

I made it to the left turn as Leone came around it. He gave me an odd look for a moment and then motioned down the hall. "I wasn't sure if you knew the way."

I kept walking. "Michael blurted out some directions before he left."

He walked patiently beside me. "They're looking at me like I've grown two heads." He cleared his throat. "Sorry if I scared you. I was high as a kite."

I grinned. "Hopefully it's because they all feel stupid for thinking less of you all these years." I glanced up at him.

He shrugged. "Their support early on is what got me through, but after a decade…"

"It became smothering?"

He nodded. "Yeah." Stopping, he put his hand on my shoulder. "But you—that was a stupidly risky move today. It could have gone horribly wrong, almost did go horribly wrong."

"I knew you wouldn't hurt me, Leone." I started walking again. I could feel his eyes on me.

"Why did you do it? If you wanted eufori…"

I shook my head. "I didn't. That's not why." I looked up at him.

His brows furrowed. "Then why?"

I could see the dining room door, so I stopped. "I wanted to give you something—after all I put you through, you still cared for me. I wanted to give you back your confidence in yourself. I know I don't deserve the leniency you gave me but…"

He jolted like I'd just smack him. "You think I'm locking you in the cells?" He shook his head and opened his mouth, then snapped it shut. "Unbelievable." He turned and went into the dining room.

I followed him in as quickly as I could manage. I stopped in the door and all eyes were on me. Muttering to himself, Leone sat in a chair halfway down the table. He gave me a hard-edged look as he picked up a bowl and started piling food on his plate.

Huffing out a breath, I went and sat at the end of the table. I paused and looked at the others for a moment.

Chase waved his mug around. "Why is sparky looking at us like we're going to bite her?" Alona shook her head and he stopped.

Leone glared at me down the table. "You saved my life—more than once."

I glared back at him. "*I'm* the reason it needed saving."

"You could have just kept walking and never looked back." He ground out.

I lifted my hand in the air, "and I'd probably still be out there wandering around with the cows."

"Wait," Chase looked from Leone to me, "is she arguing *for* being locked up or against it? I think I may have my mate's hangover."

Leone scowled at me as he took a bite.

I sat back and crossed my arms, holding his look. This went on for several minutes. None of the others spoke, I didn't even look away from him to see if they ate.

With a sound of exasperation, Leone threw his hands up and smacked both palms on the table. "That's it. I'm done." He held his hands up again. "Decades of being haunted by my past only to be tormented by my future." He stood up, knocking his chair backwards. "Fine. We'll settle it now." He stomped down the table and pulled my chair back, then picked me up. Kicking the cane out of the way, he turned to the door, then glanced back at his family. "Stay out of this."

I clung to his neck, not knowing what was going on. With his long strides, we moved through the halls quickly.

"I can't believe you're forcing this. I was waiting until you recovered, trying to push it past any and all boundaries." He turned down a hall. "I can't let it go on, I'm losing my mind. Misleading you—" another turn, "and I'm sorry, much more sorry than I can express that I can't allow you the freedom in this." He clenched his jaw and stopped talking. His pace increased.

Closing my eyes, I pushed my face into his shoulder. I know I'd pushed his buttons on purpose, and I accepted my fate, but that didn't mean I could watch as he walked me though that clear-walled hallway.

He stopped, shifted me and a door opened. When it slammed behind us, I was startled and opened my eyes. We were in a bedroom. I looked at him. "I thought…"

"Don't." He growled, then grasped the back of my head and crushed my mouth beneath his. His tongue invaded my mouth, rough and demanding.

I moaned when I brushed my tongue across the sharp edges of his fangs. I didn't know why I wasn't in a cell, and didn't care. I clung to him, holding his head. He hadn't kissed me like this since that kitchen in the little house.

When he stopped, he lowered me to sit on the bed and knelt to take off my shoes. Standing again, he kicked off his boots as he pulled his shirt over his head. Unbuttoning his pants, he stopped and leaned down. Pulling my sweater over my head, slowly allowing me to pull my arms out without force. I didn't have a bra on because of my back. He tossed the sweater to the floor, his eyes moving over the exposed skin. With one knee on the bed, he lowered me to lay back and grabbed the waist of my tights.

He didn't take his eyes off mine until he pulled them free of my legs. Moving off the bed, he knelt by my knees. With a gentle touch, he ran his hand over my injured leg, then leaned down and trailed feather light kisses along the same path. When he reached my hip, he paused, his other hand rested on the other hip. His red eyes connected with mine and he held them as he tore the sides of my underwear away from my body.

I bit my lip and watched as he slowly leaned over me. With his fangs, he gently nipped one hip, then the other. He moved up to my waist and did the same. I hissed out a breath, having never felt this intense sexual tension in my life.

"No more talk of blame or consequences." He said, his mouth against my skin. "You're not going anywhere. I'm not leaving." He licked over a hardened nipple then lifted his head and looked at me. "You're mine." He whispered.

My mind was swimming in lust. I didn't know if it was a question or statement. "Yes." I said breathlessly, just in case there had been a question in there. Reaching, I pulled his head toward mine. "Kiss me."

He growled as his mouth crushed mine. Without breaking the kiss, he moved both of us up the bed. He tore his mouth from mine and nipped my throat, then leaned down and teased a nipple between his fangs. With a groan, he looked up at me. His hand moved slowly down my body to rest between my legs. "I don't think I can wait." He nipped the side of my breast.

As his fingers moved, I couldn't focus on anything else. "Leone," I moaned, "please."

He moved them fast and watched me. I shook my head back and forth; my whole body was on fire. When he moved away, I almost cried. I looked to see he was standing taking his jeans off. If I hadn't already been as turned on as I was, just looking at his sculpted body would have made me moan.

Climbing back on the bed, he gave me a heated look. "There's that look like you want me to bite you."

"I do." I licked dry lips, "want you to bite me."

He growled and lay down on his side, pulling me so I was tight against him. "I'm going to," he whispered against my mouth. Then he leaned back, my eyes widened when he sliced across his chest with a knife I hadn't seen. Without a word, he pulled my head so I could close my mouth around the wound.

With a guttural sound, he bit into my neck then lifted his head. His breathing was erratic. When his lips touched my skin again, he didn't use his fangs, just sucked gently on my neck.

He was drinking my blood too. I found that erotically electrifying. I licked over his chest then bit him.

He hissed out a breath and grasped my hair, pulled me back so he could kiss me. It was hard and rough, almost frantic. "You're so tiny, I don't know how I'm not going to hurt you."

Biting his lip, I reached down and lifted my sore leg to rest on his hip. "Leone, please."

His red eyes held mine as he shifted my body. Reaching under me with one hand, he held me by my lower back and thrust up into me.

We both groaned.

The way he held me, made it impossible for me to move, and I realized that even now he was making sure I didn't do too much. I gasped when he pulled out slowly. Leaning forward I bit his neck, hard.

Gone was his careful movement. He held one hand behind my back, gripping it tight as he moved both of our bodies with complete abandonment.

My head was filled with my passion and his combined, and I understood what the blood bond could be. It was the most stimulating and intimate moment in my life. As my body started to shake, I pushed his head toward my throat. "Show me what you feel."

His fangs broke the skin at the same time my body shattered into a thousand pieces. His feelings grew inside me as he fed from me, causing me to orgasm again.

Throwing his head back, he stiffened and groaned deep in his throat.

Neither of us spoke or moved for several moments as we tried to force oxygen into our bodies. He released my hand and hugged me against his chest as he fought to breathe.

Before I could speak a pain tore through my whole body. My back, shoulder and leg burned like they were being tore apart. I screamed. Leone jumped up to his knees above me, but I was paralyzed and couldn't speak. Fear was etched in his face.

When the burning ebbed, I scrambled off the bed, yanking the blanket with me. "What the hell." I stopped and moved the blanket, then lifted my leg up. It wasn't stiff or sore. I looked at him, he stared at my leg. I lifted my hand toward it. "There's no pain," I frowned, "my back either." I gave him a puzzled look, then I saw my arm. An intricate design weaved its way down over my skin, wrapping my entire arm.

I jerked my head up and looked at Leone. His arm bore the same pattern. "What? What did you do?" I gave him a panicked look and then shook my head. Looking around I saw the bathroom and rushed in, slamming the door.

Clutching the blanket around me, I slid down the door to the floor. Holding my arm out in front of me, I turned it slowly.

"Beth, my love…"

"Just don't right now, Leone." I couldn't think. What did this mean? I didn't know what this meant.

"Beth," his voice came through the door again, "stop thinking about it and let me…"

"Leone." I warned.

He stopped talking for a moment.

"Chase. I need help."

He must have called his brother.

"No. Not that. She's locked herself in the bathroom and if I bust another door today Mitz will string me up. I don't know. Can Alona…" There was a short pause. "Yeah, I'd say she was upset with me. Right. Bring Daxx." He snorted. "Explanations will be self-explanatory when you get here."

I heard a clunk and wondered if he'd just tossed his phone.

"Beth, I'm sorry. I know I should have explained—but I couldn't chance losing you again. You've changed everything inside me—for the better."

I huffed out an annoyed breath. "Don't suck up. I'm having a moment." I stared at my arm again. Then straightened my leg and bent it a few times.

I heard voices out in the room.

"Well, out of all of us, I didn't think you'd take the he-man approach." Chase was here.

"I didn't force her if that's what you're implying." Leone sounded shocked.

I frowned.

"I would never suggest that." Chase murmured.

"I got here as fast as I could. Actually, I got lost." Daxx was here. "Oh, shit. Leone. You trying to follow in Troy's footsteps?"

"What? No. It wasn't an accident. She said yes."

I jumped to my feet, bunched the enormous blanket up and opened the door. "To-to us." I stammered, "to having sex, to being a-a thing." I waved my hand around. "Nowhere was a full insta-sleeve mentioned." I paused, noticing he had just pulled on his jeans and nothing else. Shaking my head, I snapped out of it. "And what the hell. If having sex with you was a miracle cure—why—why have I been trying to suck it up through the pain for the last week?"

Chase and Daxx gave him a shocked look.

Leone rubbed his hand over his forehead. "The mating bond forcibly healed all her injuries at once, right after."

"Ouch." Daxx gave me a horrified look.

"You have no idea. I now know what being dropped in a vat of acid probably feels like."

Arms crossed, Chase walked around behind me and looked at my back. "I had no idea it could do that."

I turned, so he wasn't behind me. Holding my left arm out, I scowled at him, then to Daxx. "What the hell does this mean, exactly?"

Michael came running into the room. He looked from me to Leone. "Oh shit," he cussed.

I nodded. "And then some. I'm going to start tossing energy at people soon if I don't get answers." No one moved. "*Now.*" I held up my newly insta-inked arm, my palm out, bright flashes of energy arcing off of it.

Chase backed up and then looked at Leone. "Seems like this is a mate problem. I don't interfere in other mate problems."

Daxx sighed. "Put the sparks away. Get dressed and we'll talk in Crissy's tower." She pulled out her phone and started typing on it with her thumbs.

"Crissy's tower?" I picked up the blanket and went toward the bed, hoping to find my clothes.

"I'll…"

My head snapped to Leone. "Stay right there." I scowled at him. "You might be sexy as hell, but I'm finding myself immune to that at the moment."

He sighed and looked at each of his brothers. Chase tucked his hands in his pocket and Michael shrugged. "Practice?"

Leone went over and picked up his boots. "Yeah." He stopped, keeping a foot between us. "I'm not sorry I did it, just how I went about it."

I glared at him. "Don't be all sweet right now. I'm in the middle of a life-altering event and need to process."

He smirked. "Don't give me a headache." He walked out.

Chapter Fourteen

A week later I found myself standing in the practice room. Alone. Talking to myself. I was supposed to be practicing what Clairee and her coven—of magical witches—had figured out, that was supposed to help me not drain my own health or energy when I used my magic.

It worked too, when I could focus.

I was irrevocably mated, to a giant with a gentle heart and stupid ideas. Yes, I was still mad at him. Oh and through the mate bond I would now live beyond my human life span. I didn't know what that was in numbers, but knew it was going to be a century or more than I'd ever thought I'd live.

My sleeve tattoo proved we were rare, true mates. That was kind of exciting, I supposed. Billions of people in this realm and the other, and I'd actually found a true mate. Yay me. Too bad I hadn't known such a thing existed before I'd become one, irrevocably.

The longest relationship I'd ever had lasted a week. One week. Seven days. Now I was mated for, possibly, all eternity. That was pretty serious on the wow scale.

I was being petty, holding it against him, I knew. Sure, I was attracted to him like I didn't think was possible, and his sexy red eyes, let's not forget his hot fangs—but still I'd fought to be and do what I wanted and now I was—

I blew out a breath and danced around like a boxer warming up for a match. "Don't think it, just do it. Don't think it, just do it."

"Seems to me chanting it is probably the same as thinking it."

I spun around to see Leone standing in the door. Dressed in dark leather vest and pants, looking sexy as hell. Dammit.

"I'm just distracted." I turned my back to him and looked at the metal target Michael had set up for me.

"I know." I heard his boots on the mat. "You're thinking endlessly." He stood beside me now.

"I'm still processing." I gave him a 'go away' look.

"It's been a week." His brown eyes assessed me.

I shrugged. "It's a lot to process." I held up my left arm, like I needed to remind him.

He held out his that matched it.

I frowned and backed away from him. For the past week he kept appearing and always knew when he'd affected me. It was annoying. It wasn't fair my stomach filled with butterflies every time I was near him. I held up my palms, sparks coming from them as I stepped back further.

He raised an eyebrow and walked toward me.

Scowling, I focused harder and made them arc off each other.

His expression didn't change.

My back hit the wall. He reached me and grabbed my hands and pinned them to the wall beside me.

Leaning down, he brushed a kiss over my mouth, then moved to nuzzle my neck. "I miss you." He whispered. "You show me I'm stronger than I ever thought, then leave me wanting the one thing I can't have, all over again." He kissed my neck, then lifted his head. His eyes were red.

I looked at his mouth, knowing the fangs inside would bite into me if I asked. I took a shaky breath.

He looked at my mouth, then lowered his head and kissed me gently, trying to coax my mouth to open. I did return his kiss, how could I resist that?

When he lifted his head, I exhaled trying to settle my breathing. "I just need time."

"I know. I wait every night." He said quietly.

"I don't understand it. I was everything you couldn't have—then I'm not?"

He kissed me softly again. "I'm the one that messed it up, Beth, I accept that."

"I thought, the whole time I was going to be locked in the cells—I had no idea what a mate was, never mind that you knew I was yours."

"I know. I'm sorry. My head was a mess. Then you talked me into feeding off you. I don't even crave it now—" he shook his head, "others—there's only you. Every time I feed for the past week tastes like ass. You broke me of an addiction I'd fought every day for decades—so yes, I fucked up and rushed to mark you, so I didn't lose you."

My heart was melting into a puddle as he spoke. Unfortunately, my head still needed to process. Pulling my hand free from his, I brushed my hair back over my shoulder and exposed my neck to him. I couldn't deny him that. I felt somehow it was my responsibility now.

His eyes flicked from my neck to my eyes a few times. He smirked. "Can I have you naked, beneath me while I feed?"

I shook my head. "Not just yet."

"Can I try to change your mind?"

"If you think you can."

He grinned. "That wasn't a no." He pulled me by the hips and then lifted me and pinned me to the wall with his body.

As persuasion went, this was a very good start.

His mouth moved over my throat, placing soft kisses along it.

The anticipation of waiting for his fangs to pierce my skin made me shiver. "Leone, bite me." I hissed.

He chuckled briefly and then his fangs sunk into my neck.

I sucked in a breath and realized I'd missed this. Missed being near him too.

Licking over it, he grasped the back of my head and kissed me roughly.

Wrapping my arms around his neck, I ran my tongue over his fangs. He moaned.

"God's! I'm going to need a cold shower soon. I just walked in on Troy and Daxx—in Michael's office. Doesn't anyone use their own rooms anymore?"

Leone lowered me, then turned to look at Chase. "Your timing sucks, brother."

Chase smirked. "That's what older brothers are for."

Leone laughed. "If that were true I'd still be a virgin. What do you want?"

Chase sighed. "No one is answering their phones, although now I know why. My mate has sent me to fetch everyone—apparently king translates into fetch—there's a meeting."

"About?"

Chase threw his hand up. "No idea. She won't say."

"The meeting." I pushed past Leone. "I forgot."

He looked from Chase to me. "You knew?"

I nodded.

He gave me a curious look. "What is it about?"

"Guess you'll have to come find out." I started walking out of the room.

"I sense an ambush, brother." Chase said as I went by him.

"Yeah." Leone was right on my heels

"You want to do what?" Troy looked from Daxx to Chase then back to his mate again.

"Just hear us out." Daxx gave him a hard look.

Leone glanced down the table at me. "Absolutely not."

I frowned. "Why?"

"Why?" His voice grew louder. "Aside from the fact that letting Lou out of the cells is insane, screwing around in someone's head drains you."

I shook my head. "No. It doesn't now. I've been practising." I pointed to Rafael. "Ask Raf."

Chase made a strangled noise as Leone turned slowly to look at his brother.

Leone gave him a serious look. "You've been allowing my mate in your head?" His words were slow.

"Shit," Chase muttered.

"Fuck," Troy cussed almost at the same time.

I leaned forward in the chair. "I couldn't do it to Daxx, she's immune to magic." I waved my hand toward Crissy. "She has enough going on in her head and Alona has more walls and barriers in there then a maze. Raf was at the temple when Clairee and I figured out a way to do it without draining me, so he volunteered."

"Of course he did." Quinton sat back and looked from Rafael to Leone. The tension was almost visible.

"Raf," Leone said in an even voice, "later we need to discuss boundaries."

Rafael shrugged. "Fine, but the point here is she did it repeatedly, for over an hour, without even looking tired." He smirked, "having her chatter inside your head is…"

Leone glared at him.

Rafael cleared his throat, "but you already know what it's like." He finished quietly.

"This is getting us nowhere." Alona said quietly.

Crissy knelt on her chair, getting right in her mate's face. "Vic, it's a good plan." She nodded enthusiastically.

He gave her a soft look and then sighed and looked to Daxx. "Explain it again." He held up his hand, "without interruption."

Later I needed to find out how the ranks worked in this family. Everyone listened when Victor spoke.

Daxx glanced to me, I nodded.

"Okay. We let Lou out, then follow him." She motioned to her mate. "Bethany is going to get inside his head and get him to lead us to the landmarks Troy picked out of his head."

Victor looked around at his siblings. "It's a sound plan with proper preparation."

Leone made a sound of exasperation. "Yeah, except it's my mate following him around to do this. Have you all forgotten the last time Beth put herself in harm's way to help us? I haven't," he tapped his head, "it's burned into my memory forever."

The pain on his face broke my heart. *Hey, superman,* I whispered inside his head.

Leone's head snapped to look at me.

You'll be right beside me the whole time. I whispered so only he could hear.

His expression changed. "Fuck." He got up and went into the kitchen.

Chase started to get up when Alona put her hand on his arm and shook her head. She looked down at me.

Taking a deep breath, I got up and followed where he'd gone.

He stood on the other side of a very large, very white, spotless kitchen. The fridge was the size of my closet bedroom. His back was to me, hands on his hips with his head hanging down.

"Hey," I went up behind him and put my hand on his back.

He turned and looked down at me. "I see you laying there broken every time I close my eyes."

"I'm not any more, thanks to you."

"I don't—" he shook his head.

"You can't seal me in a bubble, Leone. I can't live like that. I don't run away from problems—I solve them."

Scooping the back of my head in his big hand, he pulled me toward him, tilting my head up. "Did you ever think that's *why* you get into trouble?"

I shrugged, "it's how I am."

He made a sound of frustration. "If anything happens to you again, they're going to have to put me down like a wounded animal."

"I won't take risks."

His eyes held mine for a long moment. He cursed softly then kissed me hard on the mouth. Releasing me, he walked back into the dining room. "I want a camera and tracker on Lou. In case we lose him in a crowd."

Victor nodded.

"And," Leone pointed to me, "If anything goes down, someone gets Beth the hell out of there."

"I will." Daxx nodded to me, looking very happy now.

Leone heaved a loud sigh and glanced to Troy. "Let's do it."

Chapter Fifteen

I stood looking at myself in the mirror. I was now dressed in all black, like the brothers did.

Leone walked in.

I lifted my arms and turned around. "Daxx was so excited to give me this vest." I frowned. "Why black?" I motioned to his outfit.

"You look good. Black is easy for Clairee to hide and…" He looked down at what he wore, "the blood doesn't show." He shrugged.

I'd get to that part later on from my list of 'I need to know' things. "Crissy is cute in her black hoodie." I frowned, "I think Alona has boots for every occasion."

He nodded, "yeah she does." Pulling something out of his pocket, he held up his hand. A chain dangled from it. "I came to give you this."

I went over. It was a smaller version of the one he'd given me at that house. I looked at the one resting against his chest.

He motioned for me to turn around.

I did and lifted my hair. His hands were shaking as he put it around my neck.

"I used to sit and look at this and wonder if there was a woman out there to wear it." He said in a soft tone. "The prophecy for the kings' sons numbering nine…" He leaned down and kissed my neck after he did it up.

I turned and put my hand on it.

"My prophecy said my mate would give me what I desired the most." His eyes held mine. "For fifty or sixty years I thought that was someone to be with, someone that was mine to be with." Pain went through his eyes. "Then it turned into human essence being what I wanted the most." His mouth quirked. "But it turns out the thing I needed, more than anything, was someone to believe in me again. Without doubts."

The emotion in his voice made my heart beat faster. "Scored some points with that." I said trying to lighten the mood.

"I wasn't trying to."

"I know, hence the points." I looked down at the pendant. "I'm part of the royal family." I gave him a shocked look. "Why hasn't that sunk in sooner?"

He smiled. "Yeah you are. No one will question or disrespect you while you wear that. I'm fourth in the ranks around here because of my position, after the kings, Justice and Michael." His expression grew serious. "If someone disrespects you while you wear that, you let me know."

His tone sent shivers up my spine. I nodded.

Lifting the pendant in his hand for a moment, he smiled down at me. "Do you think when we return we could spend some time together?"

There was doubt in his eyes. Doubt that I'd caused. I smiled, "I'd like that." I huffed out a breath. "I'm nervous. I don't want to screw this up."

He lifted my chin. "You won't. I'll be right there." Lifting my arm, he looked at it. "Where's your device?"

"I was just going to put it on when you came in." I motioned to the dresser.

Going over, he picked it up and came back. I watched his large hands put it on my wrist.

"I'd like to exchange blood before we go."

I raised my brows.

"Just appease the paranoid man." He smirked. "Between the mate bond and the blood bond, I'll be able to find you anywhere."

I nodded.

He bent down and pulled a knife out of his cuff, then paused. "We need to get you a blade."

"For?" My voice squeaked.

"Back up." He nodded. His tone and expression told me this wasn't a discussion.

"I have no idea how to work one, unless it's to cut my food."

He grinned and held the knife up. "Aim. Flick. That's it." He moved his hand a few times.

"Okay. I can do that. Just hope no one we like is anywhere nearby." With shaking hands, I unbuttoned his vest. Red eyes watched my every move.

With a grunt, he leaned down and picked me up, then walked over and set me on the dresser. He stood between my knees and scored his chest with the blade.

I leaned over, wasting no time. A soft growl rumbled through his chest and then he bit into my neck. Once again, he sucked on it without feeding. As I licked over the closed wound, he bit into me again, this time feeding. He didn't use as much eufori as before, probably so I would be alert. It hurt, but not in a bad way. Later, I'd have to think about that.

Lifting his head, he licked over the punctures, then grasped the back of my head and devoured my mouth.

When he broke the kiss, both of us were breathing hard. "We'll be there in a minute, brother."

I turned to see Michael standing in the door.

Leone and I walked along the sidewalk, following a block behind Lou. I'd wanted to be closer, but he assured me with his height, he was keeping an eye on him. Michael was somewhere behind us, and Rafael behind him.

The phone app was open on all our phones and we were using ear pieces to talk and listen.

"I can't believe he didn't ask questions when you released him." Daxx said.

"If you had the chance to get away from Arius, would you ask questions?" Rafael said sounding entertained.

"Beth is trying to focus, people" Leone growled into the mic.

I touched his hand. "Beth is fine. Lou's head is mush and easy to stay in." I glanced up at him. "Unlike some hard heads I've been in recently."

He smirked down at me.

"Eloquent insult. Welcome to the family, sparky." Chase chuckled. "Is the camera working?"

"Yes, Chase. I can see what he does." Alona said quietly.

"I recognize the area." Daxx informed them.

"I'm watching from up high." Crissy added. "I like this phone thing it's like we're all together but not."

"You better be dangling up there safely." Victor warned.

"I'm okay. I'm strapped to a pole, bolted to the top of a concrete building."

I looked up at Leone, he shook his head.

Daxx, Alona and a few others had stayed at the apartment. Once we knew where Lou was taking us, she could teleport the rest there, and me out.

"There's our landmark. It's a sign on a building. He stopped and looked right at it. Good work, Bethany." Troy said quietly.

"Do I pull out of his mind or wait a few minutes?"

Leone paused in step waiting for an answer.

"Wait until he's reached his destination." Victor answered.

"Okay." Leone took my hand and started walking again. I looked at the weapons strapped to him. I'd been assured that Clairee had used a glamour spell, so only we could see what he was really dressed like. Also, apparently to others, I had blonde hair right now.

He looked down at me, one eyebrow raised. His was of telling me, without speaking, to stop thinking.

I smiled at him then focused on Lou. "He's starting to question if he should be here right now." I said into the mic.

"Can you ramp it up at all? Make it seem urgent that he gets there?" Arius asked.

I nodded, even though they couldn't see me. "As long as Leone controls where I'm walking, I can."

Leone's hand tightened around mine.

"Coming up on what looks like an entrance to a tunnel. It's supposed to be blocked off, but nothing secure enough to stop anyone." He told everyone.

"Checking." Alona said. "Yes, there's tunnels under there." She sighed. "I hate tunnels. They're like life size rats, the whole group of them scurrying around in tunnels..."

"Less loathsome chatter, beloved, we're all trying to pay attention here."

"Yes, sorry."

"Is he going down to the tunnel, Leone?" Daxx sounded anxious.

"He's looking around like he's afraid he might have someone following him." Leone told her.

"Is anyone else looking at him?" Quinton asked.

Leone looked around. "I don't see anyone taking an interest."

"Good."

I squeezed his hand, so he'd stop. I needed to give Lou a push and it would be easier if I didn't have to remember to walk at the same time. He seemed to understand and stopped, pulling me into his chest for a hug. I closed my eyes and told Lou he needed to get the news to them that the trade for Marcus ran into problems, and only he knew why.

"Don't wear yourself out." Leone warned quietly.

I heard him but didn't answer.

"He's moving," Leone said quickly, "going down the stairs."

"What do you see, ladies?" Chase asked.

"So far just stairs." Daxx informed him. "Lighting is pretty bad. Do I start transporting?"

"Not yet." Victor said calmly.

"He's going down a long hallway on the first level." Alona informed us. "I hope the signal lasts."

"I need to move closer. If I stop now he might just turn around and come back up. He's very cowardly." I looked up at Leone.

"Shit. Michael, move in closer to us. We're going down the first flight of stairs." Leone pulled me toward the stairs.

"I'll be at the top making sure no one follows." Michael assured him.

Leone guided me down the stairs while I focused.

"He just went through a door into a better lit area. Keep going, Bethany." Daxx said with excitement in her voice.

Leone paused at the bottom of the stairs and lifted my chin. I looked at him and nodded, letting him know I was doing fine. A determined expression fixed on his face, he led me down the long hall. "What do you see now?" He asked.

"A very well-lit tunnel still. I wished we had sound with this." Alona answered.

"Short notice." Quinton replied.

"I'm climbing down." Crissy said abruptly.

"You meet Daxx and go back with Bethany." Victor said, sounding like he was running.

"Okay, Victor."

"I'm three minutes away, brother, don't go too far alone." Arius said in a strained voice.

"We're stopping at the door." Leone informed him. He gave me a quick look. "Where is he now?"

There was a silent pause.

"He's entered some kind of chamber... oh..." Alona stopped speaking.

"Fuck me," Daxx whispered, "we're going to need backup."

"I'm calling the guards on standby. All of them. Sith and Bronx can get them here." Troy barked.

Leone stopped. "What are we looking at?" He stared at the floor, his jaw clenched.

"Need numbers, guys." Quinton was clearly running.

"Fifty or more." Daxx answered. "Lou is talking to a few of them. They don't look happy." She added. "I'm starting the transports. Michael is there an alley across from you, red sign with a cartoon tiger on it?"

"Yes. I see it." Michael answered.

"Okay. Good I'll bring us there." Daxx said.

"Beloved," Chase was out of breath, "come over and wait with Bethany and Crissy until Daxx gets everyone there. Strength in numbers." He added.

"All right. I'm bringing the chucks though. Not a scratch, Chase." She warned.

"Yes, my queen." He answered hurriedly.

Leone looked down at me. "Are you out of his head?" I nodded, feeling tense. "Are you okay?"

"Yes. I'm fine."

He leaned down and kissed me softly.

A sound came from behind us, I spun, palms up, arc building quickly between them.

"Whoa, sister." Rafael held up his palms.

Leone grinned and hugged me against him. "Wait here for Daxx."

I nodded.

"I'm almost there." Crissy said quietly.

"I'm running past Michael now." Alona said.

I watched as they started to file down the stairs into the tunnel. My stomach was in knots. Turning, I grasped the front of Leone's vest and looked up at him. "I will fry *everyone* if you get hurt."

He grinned down at me, then pulled the ear bud out of his and my ear. Holding them in his hand, he leaned down and kissed me. "I'll be coming back to you, don't worry about that."

"Be safe." I whispered.

He held out the ear piece for me as he put his back in. "Getting antsy here, what's the hold up?" He said to all.

Quinton laughed, "You didn't have to run three blocks."

"You need the exercise," he answered while rolling his shoulders.

"Yeah," Rafael winked at me, "getting a little squishy around the middle there, big brother."

"I'll show you squishy, you punks." Quinton mumbled.

"Be there soon." Daxx said. "Need to catch my breath."

I watched as large men filed past me in the tunnel. There was at least twenty, plus the brothers, so I felt a little better. Crissy was beside me as they vanished through the door. Alona walked over after Chase went through the door.

"Coming down the stairs. We've got a problem. Six more inbound, right behind me." Daxx said in a vibrating voice as she ran. "Too many for us to handle. I don't have my zapper. I wasn't supposed to need it."

"Beth," Leone's voice barked in my ear, "twenty feet after the door is another tunnel, its dark. You girls can lay low there until they go by. We'll get them as they reach us."

I nodded and watched Daxx running toward us. "Okay." I told him and held open the door.

"We'll be turning off our mics now, but we'll still be able to hear you." Leone said.

"Yeah, don't want to listen to the old guys grunting when they fight." Rafael chuckled.

"We'll see whose grunting next practice." Troy informed him.

"Everyone watch Leone's ass, so sparky doesn't fry us." Chase said in a hushed voice.

"Watch your own ass, Chase." Leone told him. "Your queen will take it out on you if you get hurt again."

"Fight well, brothers." Quinton said with a serious tone.

"Only as good as you, brother." Arius replied.

"Then we're all doomed, brothers. Ladies stay safe." Leone added.

The chatter stopped as we reached the darkened tunnel and ran in far enough so no one would see us.

Daxx pulled one of her blades off her back and turned toward the entrance. Alona had her hands out with nun-chuck at the ready. Crissy squatted down, her hand resting on the blade strapped to her leg.

I held my palms up, but kept the sparks within so the light wouldn't lead anyone to us.

We heard the voices and boots echoing on the stone. Barely breathing, we listened as they went by us. Waiting a bit longer until the sounds faded, we stepped out into the light again.

"We're heading up now." Daxx whispered.

Reaching the door, she opened it and looked out. Closing it she gave me a wide-eyed look. "Shit. There's more blocking the stairs. Just standing there."

"Going back to hide." Alona said and turned back the way we'd come.

As we ran into the darkened area, lights reflected from far inside it.

"Problem." Daxx paused and then shook her head. "Someone is in the tunnel we were in. Coming at you, boys."

We started moving quickly down the tunnel.

"Focus on not getting sliced open, and we will find a place to stay out of the way." Alona said quickly as she glanced over her shoulder.

We ran down the tunnel, apparently too fast because we caught up to the group that had gone past us. "How far to where the men are?" I whispered to Daxx. She'd seen it in the camera.

"Fifty, sixty feet then a short tunnel to them." Alona answered before Daxx could.

I started to feel trapped. I didn't like the feeling at all. I huffed out a breath. "Okay. We'll clear the path to get to them." I looked at Daxx and she nodded, pulling the second blade from her back, then rolled her shoulders.

"I'll watch behind us." Crissy said quietly.

"Let's party." Daxx said and started running toward the voices.

I caught up to her and lifted my hands to build the arc. Three of the men lagging behind the others turned and saw us.

"Uh." Alona made a sound. "Vile."

They grinned and pulled swords from their belts and started walking toward us.

"Damn, I want my zapper." Daxx opened her arms to them. "Come and get it, boys." She glanced to me. "Do a Davis on them."

I nodded and moved my hands up higher to build the energy. One of them looked at me and sneered. Flicking both hands down the energy shot toward them. When it connected two of them were knocked back against the wall, then slumped to the floor. The third one kept coming.

I lifted my hands. "I've got this one." Alona ran past me, her hands spinning so fast the chucks were a blur.

As she reached him she spun, the chucks connected against his body, he stumbled back. She stopped her hands and smacked him over the head with the weapons. "Take a nap." He slumped to the floor.

"Three down." Daxx said running and looking down at them. "Do we tie them up?"

I bit my lip. "I can try a spell, of sorts, to keep them down for now."

She nodded. "Do it."

I focused on the chant Clairee had taught me. Never before had I tried things like this. Dropping my hands, I looked down at them. "I hope it worked."

A noise behind us had Daxx pointing in the direction we were heading. "Let's go. I can hear the commotion, so we're close."

"Oh no." Crissy said.

"What... Oww." Daxx spun around. "They shot me in the ass." She tried to look.

I went around behind her and pulled a dart out of her and held it up.

"They shot me in the ass with a dart." She made a loud growling sound.

Crissy came over and pulled it from my hand, then wrapped it and put it in the pocket of her backpack. She nodded. "In case we need to know what was on it."

"On it?" Daxx growled again.

"No time." Alona said and grabbed Daxx' s arm. "We need to be visible to our men, before they come looking."

I nodded, knowing she was right.

"Fine. But I'm finding that asshat with the dart gun later and teaching him some manners." She stumbled briefly, but kept moving.

The other men that had gone before us were nowhere in sight. My stomach knotted as we got closer to the sound of metal hitting metal. We were almost to the chamber when two men, not ours, came running toward us.

"Round two." Daxx's voice was slurred.

Alona glanced to me, then gently shoved Daxx closer to Crissy. Alona stood beside me as I lifted my arms and built the arc again. I didn't wait this time to see if they wanted to fight, just sent it flying toward them. It hit them and they stumbled back out of sight again.

Alona looked at me, assessing if I was all right. "What I wouldn't give for your skills." She shrugged and went over and put her arm around Daxx, motioning for me to lead the way.

We entered the chamber and my heart slammed against my ribs. The scene before us was something out of a bloody fight movie. More bodies then I could count, clashing against other bodies. I glanced back to see the girls right behind me. With a nod, I moved over to go along the wall of the chamber, hoping to keep us out of the worst of it.

Rafael stumbled back into our path, then growled a warrior's sound and kicked the man that had knocked him back. Gone was the jovial man I was used to seeing. In his place was a fearsome man in battle. I crouched lower as Alona and Crissy moved behind me with Daxx. I didn't know what had been on that dart, but she was groggy.

"They were prepared for her." Alona said behind me. "Knew magic wouldn't stop her."

"Bastards." Daxx spat.

I nodded and motioned to keep moving. So far we were unnoticed by the men fighting the brothers. The brothers, on the other hand, knew exactly where we were. Rafael appeared again, a look of rage on his face as he looked at Daxx.

He pointed to a door on the far side. "Get her there." Leaning over, he pulled out Daxx's ear piece and tucked it in his pocket. Most likely because her slurred words would distract Troy too much.

I nodded and held up my hands, making the arc dance between them. A man charged at Rafael and without thought, I sent it toward him, knocking him into several other bodies.

Without pause he rushed back into the large group.

Troy started toward us, then Chase appeared and blocked a blade that had been intended for his twin. With a quick glance to Alona, he jerked his head to the door.

She nodded and started to move with Daxx again.

A large man rushed at us, I held up my hands.

"He's one of ours." Alona said quickly. "Daxx's blocker."

Giving me a wide berth, he went to Daxx.

"Tim. Get back out there." Daxx mumbled. "Kick thezze bozo's azzes." She slurred.

"We've got her." Alona assured him.

Another came at us and I paused long enough to see if anyone vouched for him. When no one did, I sent a blast of energy at him, knocking him back. Tim spun around and with powerful strides met him blade against blade.

Alona and Crissy were almost dragging Daxx now, I followed along beside them watching out of the corner of my eye, but not taking my eyes off the bodies moving around us.

A body emerged from the crowd, it was Leone. He ducked the swing of a blade and snarled, kicking his opponent back. When he stepped toward him again, a gut reflex had me sending a burst of energy to the man trying to hurt him. It hit him in the gut knocking the air out of him, making him hunch forward. Leone took advantage of it and his large boot connected with the man's head. He looked to me and raised an eyebrow. Victor appeared and used his box and the man disappeared. Both of them came in our direction.

Victor assessed Daxx, even while knocking a man flying to the floor. His eyes moved over Crissy. "Go quickly." He motioned to the door with his head.

Crissy nodded, and boosted Daxx up again between her and Alona and they started to the door once more.

Leone backed toward me, keeping his eye on the commotion. He glanced down to me quickly. "Find a place and hide. I will come for you."

I nodded and followed after the women.

As we reached the door, Troy got to us. His twin was at his back ensuring nothing happened to him. He looked at Daxx, as her head dropped down to her chest. He glanced at me, eyes red and a snarl on his face. "Go." He growled.

"We'll keep her safe." I assured him and opened the door. I stood by it as they dragged her through the door. Looking around, I noticed each of the brothers were well aware of the state she was in. Each of their eyes were glowing, revenge etched in their faces.

Closing the door behind us, I looked around. "It's a tunnel. Behind the door." I said for the sake of the men. "It leads down."

Alona nodded to Crissy and they started to go down the incline of the tunnel.

"We're going down it to see if we can find somewhere to hide." I fet rage move through me, and knew it wasn't mine. "Focus on your fight." I said, meaning it to reach all of the men and not just Leone.

Alona pulled her ear piece out and Crissy did the same. They tucked them in pockets. I nodded but kept mine in for now, thinking if the men tried to reach us, one of us should be listening.

We'd gone thirty feet with no sign of the tunnel branching off, or a safe spot to stop. A sound from behind us had me spinning around, hands raised. "Someone's come through the door." I motioned to Alona to keep going. "We're going down further." I started after them. "Leone, look for the shimmer of a magical trail to find us." I pulled the ear piece out and turned off the mic, then put it back in. I didn't know how far we'd have to go or how long he'd be able to hear me, but I had to believe they would be all right and come for us.

"It's getting darker." Alona said in a low voice.

"I don't know this tunnel." Crissy said sounding worried.

I glanced behind us. "It has to branch out at some point. We'll stop when it does." It wasn't much of a plan, but it would give us options if we needed to move again.

I stopped and looked at the device on my wrist, opening I looked at the button. "Will these work?"

Crissy shook her head. "I don't think they work well this far underground."

Closing it I sighed, "I'd rather not take a chance on that then." I paused and looked up the tunnel, trying to listen.

Alona reached into her pocket and pulled out her phone. "We're going to need a flash light." I took the phone and turned on the light and held it out in front of us.

I looked to Daxx. "Is she all right?"

"She's out cold. And quite weighty." Alona said.

"I can help." I offered.

She shook her head. "I'd rather you and your hands be free to save us, if it's all the same to you."

I nodded and aimed the phone further in front of us. I was trying not to worry about Leone and his brothers. "Think happy thoughts. Think happy thoughts." I whispered. Crissy looked at me. "So I don't convey to Leone that I'm freaking out a little bit inside here."

"A little bit?" Alona glanced back to me. "On a *freakout* scale of one to ten..." She shifted Daxx higher, "I'm at fifteen currently."

"I'm right there with you." I looked over my shoulder again. "Leone said with the mate bond and blood bond he could find me anywhere."

"Let's hope that includes in the bowels of hell, because that's where we are." Alona was not amused.

"I don't mind dark spaces." Crissy said. "If I can't see out, no one can see in."

Alona and I both paused and looked at her. Waving my hand, I motioned for them to keep going. It was a slow walk. They had to balance their weight against the steep incline and keep Daxx off the floor. "Wait here." I went by them and ran down the slope. There was a small flat space before the tunnel turned and went down even further.

I turned and shone the light back toward them. "We'll wait here." I glanced to the wall and motioned down it with my hand, leaving a trace of magic. I hoped Leone would know what to look for. I bit my lip and then took a deep breath. I couldn't convey my fears to him, his life literally depended on his not being distracted.

Alona and Crissy reached me and set Daxx down along the ledge of the concave space. Crissy sat down beside her. Alona stood up and blew out a breath. "I feel like a sitting duck here." She stepped back and leaned against the wall.

I stepped into the space and looked at the top of it, then the sides. "Maybe I can make an illusion of a wall here." I shrugged. "As long as no one touches it, they won't know."

She nodded. "I'll stand out there and see if you manage it."

I paused and sent my hand over the floor into the area, leaving another trail for Leone. Taking a deep breath, I raised my hands and focused on the stone pattern surrounding us. Lowering my hands slowly, I thought of only that.

As I stood there trying to figure out if it worked, I looked out at Alona, her face showed surprise. She stepped back in. "It looks like a wall."

I sighed and relaxed for a second. "That's better than sitting in the open."

"I couldn't see the light from the phone either, so we won't have to sit here in the dark." She slid down the wall and sat by Daxx's head. "There's that at least."

I sat on the other side, keeping my eyes on the dark tunnel leading down. I looked down at the phone. "We have no signal here."

"Perfect." She sighed, "because it's wasn't hard enough to sit here not knowing. Now they can't even call, to let us know they're all right."

"I think you'd feel it again if Chase wasn't." Crissy nodded. "Like last time."

I looked from one to the other. "That's possible?"

Alona brushed her hand down her sleeve. "Yes. I had a piercing pain in my side when Chase was injured. Stupid man."

Closing my eyes, I tried to assess if all me felt right. Aside from the fear in the pit of my stomach, which knew was my own, I felt fine. "I feel okay."

Crissy nodded. "I can't feel Victor at all, so he's fine."

Blowing out a breath. "I'm the same."

"Okay, then. The men are good." I looked at Daxx. "Think she'll come out of it soon?"

Alona made a hesitant face. "I almost hope not. She'll charge back up there threatening every one of them that is still standing."

My eyes-wide I nodded slowly. "So we'll just hope it's a peaceful nap until the men come."

"I've never seen Troy that angry." Crissy said softly.

"Is this..." I waved my hand around, "often? The fighting like that?"

Both women paused and looked at each other then looked back to me and nodded.

"Great." The light on the phone died as I said that.

"Guess my battery just died." Alona moaned.

A light illuminated Crissy's face. "Mine is at half." She turned on the flashlight and set the phone on the floor screen side down.

I handed Alona her phone back. "Has it been long?"

Alona waved her phone. "No idea."

There was a long silence. "That box thing Victor uses. Where do the people go?"

Alona smiled. "I know. I want one, but they only work for the Justice and Huntress." She shrugged, "probably just as well or I'd be zapping people to the cells that got in my way when there's a boot sale." She grinned and then her expression became serious again. "How are you doing with all of this?"

I nodded slowly. "I just sent men flying with energy balls because they were trying to chop up people I know."

She smirked, "so, all good." Nodding, she motioned to Crissy and Daxx. "We're all here if you need us. We must stick together or else the men will lock us in pretty little bubbles forever and ever."

Crissy giggled. "Victor says that a lot. That he should put me in a bubble."

Alona nodded. "I suppose, in their defense, they've lived quite a long time without having females in the way and messing with their mojo."

I snorted, "That mojo needs some squashing in a few areas."

Daxx moaned. "Anyone see the truck that hit me?" She rolled and lay on her back. "What happened? Where the hell are we?"

"You were shot in the butt with a dart." Crissy reminded her.

"I was tranquilized?" She slid up on the wall then stopped and grabbed her head. "I feel like I drank a pail of J.D."

"We ran down a tunnel to get you to safety." I informed her.

Opening her eyes, she looked around. "We're still in the tunnels?"

I nodded. "The guys told us to go in this direction, so now we're waiting for them."

She started to sit up and then leaned back again. "We'll just wait." Turning her head in slow motion she looked at Alona. "How were they?"

"Kicking ass. A lot of it." She said in a quiet tone.

"That's my boys." She closed her eyes. "I'm just going to rest here until they come."

All of us froze as the sound of boots on stone echoed in the tunnel. It was too hard to tell which direction it was coming from. Daxx straightened.

Alona touched her arm and leaned closer. "Bethany has us hidden behind an illusion."

Blowing out a breath, Daxx leaned back but kept her eyes open.

There were voices, all of us turned toward the hidden barrier and stared at it. I held my breath.

"How the hell do I know what it meant? Do I look like I'm magical? I'm still trying to figure out how to earn her forgiveness, we haven't gotten to magical conversations yet." It was Leone.

The sound of all of us exhaling in unison was heard. I went to get up when Alona touched my arm and shook her head. I gave her a curious glance, she smirked. She wanted to listen.

"Could be worse, you could have pulled a Troy and tormented her with a mark and no bond." Chase said.

"Just shut the fuck up and look." That was Troy.

"I can feel Cristy, but this tunnel just keeps going." Victor sounded unhappy.

"I've had this dream. If there's a flame filled cavern at the end of it, I'm screaming like a girl and pushing you in to save my ass." Chase sounded less amused than usual.

"What the hell is that smell?" Leone asked.

"What. I didn't see the cistern when I tackled that idiot." Troy complained.

"At least if we lose you, we can follow the smell." Chase murmured like he had his mouth covered.

"It's blue." Leone blurted out.

"Channeling cutie, Leone?" Chase sounded amused.

"No. Look. There's a trail of blue shimmering along the wall." Leone said in a low tone.

"Follow it." Victor ordered.

We could see them now, on the other side of the barrier, I looked at Alona, she was smirking. Later on, I'd have to think why she wasn't rushing into her mate's arms. She shrugged and smiled at me.

"What the…" Leone put his hand through the barrier and moved it up and down. Then he stepped through and looked down at me, his shoulders sagging in relief.

"Where the hell did he go?" Chase spun around. "He was right here."

Alona laughed and stepped out through the barrier.

He grabbed her and hugged her to him. "You, bad, bad woman."

Troy and Victor stepped through it.

Crissy was in Victor's arms before I could stand up.

Troy knelt in front of Daxx and touched her cheek. "Are you all right?"

"Groggy still." She held her hand over her mouth. "What were you rolling in?"

"Don't ask." He scooped her up into his arms and stepped back through the barrier.

Leone pulled me into his arms and hugged me. Leaning back, he grabbed my face between both hands and looked down at me. "You have to stop scaring the hell out of me."

"Can we get out of here now?" Alona asked.

"Is everyone all right?" Daxx asked in a muffled voice behind her hand.

"Few bumps and cuts, nothing serious." Troy answered. "We left them cleaning up the mess to come and find you."

Daxx dropped her hand and gave her mate a steady look. "They shot me in the ass with a dart."

He nodded. "I heard."

Victor continued to carry Crissy. "We heard every word until Bethany told Leone to follow the magical trail."

Leone hugged me under his shoulder. "Knowing what the hell that was, would have been good to know in advance."

"How many did we get? Any important ones?" Daxx asked.

Chase shook his head. "No idea. Arius said it would take him and Michael a week to sort them all out."

I looked up to Leone. "Did we get Lou back?"

He nodded. "Yes, he's not much of fighter. Fell to his knees and put his hands up when Victor went toward him."

"Despite the heart-stopping events that occurred," Victor paused and looked at me, "your part in this just gave us an advantage in this war. The more heads we have to pick through, the more locations we find." He inclined his head and walked ahead of the rest of us.

"Now what?" I asked.

Leone sighed, "Can you just not think of the next ten steps yet? We go home, wash off the stink," he glanced to Troy, "some of us more than others, then we eat."

I rolled my eyes. "Of course you eat. When don't you eat?"

He chuckled and leaned down. "Do you really want to know?"

My cheeks heated, I shook my head.

Pulling his ear piece out, he put it in. "We found them. They're all right."

I'd forgotten about that until his voice sounded in my ear. There were several responses at once. Then Arius' serious tone came over the ear piece.

"My sisters all have smooth moves. When you're finished hugging and cuddling them, I could use a hand in the cells. We have a few that are going absolutely crazy down here."

"I'll be there shortly, brother." Michael answered. "Watching the tunnel to make sure they get out with the women first."

"Wouldn't want to be the one that did that to Daxx." Rafael said in a grim tone.

Troy snorted. Then shook his head when Daxx gave him a curious look.

"Leone, is your ass intact?" Quinton's amused voice filled the ear piece.

I glanced behind him and then smiled up at him.

"Beth seems to think it is." Leone answered with a grin.

"Good." Arius answered, "I've been plagued with how being fried would feel."

Taking the ear piece out I switched on my mic and put it back in. "I can show you next practice, *brother*."

The line went quiet and then there were several laughs.

"If you like, sister." Arius answered. "Leone, a little warning next time, please."

Even Victor was chuckling now. I didn't think he knew how to.

Alona tapped me on the shoulder and held up her hand. I give her a high five.

"Beloved, we're ruining your snobbish refinement. First you play a joke on us, now high fives? Brothers, we are in so much trouble I can't even describe my fear right now." Chase said with a smirk.

"Sounds like a challenge." Rafael said in a dry tone.

Leone grinned and looked down at me. "Accepted."

Chapter Sixteen

I found my way to the dining room, without pausing once to second-guess my direction. At least something was improving.

Victor, Crissy, Daxx and Troy were the only ones there. I looked around. "I beat the rush?"

Daxx nodded. "A few went to lend a hand in the cells first."

I sat down at the end of the table. "I knew there had to be an important reason to delay eating."

Victor smirked as he took a bite.

"I suppose the amount of energy you guys use fighting balances out the amount you eat."

"What about you?" Troy piled more food on his plate. "No issues using that amount of magic?"

I shook my head. "Not as long as I concentrate on what I'm doing—in the right way. I'm so thankful that Clairee helped me to figure that out."

He nodded. "I'm thankful too, it enabled you to protect my mate when she was unconscious."

Daxx sneered. "You better tell me if you see any of them shooting me in the ass when you're poking around in heads."

"Rest assured, I will. Although Arius might object if you beat the hell out of his prisoners."

Arius came in the kitchen entrance. "I'm open to the odd beating if it is warranted." He grinned at Daxx. "In this case, it is very warranted." Arius wandered down the table putting food on a plate.

When he finished he walked down and sat in the empty chair to my left. He didn't offer comment, just started eating.

"What's the head count?" Chase and Alona walked in holding hands. He paused seeing where Arius was sitting, raised an eyebrow, but didn't comment. As he walked by his twin, he leaned down and inhaled noticeably. "Much better. Seems quite similar to what your mate wears—but overall an improvement."

Daxx smirked, then blushed when Troy gave her a smug look.

Michael came in, paused in step and looked at Arius. "Bastard, you pilfered my idea."

Arius grinned. "Not at all, brother." He waved his fork back and forth. "Great minds and all that."

Michael grabbed a plate and quickly put some food on it. He hurried down the other side of the table and sat in the empty chair to my right.

Daxx cocked her head and looked at me, basically asking what that was about. I gave her my best 'no clue' look.

Rafael and Quinton walked in, they paused and scowled at the two brothers sitting near me.

"Brother king, have we been left out of some plan?" Chase asked his twin.

Troy watched them go sit beside the two nearest me. "I think we have been."

"Should we prepare for battle?" Victor looked from one to the other, "for when her *mate* arrives?"

"Whose mate?" Leone asked coming in from the kitchen. He frowned at his siblings and set a glass of juice on the table at his seat. Pausing he looked at me, amusement on his face. "They think if they sit close to you, you can't hit them with as much energy."

Rafael nodded. "I'm serious, Michael and I were heading to the tunnel after the girls said they were coming our way—I kid you not two guys flew out of it like they were on pulleys."

Michael nodded and looked at Arius. "You saw what she did to that guy after Raf."

Grinning at me, he pointed a finger my way. "I'm on your team for everything—always."

I looked to Daxx, she was smiling and shaking her head.

Crissy giggled.

Turning, I saw Leone shrug. "There's just one problem with you sitting there, brothers."

"What's that?" Quinton asked then took a bite.

Leone started walking slowly in my direction. When he reached the end, he pulled out my chair. Leaning down he scooped me up into his arms and walked back to his seat. He put me in the chair beside his. Kissing the top of my head, he slid the juice over. "Here's your drink."

He sat down and leaned forward to look at his brothers, making a show of looking to me then back to them again. "That's a good distance, build up some momentum."

The brothers at the end of the table paused, then in unison got up and rushed back to their normal seats.

Troy toasted Leone. "Taught him well, we did, brother king."

Chase grinned. "Indeed, we did."

Mitz came rushing out, carrying a tray filled with fruit. She set it near my plate. "Let me know if you have other preferences, love."

"Thank you. This is wonderful."

She went from smiling to her eyes wide. Covering her mouth, she heaved out a breath. "Oh no."

All the men froze.

"Mitz?" Victor was standing.

She waved him off. "I just realized crimson isn't going to work. It won't be complimentary to Bethany's hair at all." She pulled a phone out of her apron. "Oh my. I have to stop the seamstresses immediately." She rushed out of the room.

All the males turned to give Daxx a cautious look.

She waved her fork around. "I was shot in the ass today. In. The. Ass. Don't even *think* of the words ball, dance, or gown right now."

All at once the men put their heads down.

I turned to Leone.

He was smirking, he gave a quick shake of his head. "I'll explain later."

I looked at Alona, she had her hand over her mouth, she was laughing quietly or crying—it may have been a bit of both.

"So," Daxx game everyone a look, daring them to say the forbidden words, "did we get anyone of importance today?

Arius took a drink, then gave her a skeptical look. "Too soon to tell. Scanning and sorting that many while they were *dancing* around made it mayhem."

"What was the final count?" Victor asked looking very serious. "I lost track. I may have actually dropped the *ball* a few times."

Daxx scowled at him.

"Please brothers, have mercy on me. I have to sleep beside her and where would we be with only one king?" Troy tried to look stern, but failed when his mouth quirked.

Michael sighed looking disappointed. "Last count was fifty-seven, but we may have counted a few twice."

Arius nodded. "I'll know more after they're properly processed."

"I'm never leaving without my zapper again." Daxx mumbled.

"Yes, another transporter would have been prudent." Victor agreed.

"It's not…" everyone paused and looked at me. "It may not be my place, but wouldn't it be easier if a few more had them?"

Alona looked animated, "Can…"

"Not a chance, woman. I've seen you at a shoe sale. Arius would have cells filled with angry shopaholics." Chase patted her hand.

I smirked then looked back to Victor. "It is war." I believed that completely after what I'd witnessed today. "Wouldn't it make sense that those who uphold the law," I motioned to Michael and then to Leone, "had one?"

Michael and Leone both turned to look at Victor.

He studied me for a moment with those cold, pale green eyes. I thought for sure he was about to shoot down that idea. Cocking his head to the side, he glanced to Troy and then Chase.

Troy lifted his hand and briefly glanced at his twin. "Those matters are yours to decide as justice."

Chase nodded. "I agree. We're left with far more important matters like herds of cattle."

Troy rolled his eyes. "I read those. We need to delegate someone to sort through the time consuming…"

"Redundancy that lands on our desks." Chase finished for him.

Troy nodded.

They both stopped and turned to look back to Victor.

He moved his head slowly, his expression thoughtful. "It is a viable solution with strong reasoning. I'll speak with our scientists about constructing two more devices."

Leone grabbed my hand and squeezed it.

Michael smiled, and toasted me.

I was still trying to process what Victor had said. Glancing to Crissy, she gave me thumbs up.

Arius sighed and pulled out his phone. He glanced at it then looked at Michael. "I'm needed at the cells. I could use a hand.

Grabbing a sandwich, Michael nodded and got up.

"May need you as well, Leone." Arius stood up.

Leone squeezed me hand again. "I'll be right there."

Chase kissed Alona. "I'm going to see what we caught today."

Smiling, she gave him a slight nod. "I'm heading to the apartment to see whether the carpet is salvageable or not."

He stood up. "Stay *in* the apartment."

She laughed. "No worries there, I've had my adventure for the day."

"Let me know when you're back, we could still get a few hours sleep before our shift." He walked out the kitchen door.

Troy glanced to Daxx.

She flicked her hand toward him. "Go see the new heads you get to play in. I'm going to lay down for a bit. I feel awful after that tranquilizer."

He kissed her on the forehead. "Call if you need anything."

Crissy looked at Victor. "I'm going over with Alona to get my lists, then I'll be in my tower."

"Very well, my heart. I'll go make arrangements for the two new devices."

Leone watching his siblings leaving, then sat looking at me.

I realized he was waiting to see what my plans were. This couples thing was going to some time getting used to. "I think I'll go help Alona. I still have some of my stuff there to go through."

Leaning over he kissed me. "I'll let you know when I'm done. Maybe we could watch a movie." He smirked. "I bought some new ones."

I gave him a surprised look. "Racking up those bonus points, huh?"

"Until you tell me to stop."

"Not a chance, superman."

He stood up and winked at me then left through the kitchen.

Alona leaned forward and looked at the tray of fruit. "Let's bring that over. It looks tasty and will go well with this wine I have." She wiggled her eyebrows.

As I was going through the boxes that held my belongings—which I was realizing weren't things I wanted to keep, or needed to. Most of it held memories I thought I had needed to be strong and remember who I was. I wasn't that person anymore, and I was coming to terms with that. Mostly in a good way.

Crissy came running out. "Victor needs me for a minute. I'll be back to get my bag and the lists." She nodded and opened the device on her wrist then vanished.

Alona came out looking distraught. "I don't think there is anyway to salvage it." She stopped and stood there with her hands on her hips. "How are you making out?"

I looked at the small pile of items I'd decided I was keeping. "None of this is relevant to who I am now."

"A royal princess of Alterealm?" She smirked.

I laughed. "I was thinking more internally than a title. I guess I am a princess, huh?" I tilted my chin up. "Princess Bethany…" I frowned, "is there a last name that goes with it? I'm mated to a man and don't even know his last name." Getting up I went over and leaned on the island counter. "I'm assuming the mating is like marriage."

She snorted and went to the fridge. "I believe it is much more eternally permanent than a piece of paper marriage." Opening the door, she pulled out a bottle of wine. "The men's last name is Whitham though."

"Whitham. Well that does sound…"

"Privileged?" She opened the bottle with a quiet pop. Setting it down, she turned for glasses. "They may have had certain privileges in their life, but as you've seen, they are the first into battle and most likely work harder and more often than all of Alterealm. Keeping the balance is not a job for pampered princes."

I sat on the stool. "I can see keeping the balance in two realms as a heavy burden."

She nodded as she poured two glasses. "And yet, the comic relief is never ending."

I smiled. "My heart was caught in my throat, and they were ribbing each other a second from stepping into a bloody war zone."

"Oh, I know, but it's their way. Most times it's endearing." She hovered her hand over the tray of fruit and selected a piece. Popping it into her mouth, she chewed slowly and then took a sip of wine. "Mmm, not bad."

The buzzer by her door sounded.

"Odd. I didn't get a warning from the guard in the lobby." Setting the glass down, she went to the monitor beside the door. Smirking over her shoulder at me, "someone is going for maximum points."

I got up and went to look.

"That is an enormous amount of roses. I can't even see the delivery person."

"You think they're for me?" I stared at the screen.

She nodded. "Yes, Leone is sweet like that. If Chase were sucking up to me, he'd buy me a greenhouse or winery."

I laughed and looked back at the monitor. "That is a lot of roses. I've never been given flowers before."

"Looks like forgiveness for dear sweet Leone isn't too far away." She watched the monitor. "You did after all, torment him by whispering in his head for a few weeks."

I covered my mouth and sighed, "That's very true."

Alona pushed some buttons and used an eye scanner. Turning, she held her hand on the door knob. Her eyes were red and she grinned with fangs in her mouth. "What about fangs? Leone's? Fangs do it for Chase." She blinked, and her eyes were green again.

I felt my cheeks heat. "Leone's fangs work for me."

She laughed. "He's definitely forgiven." She pulled the door open.

I stood there gawking at the huge bouquet of roses.

Alona motioned for the delivery man to come in.

As he stepped in, he tossed the roses at me and grabbed Alona. With a blade to her throat, he shoved her forward and another man came through the door. They were both large, scruffy and wearing devices on their big hairy arms.

The second one closed the door. I heard a beep and knew even if we could distract them, there would be no fast escape running out that door.

Alona made a sound of distress as the blade pressed against her throat.

The other one came over and grabbed a handful of hair and started walking us down the hall. He looked in doors as we went. I held his wrist, so he wouldn't rip my hair right out.

"No one here." He called out.

"The blonde has to be here. She's the one we shot."

I glanced to Alona as he dragged me back out. I couldn't use my magic energy. Not with him holding a blade to her throat.

"Shit, they're both mated." The one holding me said.

I didn't look away from Alona, if she managed to move I didn't want to miss my chance. She clutched her stomach and was looking ill. I realized she was picking up their emotions.

"You guys don't want to do this." I said quietly.

"I know her." The one holding Alona said. "That's Marcus' witch's friend."

The one holding my hair wretched my head to the side and looked at my face. "So it is." He reached and jerked the chain around my neck. "She's mated to that god damned enforcer. I hate that guy, he's the reason my uncle got life in the cells."

The one holding Alona made a sarcastic noise, then pulled her chain off. "Well, well. We're in the company of a queen."

Alona looked like she was going to throw up.

Tossing the chain to the floor, he grabbed her arm and pushed her down into the sitting room.

"I suggest you take your hands off our mates. *Now.*"

I moved my eyes only to see Leone and Chase standing at the door. Their eyes were red and if these two jerks had half a brain they would throw themselves out the window of this penthouse.

"Your majesty. Sweet digs you've got here." The one holding me said.

Chase didn't even move or blink. His eyes were on the man holding Alona.

"Enforcer." The idiot jerked my hair. "See you got yourself the hot red headed bitch."

Leone growled.

I swallowed and looked at him. *Leone…* I cried in his head. *What do we do?*

His red eyes moved from the man holding me to meet my look.

He heard me. *Think it.* I told him.

He looked to the man holding Alona and I felt his words in my head.

Do this to him with the knife.

A flashing sign couldn't have been clearer than his thoughts right now.

I winced as he pulled my hair again.

Looking to the one holding Alona as she stood there shaking. I focused hard on him. I could do this. His head was a mess.

Drop the knife. I said in his head.

He looked to Chase and Leone.

Drop. The. Knife. Now. I tried again.

Drop it. Hurry!

His hand shook.

Throw the knife away, quick.

His hand jerked, and the knife flew towards the hall.

"What the hell?" The one holding me said.

Lifting my hand, I tossed energy at the one still holding her arm and it hit him in the head, knocking him away from her.

Chase flew across the room. His body was a blur and the guy sprawled on the floor with the force Chase hit him.

"What the fuck?"

My hair was released. I spun and flicked my hands at him. The energy connected, and he bounced off the wall. I did it again. I was so upset. He smacked against the wall again and slid down it. Lifting my hands above my head, I was about to hit him a third time when someone grabbed my hands.

"Beth, he's down." Leone turned me and wrapped his arms around me.

"Alona." I cried against his chest.

"Chase has her."

I turned and looked, he was on the floor with her, holding her face between his hands. His eyes were yellow.

"He's pulling the bad emotions from her." Leone said softly.

Alona sobbed. Her whole body was shaking. Chase helped her to stand. She pulled out of his arms and went over and kicked the unconscious man in the head. Turning she ran down the hall to the bathroom.

Chase went after her.

"They are the ones that shot Daxx. They said something about…" I leaned back and looked up at him, then ran down the hall to the room Crissy had been in. Her back pack sat there. I fell to my knees and opened the pocket. The dart was till in it. I turned, Leone was behind me. "They tracked this." My mouth dropped open. "Call Troy. They can track Daxx."

Leaning down, he took the dart and then my hand.

I could hear Alona throwing up when we went back into the hall.

Leone set the dart on the counter and pulled out his phone. He wrapped his other arm around me. "Michael—at the apartment. No, the fucks that shot Daxx were here. They tracked the dart…" His hand moved up and down my back.

I jolted when Michael appeared beside us.

Leone dropped his phone on the counter. "Get Victor here for them," he motioned the men on the floor, "before I call Troy. They may still be tracking her."

Michael tapped his phone. "Get to Alona's apartment. *Now.* Bring your transport device." Before he turned around Victor stood by the door.

He didn't say a word, just went over to the guy that had held Alona. Lifting his head, he looked at him and then pop, he was gone. Getting up he went to the one that had held me and did the same. Straightening, he looked at me, his pale eyes assessing I was all right. "How did they get in?"

I pointed to the roses on the floor. "We thought they were from Leone." I started shaking.

Alona came out of the bathroom, Chase holding her close to him. "It was my stupidity." She froze. "Oh my god. Someone please go and check on the guard in the lobby. He would never admit someone without my say so." She held a shaking hand over her mouth.

"I'll go check." Michael vanished.

Leone pointed to the dart. "It was in Crissy's bag. She left it here. They tracked it."

Victor's expression changed to one of vengeance. His mate could have been here also.

Chase swore and pulled out his phone. "Where's Daxx? Get there. Get her to Clairee and Romulus, now. Grab the science geek too. There's some sort of substance they can track on the dart." He shook his head. "They're at the cells now. They got into Alona's apartment." Chase eyes were yellow now. "Don't ask. They're not injured." He nodded and hung up.

Victor went down the hall and into the room. Coming out, he held Crissy's backpack. With a brief nod to Leone, he picked up the dart. "I'll get this tested immediately." He vanished.

Before anyone could speak again, Michael appeared.

"The guard is conscious, now. I called an ambulance. He's calling someone to fill in for him. He thinks he slipped and hit his head…"

Arius appeared. "What the fuck is going on? Two unconscious men appear in my cells, then Michael calls me to tell me some guard fell and hit his head?" He looked to Alona.

She held up her hand. "I'll be all right. I just sucked up all their vile emotions." She shuddered.

"His head was a mess." I said quietly. I rubbed my head. "Did he leave any hair? It's still stinging."

Michael scowled. "He held you by the hair?"

Leone moved my hand and gently checked my scalp.

"Dragged her up and down the hall by it." Alona said with a shaking voice.

I looked to her. "That's better than a knife to my throat. Are you okay? I couldn't blast him until I got him to drop it." I leaned back against Leone. "Which I wouldn't have thought to do without Leone…"

"Wait." Arius growled. "A knife…" he stopped and bent down and picked up Alona's chain and held it up.

Chase came over and took it.

"My chain." I looked around, not sure where it had been tossed. "They knew who the symbols belong to."

"I've got it." Michael brought it over and handed it to Leone.

Arius growled again then vanished.

Leone looked to Chase. He motioned at Michael. "Go make sure he doesn't kill either of them. We need answers."

Michael nodded then was gone.

"Chase. I want to go home." Alona leaned into his arms.

He nodded and kissed the top of her head. "We'll meet when Victor gets the test results." Chase gave Leone a hard look. "Stay away from the prisoners."

Leone snorted. "You as well."

They were gone.

Lifting my chin, Leone searched my face. "Are you all right?"

I sighed. "Shaking. Scared but I'm okay." I hugged him. "Take me back please. I want to soak in the tub."

Wrapping his arms around me, he leaned down. "Mine or yours? Tub?"

"Yours. I don't want to be alone right now."

Tilting my chin up, he looked at me. "You never have to be again."

Chapter Seventeen

Leone knocked on the door. "Beth. When you said you didn't want to be alone, you know, I thought we'd be in there together."

I grinned at the closed bathroom door. "I know I'm sorry. I just—I had a bashful moment."

"Did you use lots of the bubble bath Mitz brought?"

I looked at the bubbles piled up higher than the tub and poked them. "You could say that."

"Then cover up with those." He paused. "Please don't make me beg to be in the same room as my mate. It's very emasculating. Superman shouldn't have to beg.

I laughed. "What would your brothers say if they heard you right now?"

The door handle jiggled then there was a crack, and he was standing in the doorway.

He held up the broken handle. "Now look what you made me do. Mitz is going to string me up." He stopped talking and looked at the mound of bubbles in the large tub. "Did you use the whole bottle?"

I lifted bubble covered hands. "It's a big tub. I didn't know if a cap full would be enough."

Laughing he walked toward me. Stopping he looked at his hand and dropped the broken handle. Coming over he sat on the edge of the tub. He grinned. "I'd need scuba gear to even find a trace of you in these bubbles."

I tried to distract him from my miscalculation. "You said you'd be right back, did you go to feed?" I don't know why I asked him that. Between the bubbles and the awkwardness of having a conversation while naked in the tub, made me blurt out the first thing.

"No. I grabbed a bite when I was helping in the cells."

"Eww. I hope you brushed your fangs afterward."

He laughed. "I took your chain to be repaired."

"Oh."

"How's your head?"

I touched a bubble coated hand to it. "It still hurts."

Dropping to his knees, he moved behind me and touched my head. "You know, I have this pretty amazing blood that would take care of this."

"Yeah, I heard that somewhere." I grinned. I hadn't realized he could be, fun. It was something I needed in my life, and hadn't had much of up to this point.

Brushing my hair away from my neck, he leaned down and kissed it. "I'm still a little hungry—I did use a lot of energy today."

"Really?"

"Mmm." He kissed my neck again and then stopped. "You're not going to toss energy at me, are you? You battered the hell out of the one guy at the apartment." He leaned on the edge of the tub. "Can you do it when your hands are wet?"

I lifted them out of the water and looked at them. "I've never tried. It's energy though, not actual fire." Turning them away from us, I focused, and the arc appeared. "Guess it works." Sending a small burst at the mound of bubbles it sent them floating in the air.

"Mitz is going to make me clean this up." He moaned.

I laughed, then did it again with more force and the bubbles clung to the wall, sliding down it slowly.

"Hey. That's enough." He got up and gave me a wide-eyed look.

Grinning I did it again on an angle and sent it toward him. It flew up hard enough that water and bubbles soaked the front of him.

His jaw dropped. "That's it." He stepped into the tub, clothes and all.

"Leone. You're crazy."

He knelt in the tub in front of me and pulled his shirt over his head. "I'm done being patient." He said as he grasped my waist and pulled me into his lap. "Keeping my distance has been slowly killing me." He kissed my mouth, then trailed his lips down my throat.

I clung to his shoulder, moving my head to the side, giving him access to my neck.

Lifting his head, his red eyes searched mine.

I grasped the back of his head and pushed it toward my throat. "If you need to feed. You feed from me."

With a soft growl, he leaned down and sank his fangs into my neck.

Leone kissed me as I sat at the table. "I better go talk to Mitz before she finds the mess on her own." He whispered.

Alona turned to look at me after he walked out. "Mess?"

I felt my cheeks heat. "Bubbles." I said quietly. "I used a bottle, and the more we try to wash it down the drain the more bubbles it creates." I started laughing picturing Leone swearing he'd fought killers easy to take down than those bubbles.

Covering her mouth, she chuckled. "I guess the roses worked."

We both started laughing.

Chase and Leone came out of the kitchen. Chase frowned and leaned closer to his brother. "Were they into the wine again?"

Leone shook his head, "not unless it was in the last minute."

Alona waved her hand at him. "It wasn't wine this time." She glanced to me. "It was bubbly."

Leone gave me a shocked look.

I started laughing again.

Chase motioned between his mate and me, "These two are going to be trouble together, brother." He smirked. "I love it."

Troy and Daxx came in, she came around to our side of the table. "Are you two okay?" She gave us a funny look as we tried to settle down.

I nodded. "Yes. Are you?"

She scowled across the table at her mate. "He won't let me go to the cells."

Leone sat down. "Rest assured Daxx, Beth battered one for you. Bounced him up and down like a ball." He held my hand gently. "If I hadn't stopped her, I don't think he'd be alive to pay for his crimes."

Daxx crossed her arms and gave me a quick nod. "Good."

"We had to stich up the other one's head. Seems Alona's boots are a weapon all on their own." Arius said as he came out of the kitchen.

"He broke my necklace." Alona said picking up her cup.

Victor walked in, with Crissy in his arms. Kissing her mouth softly, he set her on her chair. Then turned to give Alona and I look of appraisal. Assuring himself we were all right, he sat down.

Mitz came in carrying a tray. She glanced at Troy. "I'm going to need a bigger maintenance budget at the rate things are progressing."

Troy took the tray and set it on the table. "Has something happened?"

Shaking her head, she checked the coffee urn. "Nothing of consequence. Doors broken, water damage…"

Leone and I looked at each other, smirks on our faces.

"Book shelves crumbling like a deck of cards…" Mitz shook her head.

Victor cleared his throat and Crissy giggled.

Picking up the sugar bowl, Mitz turned. "I don't even know how a solid wood dresser can break," She waved her hand. "Never mind a desk." She went into the kitchen.

Daxx coughed and quickly went around and sat down.

Chase gave Alona a heated look.

"Well that was too much information." Arius said quietly.

"What is?" Michael came in with Rafael.

Arius waved his hand to the end we sat at. "The damage these mated couples are doing to their furnishings."

Rafael stopped and looked at the four couples. "Way too much information."

Quinton came in shaking his head. "Ellis is like a caged animal right now. He hasn't heard back from Emil in a few days." He sat down. "We need to tell him what his father and brother are up to."

"I was waiting for the rest of you to get here before speaking," Victor pulled out his phone and tapped the screen a few times. "Kinsley has managed to get a few photos of her surroundings to me." He handed the phone to Chase.

Chase flipped through them, his expression bleak.

Alona glanced over his shoulder and shook her head. "That island needs to become our priority I believe."

Leone looked at them and then offered me the phone, I shook my head. I was still trying to process the fact that those men earlier had known me.

He handed it to Arius.

Arius focused on the screen. "There are so many women there." He looked up to Troy as he handed it to Rafael. "We need to focus on finding those they haven't found as well."

Troy nodded.

Daxx glanced to Victor. "How is this Kinsley getting photos and information in and out? I doubt she's just wandering around snapping pictures."

"Kinsley," Michael said quietly, "is quite resourceful and…"

"Distracting." Rafael finished for him. "You'd never suspect her being trained as a guard, and even if you did she could divert that thought with little problem." He handed the phone across the table to Quinton.

Daxx gave Rafael and hard look. "Figures you'd know her."

Rafael held up his hands. "It's not what you think. I help train the guards, that's how I know her. I didn't even know that's who they were talking about sending in until recently."

Quinton grunted and handed the phone to Michael.

Tapping the screen, Michael sighed, "we need to process these and start taking stock of what we're looking at once we get in there."

"It's not going to be an easy task, brother." Victor said crossing his arms over his chest. "Her reports have been quite detailed. There is only one area that isn't heavily warded and to get to it would involve dropping in from above or climbing a treacherous cliff. The only way off unnoticed is to jump into the water below."

Michael handed the phone to Daxx, she took it and gave it to Troy.

"I'm pissed off enough today, I don't need more anger I can't vent."

Troy looked at them, his brow furrowed. "I'm inclined to agree with all suggestions. If we are able to get any viable information from the new group in the cells, about the other sites, we'll act on them. But, finding women they haven't, and figuring out a way onto this island must take priority." He handed the phone to Crissy.

She took it and looked at the pictures then stood on the chair. "Victor. It's Emil's daughter." She held the phone in front of his face. "See the hair so light it almost looks white?" She nodded.

"Shit." Chase stood up. "I'll call him." He went out into the kitchen with his phone already to his ear.

Victor took the phone and held Crissy's hand as she sat down. He looked at Quinton. "You had better go get Ellis. Emil will be back shortly, and we'll have to bring them in on this."

Quinton nodded and stood up.

"We'll meet at my office." Victor called after him.

Chase came back in and sat down. "Emil is getting in touch with Abraham, then they'll meet here."

"I still don't know what the frozen clocks mean." Crissy said quietly playing with a red rubber ball in her hand.

Arius coughed. Setting his glass down, he looked at her. "You're seeing clocks?"

She nodded, "and water and herbs—but the clock is the most fascinating." She turned to Victor then pointed to the kitchen. "I'll be in there." She stood up and jumped down from her chair. "I need to sort."

He gave her and understanding look and nodded abruptly. He watched until she was out of the room and looked back to us. "Before Emil descends upon us as a protective father—" He leaned on the table. "The substance on the dart was," he waved his hand, "expired. So the labs feel it has a short time frame to be traceable." He motioned to Daxx, "hers was too diluted almost immediately to be followed and there are no traces on the backpack."

"So essentially, they had a great idea but botched it up?" Leone asked.

Victor looked from Daxx back to him. "More or less. Had they gotten the property's strength correct, it could have been an entirely different situation."

Troy looked at Daxx.

She sighed. "I know what that look means. I'm going to have a guard strapped to my ass indefinitely. Again." She nodded to Alona.

Alona sighed. "I suppose I'll need more puzzles."

I gave Leone a curious look.

His dark eyes searched mine for a moment. "You will also have a guard when I'm not with you." He motioned to

Alona, "especially if you're going to be helping the girls search for women before these maniacs find them."

I opened my mouth, then closed it and looked at Daxx then Alona. They watched me waiting. "Of course, I'm helping. I've been among these creeps. No woman should be near them."

Leone sighed. "I was afraid you'd say that." He turned to Chase. "Any more pirates to spare?"

Chase laughed. "I'm not going to have a single personal guard left. Who will protect me?"

Troy laughed. "Since when do you need a guard to protect you?"

"I don't." Chase shrugged, "but that's beside the point." He nodded to Leone, "I'll see who would be appropriate." He glanced to me. "Just don't let her break him." He took Alona's hand. "On that note, my queen and I need to go rest, or no one will be on watch later." Motioning to the clock on the wall, "do you see the time? It's almost dawn and I haven't closed my eyes once."

Alona stood up. "Is that why I feel like I'm drooping?"

After they walked out, Troy looked around. "We have three so far in the cells that have information in their heads that may be quite valuable." His hazel eyes paused on me. "Bethany, can you *see* when you're inside their head or just in the moment?'

I sat back and sighed. "It's more in the moment. I can't dig around in memories or anything. Basically, I talk inside their head and feel what they're thinking and feeling."

Leone snorted. "I can vouch for that." he gave me soft look, "the constant voice inside your head part." He toasted me with his glass.

I clasped my hands in my lap. "You didn't mind earlier." I said in a whisper.

Coughing, he set the glass down and gave me 'I can't believe you said that' look.

I shrugged.

"Ignoring that." Daxx turned to her mate. "What kind of valuable information?"

Troy rubbed the back of his neck. "I don't have anything definite yet. There's a lot of minds to comb through down there right now. Places, mostly. Some of them so out of place that they make me think they aren't just hideouts for small factions."

"We need to cut the head off the snake." Rafael motioned around him. "If we can find Hubert or one of his *generals*," he rolled his eyes, "then we can slow this down."

Michael leaned forward. "When we find Willis Hubert. He is mine." His voice dropped, "I owe him." He touched his scarred cheek.

I looked at Leone, he shook his head quickly, so I wouldn't ask.

"We'd never deny you retribution, brother." Victor told him in a hushed voice.

A chill went down my spine with the sudden mood change. "So, so these out of place locations." I looked from Victor to Troy. "You think they might be hiding there? The leaders?"

He gave me a half nod, half shrug. "That's what I'm hoping."

Victor glanced to his phone. "I have to go. Quinton is having a hard time wrangling Ellis." He stood up. "Keep me informed about any information you feel is relevant. I am past ready to end this uprising." He glanced into the kitchen for a moment and then turned and left through the other door.

Michael stood up. "I'm going to go lend a hand there. Brothers wanting vengeance is something I'm good at." He shrugged. "The father part is new, and I suspect going to be harder to manage." He turned to the door.

"Just don't let Emil try to go to the island." Troy said quickly.

"I will try, brother." Michael said walking out.

Crissy came running out of the kitchen. "We have to go. Now. Now." She ran down the length of the table and spun. "She's in trouble. So much water." She ran out the door.

The men were up chasing after her.

When I reached the door, Rafael had caught up to her and was walking back toward us. "She saw a woman drowning…"

"Shit." Troy leaned down, his face close to hers. "Is she from the island?"

Crissy shifted back and forth on her feet. "I think so. There's so much water, she's going to be cold."

My heart was beating so fast in my chest, I thought I might pass out. Leone grabbed my hand and squeezed it.

Arius turned and started running down the hall, "I've ported to all those islands. I'll go start looking." He called over his shoulder. "Raf, find a boat to borrow. Call when you have one."

"On it." Rafael vanished.

Troy motioned down the hall. "Leone, go fill Victor in. We may need more backup and he's ported to that whole area."

Leone gave my hand a quick squeeze. "Beth, go with Daxx and get Clairee, see if she can tap into anything."

I nodded, not knowing what else to do.

Troy kissed Daxx quickly. "Crissy and I will go meet Rafael with the boat."

Daxx nodded quickly. "Just find her, Troy."

"That's the plan." He took off in the other direction, Crissy right on his heels.

Daxx looked at me. "Welcome to Alterealm." She went back into the dining room.

I bit my lip and looked in the direction Leone had gone. So much in my head right now, it was frightening. I could only hope this woman survived and it wasn't too late.

KEEP READING FOR AN EXCERPT OF

Beltane Magic

Book I
Magic Seasons Romance

By Jacqueline Paige

⚭ **Chapter 1** ⚭

Leena drove slowly through the massive trees, their branches were like gnarled hands, long, pointing greyed fingers reaching toward the others across the road. Light sifted through, casting web-like patches of brightness on the road. Soon leaves would fill in the spaces, blocking the light. She wanted to stop and just drink in the scene.

A few lingering titian-colored leaves were sparsely scattered along the sleeping limbs; having determinedly held on through the winter. To some it would feel eerie, or a detail they wouldn't stop to notice, to her this was nature at her most beautiful time of awakening after the long, restful winter.

She sighed and glanced back to the road. Why was she the one to get there last, after driving through this middle-of-nothing alone? Oh right, she was the big supervisor; the one who needed to stay behind and finish up while her three friends and coworkers had piled into another car, four hours earlier. Well, at least they'd be sure to get a cabin in a good location. One close enough to everything to be easy to get to, but far enough away that private time wouldn't be a problem.

Leena glanced in the rear-view mirror before stopping the car in the middle of the road. Of course, no one would be behind her on this scenic route, which was beginning to look more like a path through an enchanted forest. She picked up the map to study it again. Somewhere there was supposed to be a bridge and slight incline. She was pretty sure the drawing with arrows pointing down meant downhill. She grinned. Justin made this map, and unless he'd changed since last year, she knew in her gut that his description of a thing and hers were not going to be even close.

Justin and his wife, Gwen, organized several small events throughout the year and they were never in the same place twice. The places were always completely secluded, and completely appropriate, for the small gatherings. She admired them for that.

She wondered how they managed to find some of the places; most were so remote that explorers were probably the last people to have set eyes on them. Knowing this made her look forward to this first gathering after the winter months, just for the surprise.

Double checking the printout from Gwen's email one more time, she started moving forward again. She held her breath as the car carefully crept around the corner. In this atmosphere, she almost expected a dragon or another fanciful creature from the fairy tales to jump out on the other side.

That was the bridge? It looked more like a few logs tossed in a line. She glanced in the mirror again. It had to be. There hadn't been anywhere to turn off from this road, it seemed to get narrower with each mile she traveled. She didn't want to think what she'd do if she met another vehicle at this point.

Driving slowly and hearing the crunching under the tires of her car did nothing to reassure her. Nor did she allow herself to look out the window and see what exactly was under this primitive bridge. She hadn't realized she was holding her breath, until it rushed out in a whoosh as the back tires cleared the last log and were once again on the dirt path that passed for a road.

Her stomach was knotted with tension from the drive, and fluttery with excitement. The Beltane gathering was finally here. Most called this a festival, but to her, it was more.

Being reunited with those she saw only a few times a year, or some she'd only ever seen at an event.

For some this would be the only time they could be who they were inside, be how they wanted to be and feel accepted.

Leena felt she was luckier than most, she had three *true* friends. They didn't have the exact beliefs as one another, but in the last five years as the friendship grew stronger, they found ways to blend and merge those beliefs into something strong and unbreakable.

This was a slight incline? She almost hit the brakes but was afraid she'd slide off the road. It looked as if it dropped right off to nothing. The email said private and secluded. However, they didn't mention that people would be too afraid to venture over the bridge, and if they did, surely this hill winding down into a dark path of overhanging trees would deter them from going any farther.

It was probably breathtaking once everything was reborn and newly grown. As it was not yet May, it was still covered with the brown and grey of winter's slumber. She smiled, soon a thousand different shades of green would cover the ground, and life would breathe anew. Leena loved spring, loved the rebirth after long cold winters. Being of a pagan nature, she understood that winter was needed to revive the Earth, which supported so much life, but this still didn't stop her from being as thrilled as a child seeing the first signs of spring every single year.

This path would be eerie in the darkness with the trees casting shadows, and it would scare many, she thought. Well, those who did not believe as she did. Nevertheless, she loved nature in every form, as it chose to present itself.

These next three days would be spent with many of the same heart and mind celebrating the new season; celebrating Beltane and thanking the Earth for blessing them with the bounty of the seasons to come. The excitement of the gathering brought a smile to her face. Together again with her chosen family, not the ones of her blood, but with her friends and fellow pagans, she could revel in the seasonal change.

As she pulled through a gate covered with dry vines she smirked, because it left the impression of entering a haunted space. A short distance away was the best part of her pagan family. Coralee, Rachel, and Kasey stood by a little shed waving to her. Pausing, she took a moment to just sit and be thankful for friends such as the odd trio walking toward her.

The four of them together had all the bases covered in terms of looks. Coralee was a few inches taller than Leena's five foot ten, with long, dark red locks of "frizz," as Cora herself liked to call her own hair. Rachel, whose pale complexion seemed even lighter than normal next to Cora's dark skin, stood a little over five and half feet and had straight, jet black hair barely past her jaw line. Kasey was the shortest of them, and this week, wore her blindingly bright, wavy blonde hair in short spikes all over her head.

Leena glanced quickly in the mirror to make sure she didn't look as frazzled as she felt after the adventurous drive. Her scant makeup seemed intact, and her lifeless brown hair was, as always, perfectly flat.

Many on her spiritual path would spend a lifetime trying to find a close friend with similar beliefs. She had been lucky to find three five years earlier. And she thanked whatever forces were responsible for this every day.

Cora grinned and leaned in the door as she opened it. "How'd you like that bridge?"

"It seemed like trees that fell in place. My heart still hasn't slowed since I drove over it."

Rachel laughed. "We debated on parking and walking over, but didn't want to interrupt Kasey, who was praying to every goddess she could think of."

"It didn't help when you said if it failed, we'd be rafting instead." Kasey mumbled quietly, as she tried not to grin.

Leena got out and stretched. "I need the bathroom. Now. Then I'll go check in with Gwen." She watched as the three all smirked. "There is an actual bathroom here, right?"

Cora nodded. "Yep, there's one bathroom for the guys and one for the girls." She grinned when Leena's eyes widened. "It should be interesting with roughly a hundred people in attendance, according to Jean at registration."

"Let's hope they're mostly men then." Leena reached in and grabbed her purse.

"Yes! Mostly men works for me." Rachel grinned.

The others were laughing as Leena headed in the direction Cora pointed, shaking her head. "We'll take your stuff to the cabin and meet you at registration."

After exiting the bathroom, which she was sure at some point had been a storage shed, Leena paused to look around. The cleared area wasn't huge, but it was big enough to have a large open space with a few covered picnic areas in the center. There were small cabins around the outskirts of the clearing that looked much newer than the bathroom shed. They were far enough from the surrounding trees to give you a sense of privacy without having to hide in the bushes to get it.

She smirked as Charlie, the regular event handyman, walked past, carrying a shovel and mumbling to himself. Charlie was a familiar sight at the gatherings. Although in all the years she'd been coming, she never actually remembered saying more than a handful of words to him. She watched the older man attack the ground with the shovel for a moment.

Outside the clearing were trees of every size and type. It was almost as if they were holding the small area in their arms, keeping all those inside safe and protected. Perfect, as always. It would take a solid day or more to hike up out of this valley through all the trees, without getting lost; and you couldn't hear any traffic or unnatural noise. To the east, she could hear running water and made a mental note to find the time to check out the river. It was obviously swelling with the spring thaws and rushing madly between the banks. Smiling, she headed back toward the larger building. She hoped it held a kitchen that was a bit more modern than the bathroom.

With registration taken care of, the four headed to the cabin. Leena was surprised to see it was actually larger inside than it appeared. Dark and weathered wood on the outside contained a soft cream interior, making the area seem larger. One window at the back and the glass door allowed natural light to brighten the space. She was thankful when she noticed the wooden door to shut at night and they wouldn't have that "being watched" feeling. There was a set of bunk beds on each side of the room. Well, it wasn't the Hilton, but it would be dry and reasonably private.

The four women allowed themselves the luxury of a cabin at events. It was easier than hauling tents and other gear, they had all agreed after their first time sharing a tent. The tent came close to going up in smoke during one silly moment, lighting candles for a ritual.

Turning again, she noticed the little folding table they always brought was sitting by the door. "Shall we cleanse and protect our little space?" She grinned, because the others were already digging in bags and cases. Mixing beliefs and magic, always proved to be interesting among the four, for you never knew who was going to do what.

Cora stepped to the table first and placed a small cloth voodoo protection doll in the center, "To protect those who dwell within." She stood with her eyes closed.

Kasey opened her hand to sprinkle shiny dust around the table. "A touch of moon dust to see us safe during this full moon." She joined hands with Cora and waited.

Rachel stepped up to place a light blue candle on the table, then grinned and held her hand over it. As the wick burst into flames, Rachel smiled. "Blue light to protect us and ours."

Leena stepped into the space between Kasey and Rachel and placed an abalone shell onto the table. Smiling at Rachel, she rubbed her hands over the shell letting crushed herbs fall. They began smoking as they settled in the shell. "Lovage to cleanse, purify, and release this space of all negativity." She clasped hands with the others and smiled.

The air in the small cabin stirred and swirled lightly, taking the scent of the Lovage throughout. From one hand to the other, through the four, a tingle could be felt.

Leena dropped her hands and smiled. "At least you kept the snakes and critters at home this time, Cora. I wasn't ready to hold Kasey still again."

Cora laughed in her deep husky way. "I promised not to bring living things after that first time. It's tempting, but I'll save you from that fun." She bundled her jacket up. "I'm heading to see if they need any help in the kitchen before the opening circle. Anyone coming?"

Rachel picked up her poncho. "I'll head that way with you. I want to see if they expect any children this time around and if I can help with the kids' program."

Kasey flopped down on a bunk with her notebook. "I'll be here trying to describe that drive through the stalking forest."

Smiling, Leena found her warm cape and headed back to the door. "I'm going to wander. Don't forget to show up for dinner, Kase." She grinned when the blonde head didn't even lift in acknowledgment as the pen in her hand was already flying.

Ambling around the site, Leena was lost in her own thoughts and almost walked past someone talking to her.

"You don't say hello anymore?"

Leena turned to look up into deep green eyes. "Chris! Sorry, I was in my own little world." She accepted the hug from the tall, dark-haired man. "I haven't seen you since

Kasey dragged me to your Wiccan church. How long have you been here?" He grinned down at her as she quickly stepped back from him.

"Got in an hour ago. Wasn't sure we'd make it over that bridge with the van. But we survived."

She followed his gesture to see his usual group of festival buddies. Tall, dark-haired, dark-eyed, brooding Dade. "Dade. Great to see you." She almost hesitated as he stepped forward for a brief hug.

"Let her go so she doesn't forget me!"

Grinning, she turned to see Steven, with his friendly smile and his chaotic, dark red hair. "Of course, I won't forget you. How are you?" She hugged him a little longer than the others, because he always felt safe. He was just as big as other two men, but he felt harmless.

"Do I get hugged, too, or do I have to know you forever and a day?"

Startled, she turned towards the unknown voice.

Dade laughed. "Well, you knew her about twelve years ago. If you hadn't been running around the planet, you might get hugged."

She studied the large man. He had to be well over six feet, probably by at least two or more inches. He had a build like a bodybuilder—a very nice build. His blond hair was neat, although with it that short, did it have a choice really? When she stopped at the pale blue eyes, she knew exactly who she was looking at. "Well, Owen Grey, it has been a long time." She offered a hand.

He smiled at her and took her hand. "I haven't seen you since you started high school." He studied her. "How have you been, Aileena?"

She wasn't sure she was comfortable with the way he was looking at her and tried twice to pull her hand free. "I've been good. Get tired of the rest of the world? Did Dade drag you here?" She offered a slight smile.

"Oh, he didn't drag me. I all but begged to come with him. I'm doing some research for a new book, and this is where I need to be."

He unknowingly found her weakness. Books. "Really? I've read most of your work, Owen. It always surprises me what comes out of your mind. What are you researching here?" She knew his work was mainly fantasy fiction, but she was uncomfortable knowing that he would be looking for ideas in one of the few places she felt safe.

"I've been toying with the idea of adding some mythology into a book or two. Dade is the one that convinced me that mythology and the many practices of the occult are very misunderstood... so I'm hoping to mix fact with fantasy and come up with a good story." He watched her relax.

"Well, I'm sure you'll make it work." Giving him a polite smile, she turned back to Steven. "See you at the opening circle?" At his nod, she started to walk away.

"Leena." Dade put a hand on her arm to stop her. He lowered his head and voice. "He won't expose anyone."

She stopped and sighed. "No, I guess he wouldn't, having been friends with you and your family for so long." She felt guilty at her first impression. "I'll see you later, Dade."

Owen stood with his hands in his pockets and looked at the woman walking away as Dade stepped back over to him. "You didn't tell me she went from cute to mysteriously sexy, Dade."

Dade laughed. "You didn't ask, bro." Dade slapped him on the back, "but I'll tell you, there's no chance with that one. No one gets close enough to get a chance. She went through a bad marriage and has never been the same since."

Owen grinned. "Good thing I came back then. A woman like that shouldn't be alone."

Steven and Chris started laughing from behind them.

Chris, still chuckling, walked over and patted him on the arm. "Good luck to you then, Owen. You'll need it. Even more when she has her women swarming around her. Those four together will boil your blood, in *every* way known to man." He grinned. "This is why we spend as much time with them as possible."

Dade and Steven nodded as they headed back to the van to get the rest of the supplies.

KEEP READING FOR AN EXCERPT OF

The Chronos

The Alterealm Series

Book 5

By J. Risk

COMING SOON

Prologue

Looking over my shoulder again, I kept running. I didn't see anyone following me yet, but I wasn't taking any chances. For two weeks I'd watched, waited and planned for the opportunity to get off this island. It was now or never. I couldn't be here another minute.

I pulled at the hard, red cuff around my wrist, trying yet again to pull it off. If I could access my ability I might have a better chance. It was seamless, I'd spent the last two weeks trying to get it off. Stumbling over a branch, I looked back up and tried to figure out where this lead to. There was no path in this direction. They never patrolled this way, ever. Not once had the guards come this way. I didn't know why, but I intended to find out.

My lungs screamed at me to slow down, but my mind told me not to, so I kept going. At any moment I expected to hit another invisible wall. I'd encountered more then one as I tried to assess how far they went. I knew hitting one at this speed would probably knock me unconscious, but I had to at least try.

I ducked around low branches as I tried to keep going in a straight line. It scrapped across my cheek. Wiping at it, I glanced over my shoulder again then my footing slipped. I slid across the ground on my hip and then sat there stunned and panting. The ground dropped off.

Getting to my hands and knees, I cautiously crawled toward the edge. Reaching it, I put my hand out looking for the barrier I couldn't see. My hand wasn't stopped by anything.

Inching forward, I leaned over and looked down. It was a straight drop into the water. It had to be a at least a hundred feet, from my vantage. Now I knew why no one came this way. There was no where to go.

Arms shaking, heart pounding I leaned over further to see if there was a way to climb down it. Shaking my head, I sat back on my heels. Even with ropes and a harness, there's no way I'd try climbing down that.

Now what? I looked behind me and held my breath, listening. I still heard no one. I looked around the edge of the drop off. If I took the time to go along it, that gave them more time to realize I was gone.

Leaning over again, I looked down. Could I do that? I was a good swimmer; just wasn't sure I could jump. The barrier was also an unknown factor. If I could find the courage to jump, there was no guarantee I wouldn't hit a barrier on the way down, or in the water. I could literally be plunging to my death in so many ways.

"There's no where to go this way. Head back and check in the bushes, she's hiding somewhere."

I lay flat on the ground. They knew I was missing. My heart was beating in my throat as I tried to keep my breathing quiet. I looked out over the water. It was quite a distance to land.

"Told them they need to put trackers on them. I'm sick of wandering around here with the damn insects looking for women that think they can get off the island."

I nodded my head, I could do this. Had to do this. Getting up slowly, I stayed low and looked through the trees to see if my location was visible. I didn't see anyone. I straightened and backed up a few feet. Leaning over on my knees with shaking hands I swallowed the fear lodged in my throat.

"Fuck, I'm getting eaten alive here."

I jolted toward the edge and launched myself over the side, hoping I'd clear any rocks near the shore. I'd like to say it was a long enough descent I had time to look, but it was over in a flash. Icy water closed over me as I dropped into the depths of it.

The shock spurred me into kicking toward the top as hard as I could. When my head broke the surface, I gulped in fresh air. I'd done it. I was off the island. Bobbing around I turned to look in all directions. There were rocks sticking out half way to land. They were marked so boats would see them. I could rest there on the other side so no one looking from the island would see.

I tread the water and briefly debated on taking off my shoes, then decided when I made it to land I'd need those to put as much distance between me and these insane people. Kicking was hindered by them, but I started toward the rocks as fast as I could manage.

The water was a lot colder than I'd imagined it would be. I was already feeling my muscles cramping from it. Turning I tread the water on my back for a moment to check the distance from the island. It wasn't as far as I'd hoped. I did it for a bit longer, hoping to catch my breath, while scanning along the shore to see if anyone was looking there yet. There wasn't.

Flipping back over, I pushed my body further. The shoes had to go, they felt like cement weights now. I tried to keep my head above the surface to take them off. The laces were wet and wouldn't undo. I ended up sputtering for air several times trying to free my feet.

Coughing, I had to pause between shoes. I was wasting energy doing this. Taking a deep breath, I sunk beneath the surface and fought to get the second shoe off.

Hands grabbed me, I gulped in water, trying to struggle out of their hold. Kicking out against them, I reached the surface and started swimming with all my strength. I was not going back.

I heard someone say something but wasn't about to stop and see. The sound of a boat registered, and I swam faster. My side was hurting, legs felt like they were moving slower. I went under again and had to fight to not gasp for air while under the surface. Kicking I managed to get my head above the surface. I didn't know how much longer I could do this.

A hand touched me again. I kicked out and connected with a body. I heard a man swear as I dropped below the water once more. He pulled me up and held me firmly with his arm wrapped around me. His grip was tight. He was swimming and dragging me. I fought, coughing and swallowing more water than air.

I held onto his arm, trying to rid my lungs of the liquid, gasping for air. He turned, and I found myself at the rock I'd been heading toward. I clung to it, still trying to breath so I could get away. Large arms surrounded me, his body pressing me against the rough surface.

"I'm not here to hurt you." He said between breaths against my ear, "your safe. We're here to get you to safety."

I turned to see a boat coming toward us. "Safe to where?" I coughed when water filled my mouth again as a wave hit the rock.

"Away from that island." He said calmly, his uneven breathing against my cheek.

I rested my face against the rock, drained, I couldn't swim any more.

"Arius, let me coast as close as I can." Another man called out.

I heard the motor of the boat stop.

"Thought she was going to out swim you." A third male said.

He lifted his head away from me, "it was close." He huffed out a breath.

"I brought a blanket." It was a woman's voice.

I didn't know if this was another lie or scheme to get me back on the island. My body was numb, I was shaking from the exertion and had no more fight left.

I felt myself being pulled through the water and lifted up.

A woman's face was in front of mine. "I saw you. You are so brave." She nodded and wrapped something warm around me. "Your safe now."

That was the last thing I heard just before I closed my eyes.

About the Author

J. Risk is a pseudonym used by Jacqueline Paige

I wanted to write a story that would fit into new adult levels as well as adult. Something that was serious with fun elements-- paranormal / fantasy that everyone could read and enjoy.

I've decided to use J. Risk as the pen name for this to separate this series from my other writing which is definitely adult reading material.

Jacqueline Paige lives in Ontario in a small town that's part of the popular Georgian Triangle area.

She began her writing career in 2006 and since her first published works in 2009 she hasn't stopped. Jacqueline describes her writing as *all things paranormal*, which she has proven is her niche with stories of witches, ghosts, psychics and shifters now on the shelves.

When Jacqueline isn't lost in her writing, she spends time with her five children, most of whom are finally able to look after her instead of the other way around. Together they do random road trips, that usually end up with them lost, shopping trips where they push every button in the toy aisle, hiking when there's enough time to escape and bizarre things like creating new daring recipes in the kitchen. She's a grandmother to eight (so far) and looks forward to corrupting many more in the years to come.

Jacqueline loves to hear from her readers, you can find her at

http://jacquelinepaige.com

www.ingramcontent.com/pod-product-compliance
Lightning Source LLC
Chambersburg PA
CBHW021138110726

47900CB00002B/415